# Open Fire

The driver of the Caddy swung his big car around and started back toward them, the AKs blazing again from the windows. Realizing he was in the line of fire, the kid stopped in the middle of the street, too panicked to run.

When one of the gang bangers yelled out in Spanish for the kid to run, Erik Estevez dashed out into the street. The Caddy's gunmen spotted him and sent a long stutter of 5.45 mm slugs his way.

Putting on a burst of speed as he reached the middle of the street, Erik snatched up the kid. When he reached the sidewalk, he dived for cover, shielding the kid with his body. Another short burst went over their heads as the Caddy roared on down the street and disappeared.

*Also available in this series:*
**Undercover War**

# BLACK OPS

## MICHAEL KASNER

## ARMAGEDDON NOW

### A GOLD EAGLE BOOK FROM
## WORLDWIDE.

TORONTO • NEW YORK • LONDON
AMSTERDAM • PARIS • SYDNEY • HAMBURG
STOCKHOLM • ATHENS • TOKYO • MILAN
MADRID • WARSAW • BUDAPEST • AUCKLAND

This one's for Byron—Thanks, Buddy

First edition May 1996
ISBN 0-373-63811-6

ARMAGEDDON NOW

# ARMAGEDDON NOW

*Los Angeles, California*
*January, 2000 A.D.*

Frank Buckley, sitting in the copilot's seat of the silver-and-green traffic helicopter, spoke into his throat mike. "It looks pretty good for the opening lap of the daily grind down there," Buckley said. "There's only one major accident so far, but it involves a tank truck on the Santa Monica Freeway, and the toxic-spill control team is at the scene. So, if you don't want your DNA to start growing warts, keep away from the Culver City off ramp and plan to take an alternate route."

His eyes swept over the streets and highways below as he wrapped up his report. "That's it for now, but stay tuned for some easy, nerve-soothing rock on KXTK. Jack will be giving you the smog-and-ozone report and Debbie will have the needle-exchange locations today. This is Mr. Traffic, Frank Buckley, saying, remember that wherever you go, whatever you do, play it safe and wear your Kevlar."

As soon as the mike went dead, Buckley shook his head. "Jesus H. Christ!" he muttered under his breath. "I can't fucking believe I left Oregon for this shit."

The pilot was a native Angeleno so he didn't know what his passenger was talking about. "What's the matter with you anyway, man? It's a beautiful day." He pointed to a skyscraper maybe all of five miles away. "You can see all the way to South Gate."

Buckley grimaced as he remembered being able to see Mount Hood from Portland, some sixty miles away, even on an overcast day. "Right."

The chopper banked away to the north and Buckley saw a thin column of smoke reaching up into the sky from a block of charred ruins. All the other New Year's Eve fires in Greater L.A. had been extinguished, but there were still smoldering embers deep inside the debris of what had once been the Tower of Power church. Since the fire had been contained by the streets surrounding the block-sized complex, it had been allowed to burn itself out rather than waste precious water when it had been needed elsewhere that night.

Other than that, the City of Angels didn't look too bad now that the long-awaited Second Millennium had finally come and gone. Less than a week into January, L.A. was back to what passed for normal in the year 2000.

As ANTICIPATED, what the media had tagged the "Millennium Madness" had exploded on New Year's Eve 1999 all over the world. While all the major networks gave it ample air time, CNN covered the event as if it was a war.

The month leading up to the big night had been bad enough. In the United States, self-styled prophets of every stripe had done a landslide business. Otherwise perfectly rational people had abandoned their homes, bought camping gear, food and guns, stuffed their pockets with gold and silver coins and followed these doomsayers into the wilderness to await the Second Coming.

National Guard troops in several states had been called out to turn the mobs back from overcrowded national parks. Other mobs transformed farmers' fields into muddy tent cities. Deadly gun battles between farmers and trespassers had been commonplace, with the farmers usually losing. Citizen militias were quickly formed in many rural areas and they could present a more united front, but people still died by the dozens in what politicians always called the "Heartland of America".

In Death Valley, California, two rival "born-again," doomsday-is-upon-us, armed to the teeth, fundamentalist Christian groups had clashed while anxiously awaiting the promised New Year's Day Apocalypse. The body count had been in the hundreds, and hundreds more had been wounded.

Farther to the south, a huge religious riot in Mexico City had killed thousands on Christmas Day. Someone claimed to have seen a vision of the Blessed Virgin with blood dripping from her eyes like tears.

When the word of the "miracle" got out, tens of thousands of the faithful gathered in the square in front of the National Cathedral to witness this sign of the end times. And, as could have been predicted, a riot broke out and the police had finally been forced to intervene to put an end to it.

Yet another charismatic religious leader in Panama had led thousands of his childlike followers to watery deaths in the Gulf of Mexico. He had promised them that they could walk on water to the Holy Land and be on hand for the Second Coming. Bodies washed up in the surf for days afterward.

In a much less organized fashion, people had committed suicide all over the world in droves rather than wait to see if the predictions of doom would come true. And it hadn't just been the Christian world that had gone insane as the year 2000 approached. Even though they used a different calendar, Islamic, Hindu and Buddhist nations had also suffered unrest. India and the Middle East had been particularly affected.

The body count caused by riots in Bombay and Calcutta had rivaled those of a war. But it was the Middle East, as always, that had racked up the largest numbers of dead and wounded. Smoke was still rising over more than a dozen major cities that had been looted and set on fire. That had just been the beginning. Then came the big night.

For some reason, though, the Millennium Madness had been relatively mild in California. The body count was low compared to places like New York, Alabama and Utah. Late-night comedians said that this was because life in the Golden State was so weird anyway, no one had noticed the Millennium was happening.

That might have been true, but there had still been rioting, looting and mindless destruction in many sections of Greater L.A. on the big night. The single most destructive incident had taken place at the Tower of Power, the city's largest fundamentalist church. The massive edifice to human fear and the hope of redemption was a postmodernist assemblage of timber and glass that could only be found in Southern California.

Early that evening, a crowd of rowdy New Year's Eve partyers had gathered at the massive church. Most of them had come to taunt the fear-crazed Christians trying to force their way into the already-crowded building. Others were there to have a ringside seat at the Apocalypse that the church's self-styled bishop promised was coming at exactly the stroke of midnight.

When the sixty second countdown to midnight began, the spectators started blowing the horns on their cars and pickups and pelting the church with empty beer cans and bottles. When they ran out of empties, they pried bricks from the decorative walkways and hurled them. The sounds of breaking glass could be heard over the fervent hymns of the huddled worshipers inside.

Finally some of the men in the congregation came out to do battle to protect their church. No one knew who fired the first shot. When a drunken teenage blonde clutched her ample breast, screamed out and fell over dead from a gunshot wound, the combat began in earnest. A few minutes later the dead girl's boyfriend took a spare can from the back of his four-wheel-drive pickup, splashed gas on the massive oak doors of the locked entrance and set the church on fire.

Others added their spare gas to the fire, while some had the forethought to light additional fires at the side exit doors. The church building fund had been a little short during the construction, and the sprinkler system hadn't been installed. A bribe to the building inspectors had taken care of the matter at the time, but the bishop had never seen fit to make up this omission. God was on his side and would protect his flock. As a result, in ten minutes the building was engulfed in flames and the worshipers couldn't have escaped even if the crowd had let them. By the time the fire trucks arrived, it was all over.

The site where the church had stood looked as if it had been the target of an air strike. The hundreds of cars in the vast parking lots were all burned out, as well. Medical teams were still searching through the rubble, looking for the charred remains of the more than one hundred people who were still unaccounted for.

BUT NOT EVEN Millennium Madness lasted very long in Greater L.A. The frantic pace of life in Southern

California demanded that something different be experienced every day. Even if it was the same old daily grind, the promise of something new happening drove all thoughts of the past, even the most recent past, from the minds of the Angelenos. And that's what Frank Buckley, Mr. Traffic, was paid to do—keep them informed of what was happening in their megacity, even if it was only the traffic.

The pilot was cruising to the east to check on the traffic in West Covina when Buckley caught sight of a phalanx of cop cars and ambulances parked in front of a small cinder-block building in Monterey Park.

"There!" he yelled at the pilot, pointing at the building. "Put it down."

As the chopper descended, Buckley called in to KXTK. They didn't want to miss this—whatever it was—any more than he did. They told him to check it out and report back. What a stroke of luck, Buckley thought, imagining a life of no more traffic beat.

The pilot put the small helicopter down in a parking lot next to the building, which had a sign in Korean, accompanied by the English version, reading Korean Social Club. The sign was riddled with automatic weapons fire to the point that the words were difficult to read.

As Buckley approached, a pair of ambulance attendants wheeled out a gurney bearing a bloodied body bag. Their pale faces were a study in barely repressed nausea and the man at the head of the gurney had silent tears running down his cheeks. Curious about what could have provoked such a response from hardened paramedics, Buckley forced his way to the front door and looked inside.

The interior of the social club was an abattoir. The floor was covered an inch deep in not yet clotted blood. Body parts and human organs smeared the walls as if it was a set from the slasher movie to end all slasher movies. Most of the dead appeared to be elderly, but there were shredded children's bodies in the carnage, as well, probably the cherished grandchildren of the older people.

The smell of fresh blood and voided bowels and bladders mixed with an acrid overlay of explosive residue and gunpowder to create something Buckley had never smelled in his life. He soon found himself joining the ranks of pukers at the corner of the building. His pilot silently joined him.

Once he recovered, Buckley told the radio station that he was onto the biggest crime story of the new century. They sent a cameraman from their TV affiliate and had Buckley stay at the scene. Alternately broadcasting on the radio and the TV, he had a stunned audience all to himself until the major networks showed up an hour later. Even then, knowing a good thing when they saw it, CNN gave him a year's contract on the spot and he continued his coverage for them.

To millions of Americans, Buckley's face would always be associated with the mindless racial violence that would become known as Armageddon 2000. It would become his allotted fifteen minutes of fame, and then some.

**2**

*Los Angeles*
*January 8*

Frank Buckley's coverage of the Korean Social Center massacre was a two-day wonder in L.A. It was a major crime, but there was too much daily violence in the City of Angels for it to hold public interest much longer than that. The story that pushed it into the background was another massacre, an incident that the police reported as a drug deal gone bad.

A dozen black men, all of them with extensive police records for drug offenses and gang-related crimes, were gunned down in an empty warehouse in the Hawthorne district. What made this killing different from all of the other drug deals gone bad was that the bodies had been literally shot to pieces. Hundreds of rounds had turned them into bullet-torn, blood-soaked forms hardly recognizable as human bodies. The only clue to who had murdered these men was spray-painted Hispanic gang graffiti on the walls. The paint had still been wet when the police arrived.

When Buckley reported on that story, he noticed that the ground around the kill zone was littered with the same kind of empty cartridge cases he had seen at the Korean Social Club shootout. Reaching down, he picked one up and put it in his pocket. When he showed it to one of the more experienced CNN staffers, it was identified as a 5.45 mm cartridge used in Russian-designed assault rifles and light machine guns. With the amount of ex-Soviet arms and ammunition on the world market, it wasn't too surprising that some of it had gotten to L.A.

THE HAPPY WEDDING PARTY wound its way through the streets of West Covina toward the small Catholic church in this predominantly Hispanic neighborhood of East L.A. Most of the celebrants were either mildly drunk or stoned, but they had every reason to be. This was a joyous occasion, a modern-day Romeo and Juliet story come true. The leader of one prominent gang was marrying the sister of his arch-rival gang leader. Some of the male guests were packing, true, but this was to be a peaceful occasion.

The dark-eyed bride was radiant in her flowing white satin dress and veil. The fact that her stomach was starting to protrude slightly was of no importance to anyone; she was getting married and her child would bear its father's name.

The ceremony was short and the celebrants quickly moved out into the walled courtyard behind the church for the reception. When the sun set, the party was still going on. Considering the condition of the bride, there was no need to rush off on a honeymoon to consummate the marriage.

Shadowy figures in dark gray-and-black urban combat suits and face paint stealthily approached the brightly lit courtyard. A solitary gang banger was standing guard under a shot-out street lamp, keeping a watch over the guests' cars. Since he was supposed to be on duty, he was drinking only beer, instead of tequila like everyone else at the party.

As he stared out at the street, a black-and-gray shadow silently approached him from behind. When the shadow got within arm's reach, a piano-wire garrote was slipped over his head and tightened around his neck. A twist drew the thin wire through his throat as if it was warm butter. He didn't even have time to try to claw the wire away from his neck before he gurgled on the hot blood pouring into his lungs, kicked his feet and died.

Rolling the body under the car, the camouflaged figure motioned with one hand, and half a dozen more camouflaged men joined him along the outside of the courtyard wall. Pulling grenades from their assault harnesses, the commandos prepared to lob their weapons and looked to their leader for the signal.

His hand went forward, and the grenades arched up into the air over the wall and fell to the ground in the courtyard. Before they could even detonate, the commandos opened up with their 5.45 mm AK-74 assault rifles on full-automatic fire. Emptying their magazines in long bursts, the shooters quickly changed magazines and continued firing.

Solitary shots answered their barrage but didn't shut down the murderous volume of fire. When the new magazines ran out, a final volley of grenades covered the commandos withdrawal as they faded back into the darkness. When they reached the van parked on a side street three blocks away, they quickly ducked inside to doff their camou uniforms and stow their weapons.

When the face paint came off, it was revealed that all the commandos were Oriental, except for their leader, who was a blond Caucasian.

"Your men did well, Kim," the Caucasian told his second-in-command. "You're ready to go out on your own now."

The Korean smiled thinly. "Thank you for all your help, Mr. Jones," he said. "We will have the rest of the money for you tomorrow, as we agreed."

"And I will have the ammunition you ordered ready for pickup at the same place."

Kim nodded. "Good."

Kim's grandparents and his brother's children had been victims of the massacre at the Korean Social Club, which had been hit by the Mexican gang. The attack on the church tonight hadn't avenged them, not by a long shot. Many more Mexicans would have to die before Kim would feel that his family's honor had been satisfied. To do that, he would need all the ammunition he could get for his new Russian assault rifles.

WHEN THE POLICE ARRIVED at the little Catholic church, all they found were the dead and dying and spent 5.45 mm AK-74 cartridge cases.

The black-haired bride was still alive, cradling her husband's bullet-ridden body in her arms. He had thrown himself in front of her and taken a full burst of AK rounds. Brushing the blood-soaked hair back from his forehead, she softly crooned a Mexican love song into his unhearing ears.

She looked up when the paramedics came to check him for vital signs. "Why?"

"I don't know," a medic told her. "I'm sorry."

She relinquished the body and smoothed her bloody wedding dress as she stood.

While the police interviewed the survivors, the phone in the little church rang. When the priest answered it, a muffled voice speaking accented English told him that the attack had been in revenge for the massacre at the Korean Social Club and promised more deaths.

Word of the phone call spread quickly. The bride's brother had only been wounded and, as the medics patched him up, he gathered the few survivors of the massacre around him. "We will have our revenge," Ramon del Castro vowed. "We will kill those fucking gooks and we will kill them dead."

"Mario—" the gang leader turned to one of his lieutenants "—do you still have the phone number of the gringo who offered to sell us those Russian guns?"

"Sure."

"Go out to my car and call him now. I want them as soon as possible. Pay him whatever he wants, but get them."

"Okay." Mario turned to go.

"And don't take no for an answer. I want those guns."

"I'll get them for you, man," Mario promised. "Don't worry."

THE MAN answered the phone on the first ring. "Smith here."

"Mr. Smith, this is Mario. You know, we talked about the Russian goods before." The voice spoke Mexican accented English.

"I remember you," Smith answered. "I take it you're now interested in what I have to offer."

"Right, man, we need to talk. Real soon."

Smith glanced at his wrist. "Will tomorrow morning at eight be soon enough?"

"Yeah, I'll meet you at the horse track parking lot."

Smith frowned. "Why don't I meet you at the cannery instead?"

"Hey, man, we're not trying to rip you off. We just want to deal."

"We'll deal, all right, but on my ground."

"Okay, man," Mario said. "Whatever you say. No problem."

Smith replaced the phone on its cradle and reached for his cellular phone on the bed. After switching the instrument over to the built-in scrambler, he quickly punched in a number. "We're a go tomorrow morning at eight," he said. "At the cannery in West Covina."

AT THE APPOINTED HOUR the next morning, Smith and his accomplice, Jones, waited at the abandoned cannery for their contact to show up. Both men were openly packing silenced MAC-10s so there wouldn't be any problems with the deal. They had arrived in two vehicles, one of them a van with blacked-out windows. The van was an older model, but its plates were current and all the lights and turn signals worked. As long as the vehicle was driven within the speed limit, the police would have no reason to stop it.

Mario was late, but Smith had come to expect this when dealing with his new customers. When you sold to street scum, you could hardly expect them to act like professionals. Smith had been in the gun business for years, but mostly he had dealt with revolutionary organizations from both sides of the political aisle. Selling to American street gangs was new to him, but the pay was right and he didn't care who his customers were.

When Mario finally arrived with three of his home boys, Smith walked to the rear of the van and opened the doors. Inside were four long wooden crates and five smaller ones, all bearing Cyrillic writing. Opening one of the long crates, he reached in and took out a brand-new, folding-stock AK-74 assault rifle. The weapon was clean and glistened with a light coat of gun oil. Snapping the stock open, he reached back into the crate and took out a curved ammunition magazine containing 30 rounds of 5.45 mm ammunition.

Snapping the magazine into place under the receiver of the AK, he pulled back on the charging handle to chamber a round. Flicking the safety up to the safe position, he handed the assault rifle to Mario. Jones moved back slightly to cover the gang banger with his MAC-10.

Mario took the AK, switched it down to full-auto and aimed it at the pile of rubbish against the back wall of the cannery. Leaning into it, he ripped off a short burst. Smiling broadly, he finished up the magazine.

"Remember," Smith told him, "when you need more ammunition, call me."

"How about those grenades, man?" Mario asked.

"We'll talk about that as soon as this shipment is paid off."

Mario motioned for one of his companions to come forward. The man had a battered briefcase in his hands. "Here's half of it," Mario said, handing the briefcase over. "We'll have the other half by the end of the week, like Ramon said."

Smith accepted the briefcase without counting the money. "Call me when he has it."

Smith and Jones watched Mario and his men drive off in the van. "That's another fifty of them out there." He smiled as he shook his head. "The stupid bastards."

"Who's next?" Jones asked.

"I need an order from one of the bigger black gangs, but they may require a little more prompting first."

Jones laughed. "What's the matter, can't they figure it out for themselves?"

"They're a little slow," Smith admitted. "But they've been killing each other for so long they don't understand that the last incident was different. We're going to have to leave a body behind for them to figure it out for themselves."

"Who are we going to use for it, the Koreans or the Vietnamese Red Cobras?"

"I think the Koreans again. There's so much bad blood between them already that it'll work both ways."

"When are we going to get the Chinese gangs involved?"

"I made a major contact yesterday and expect an order soon."

"Good. As soon as they're in, we can leave this fucking place." Jones was not impressed with L.A.

"San Diego will be just as bad, if not worse."

Jones shuddered. "Jesus."

THIS TIME, when Buckley arrived at the crime scene, he was mentally prepared. Bodies of young blacks were being carried out of the building. Others were being patched up by paramedics. The building had been a club organized by one of the local churches to try to keep the neighborhood teenagers out of the gangs. The fact that it had become a popular gang hangout instead was only a fact of life in East L.A.

Once more, the scene was of carnage, but not of complete savagery this time. Here the firefight must have gone both ways because there were survivors. Not many, it was true, but survivors nonetheless. The presence of empty cartridge cases littering the floor of the club showed that this time the targets had been able to fight back. That explained the survivors.

Buckley saw a paramedic working over the body of a man dressed in pants and a jacket printed in broad, jagged stripes of black, dark gray and light gray. It looked like a camouflage uniform, but not like any camouflage he had ever seen before. A military-style assault harness with ammo pouches, also in camouflage colors, was buckled around the man's waist. Beyond a fighting knife sheathed on the harness, though, he saw no other weapons.

He got close enough to see that the man was an Oriental, probably Korean.

Even though Buckley was not a native Angeleno, he knew the record of racial animosity between the Koreans and the blacks going all the way back to the so-called ''Rodney King Riots'' of 1992. They had been killing one another fairly regularly since then, but never had there been an incident like this. The killings had always been random acts before—during a liquor store holdup, or a shopkeeper wasting a thief. The recent spate of killings, though, was on a more massive scale, and displayed all the hallmarks of having been an organized extermination operation. If that was the case, an already shaky racial situation had taken a dramatic turn for the worse.

A race war between the black and white populations of Southern California had been predicted for years, by both blacks and whites. As far back as the Watts riots of 1968, threats and counterthreats of blood in the streets had been part and parcel of urban American minority politics. So far, though, the race war hadn't materialized. Regardless of what was preached and threatened by self-serving politicians and self-appointed minority leaders, the average American of any race was much too smart to get sucked into that dark hole of no return.

Now it looked as if that had changed, although it wasn't the long-expected black-white race war that had broken out. It was a war within the minority communities themselves, and that was even bigger news.

Making sure that his cameraman got good close-ups of the camouflaged corpse, Buckley did a voice-over raising the question of whether the long-awaited race war had finally begun. When the segment was edited and aired, it rated even higher than his first piece. Buckley had found his niche in the broadcasting business: covering race wars.

**3**

*Los Angeles*
*January 14*

By the third shooting incident, the FBI, the DEA, the ATF, the Civil Rights Enforcement Division of the Justice Department and every state agency anyone had ever heard of was on the scene in Los Angeles. Depending on which official spokesperson was on the airwaves, the attacks were being described variously as random violence, civil rights violations, racist group attacks, drug wars, gang shootings or organized crime. With the exception of Frank Buckley, no one was talking about a race war yet.

Self-appointed civil rights and minority group "leaders" flocked to Southern California in chartered aircraft, and no news broadcast went by without a new pontification from one or more of them. Some of them blamed a climate of institutional racism, some official government discrimination and others blamed poverty or drugs. Even though there had apparently been no white involvement so far, they all blamed bigotry on the part of the so-called majority population for the incidents. The fact that whites were a decided minority in L.A. county wasn't factored into their comments.

Hollywood actors and TV stars got in on the act, as well, getting free publicity by appearing at the sites of the latest killings. An aging acid-rock group even organized a "free" concert against racism, with donations accepted at the gate and the proceeds intended to "heal the wounds." Immediately after the concert, however, the band absconded with the till and departed for places unknown.

The killings were a PR man's dream come true, but nothing anyone said did anything to stop the killing. In fact, the killings only escalated. Every time the cops tried to stop the attacks by raiding known minority gang hangouts for weapons, the civil rights leaders went ballistic. It got to the point that representatives from the various groups were riding around in every patrol car to make sure that no one's civil rights were violated.

Despite those efforts, the killings continued.

AT THE OLD OAK DESK in the rear of his rare-book store in Huntsville, Alabama, Judson Rykoff slowly scrolled through the sales list of out-of-print books on his computer screen. Professor Ron Crawford of Montreal's Concordia University always presented him with interesting challenges. This time the good doctor wanted a mint copy of H. R. Robinson's *The Armor of Imperial Rome*. Unfortunately Robinson's 1975 classic tome was a hard item to find in any condition. It had been an expensive academic publication in its day and most of the copies had ended up in university libraries, where they had been thumbed half to death.

His only hope of finding a copy in the required condition was in England, where the book's original high price wouldn't have been an obstacle to the true aficionado of ancient arms and armor. And while there were few who met that condition in North America, Crawford was an exception. After purchasing a Sumerian bronze ax from a collector in Oregon several years ago, he had gone headfirst into the study of ancient arms and armor. Rykoff had benefited from this mania by chasing down obscure and rare works on the subject from all over the world to feed Crawford's ever- growing collection.

A signed first edition of Sir Richard Burton's 1884 work *The Book of the Sword* had been one of Rykoff's better scores for the professor. The Robinson book, although only twenty-five years out of print, was proving to be even more difficult than the Burton had been.

He was reaching the end of the list when the modem chimed to indicate that he had an incoming message. He quickly cleared the book list off his screen and downloaded the message. The man on the other end of the modem wanted an autographed first-edition copy of Hemingway's *Fifth Column* delivered to an address in Los Angeles no later than the day after tomorrow.

A slow grin spread over Rykoff's face. Hot damn! His shop was known to be a Mecca for Hemingway freaks, but this was no routine request for one of Papa's books. A request for an autographed first edition of *Fifth Column* was always a call for him to put his life on the line again to try to make the world a little better place for ordinary people to live.

When he wasn't selling rare books, the forty-two-year-old, ex-Special Forces major headed up a small group of like-minded individuals who had taken upon themselves the task of seeing that terrorists didn't stay in business very long. This was an unusual occupation for a man approaching middle age, but his other secret pastime was almost as strange. When not selling books or offing terrorists, Judson Rykoff wrote paperback thrillers under a pen name. Since he was in between books, he was ready for a little live action.

Crawford's book would just have to wait.

MELISSA BAO was in her darkroom developing prints for her own private portfolio. As was her custom when working in her darkroom, the petite Chinese American was stripped naked except for a small apron. It could get hot and stuffy in the small room and she didn't like getting the smell of the developing chemicals on her clothing.

The red light made the fresh scar running from her right shoulder blade to her waist look more prominent than it actually was. The plastic surgeon had done a good job of repairing the knife wound and promised that when it was completely healed there would only be a hairline scar left. Considering that it had been given to her by a woman intent on killing her, it was a small enough reminder to always watch her back, even in the ladies' room.

Snapping on the white light, she took off the apron and replaced it with a colorful silk wrap before stepping out into the hall. The modem was beeping when she walked into her studio. She downloaded the message and read that she was being offered an assignment to photograph the Chinese New Year celebrations in L.A. for *Insider Magazine*. Her flight had already been booked and a phone number was provided for a pickup at the airport.

She smiled when she realized that this was Jud's work, which meant that he needed her for another CAT Team mission. And the reference indicated that he wanted her to go undercover among the Chinese population of the city.

Though it had only been a couple of weeks since her last assignment with Rykoff, she was anxious to go to work with him again. That way she could continue her campaign to get closer to the mysterious leader of their secretive little band. The general chaos of the Millennium had made it too difficult for her to make her surprise visit to Huntsville over New Year's, as she had planned.

After printing out the message, she quickly dressed and started packing cameras and film in her travel bags. Her plane ticket would be waiting for her at

SeaTac and she would pick up whatever she needed to wear when she got to L.A. Her work for Rykoff always had a generous expense account attached.

JACOB MACLEOD was elbow deep in the crankcase of his vintage 1954 Panhead Harley-Davidson motorcycle. Though it was January and cool along the Gulf Coast of south Texas, sweat was rolling down his cheeks as the muscular black man tried for the tenth time to get the crankshaft bearings seated properly in the split crankcase of his Panhead's engine.

Lapping the cases on a Panhead engine was the most tedious and painstaking part of overhauling an early Harley. But it was also not something that could be hurried. Screw it up and you would have to buy two new crankcase halves, as well as a new crankshaft.

He was trial-fitting the bearings when the modem started signaling an incoming message. He tried to block out the sound, but failed. "This had better be fucking important," he growled to himself as he wiped his hands on a rag before reaching for the keyboard.

The message that appeared on his computer screen invited him to take part in a salvage diving operation off the coast of Santa Catalina Island. The operation was to try to recover a World War II Navy F4F Wildcat fighter that had been lost at sea during a carrier landing accident. The message went on to say that the fighter had been assigned to the famous Skulls Squadron.

The invitation to take part in the dive wasn't an unusual request. When Jake wasn't fixing ancient Harleys and riding with the local Harley bikers' club, he ran a scuba-diving school and charter boat service in Corpus Christi, Texas. The mention of the Skulls Squadron, however, was the giveaway that this wasn't a routine message. The bikers' club he rode with was also called the Skulls. Jud Rykoff had another mission on and needed the ex-SEAL in an undercover capacity.

Wiping his tools off, he quickly packed them and the disassembled engine away. The cases could wait for a few days, or even weeks, for that matter. Jud had a mission and he was ready to go.

ALEXANDER SENDAK slowly walked around his bonsai yet another time, his shears in his hand. Damn it anyway, he thought, squinting against the sun's glare coming through the picture window of his Rocky Mountain cabin. The strong light reflected off the snow was throwing him off his stride. This particular bonsai, a California bristlecone pine, had always been a bitch to work with. The trees were gnarled and twisted, and it was difficult enough to force them into an artistic shape without the extra irritation of the glare from outside.

"Alex?" Catherine called out from the kitchen. "Your modem's beeping."

"Okay, okay," he mumbled, carefully laying down the Japanese bonsai shears. The damned clippers had cost him a mint, but he had to agree that their samurai-sword-sharp blades cut without damaging the surrounding tissue or creating unsightly scars on the delicate limbs.

Downloading, he saw that he had a message from a sports-medicine surgeon in Los Angeles confirming his referral from his doctor in Huntsville, Alabama, to have his bad knee examined. He was to be at the clinic in two days for his appointment. He smiled as he typed out his confirmation of the message.

Sendak did have a bad knee as a result of a training accident in the Army. In fact, it had terminated his career as a Ranger sergeant assigned to the Army's elite Delta Force Blue Light antiterrorist unit several years ago. Now he ran a mountain-climbing school in the Rockies, skied and grew exotic plants in his spare time. Even though this was the height of the skiing season, he would take the time off to have his knee looked at. Particularly when the doctor would be Jud Rykoff.

When Catherine came out of the kitchen and saw the look on his face, she frowned. "It's the major again, isn't it?"

He simply nodded.

"But you just got back from Cuba," she said, trying hard to keep the note of disappointment from her voice. "And it's the middle of the season."

"I know," he said softly. "But you know he never calls unless it's important."

"When do you leave?"

"I have to be in L.A. the day after tomorrow."

She turned away and went back into the kitchen to check on her baking. She wasn't Sendak's wife and she had been told the ground rules before she made her decision to move in with him. Nonetheless, she couldn't help but wish that the major, whoever he was, would stay the hell out of her life and leave Alex alone, as well.

Every time he came back from one of his trips, he had more stories to tell about that Chinese woman he worked with, and Catherine was getting very tired of listening to them. Maybe it was time to reevaluate her commitment to this relationship. She loved the tall blond skier and mountain climber whose house and bed she shared, but she was tired of sharing him with his work.

She would give him this one last time and talk about it when he came back. For now, she knew his work was dangerous and knew better than to talk about it before he left.

ERIK ESTEVEZ unconsciously brushed his long dark brown hair away from his green eyes as he explained to the blond woman for the third time how a light plane's trim-tab controls worked. Unfortunately she was a little too dim-witted to comprehend trim tabs, and her costume of short shorts split all the way up to the waistband and a minuscule halter top wasn't helping him explain them clearly, either. There was no way she could have been wearing any panties under those shorts, and her semihard nipples were almost poking through the thin fabric of her halter top.

"But," she said, a hint of whine in her voice, "I don't see how a little thing like that can make this big old plane go up and down."

Estevez had the urge to tell her that lots of little things made big things go up and down all the time—he was looking at two of them right now. But he suppressed that urge. Sometimes playing flight instructor raised hell with his gonads and this was one of those times. Maybe he should simply bag it for the day and invite her to dinner and a few drinks at his place. The problem was that if he did that she'd want a discount on her lessons after going to bed with him and he really needed the money right now.

As always, though, he took the easy way out. He could always pick up a few extra bucks by doubling up on his charter-flight schedule. He had been sleeping alone since he got back from Cuba two weeks ago, and the scent of her body was getting to him big time.

"Look," he said. "I know airplane controls can be a little complicated, but I have an idea. Why don't I try to explain it over a couple of fajitas and a pitcher of margaritas? I know this great little place not too far from here that does the greatest margaritas north of Mazatlán."

The blonde looked at him and smiled. "That would be fun, Mr. Estevez. I just love margaritas."

I'll just bet you do, he thought. "Call me Erik," he said, with an answering smile. "Please."

On the way into his office to shut down for the day, he saw that the incoming message light on his modem was blinking. Choosing to ignore it, he was reaching for the off switch when the woman saw it, too. "You'd better check your message," she said.

"Oh, yeah."

Downloading, he saw that someone wanted to charter a flight to L.A. the day after tomorrow. He also wanted to rent the plane for an indefinite time.

Damn it anyway! Even though he would lose a bill-paying customer, he didn't want to go out of town. Then he reread the message and saw the code word Custer at the end of it—and knew what it meant. Rykoff had something going down in California and he needed a pilot. He smiled broadly. He still had tonight with the blonde, and if he handled it right she'd be waiting for him when he got back.

**4**

*Washington, D.C.*
*January 14*

In a small, solitary second-floor office in the outer ring of the Pentagon, a man worked at the keyboard of the computer parked in the middle of his cluttered desk. Winston Steadman was forty-four, and his dull brown hair, slight build and conservative attire left him indistinguishable from thousands of similar bureaucrats in D.C. But the small second-floor Defense Procurement Agency office was deceiving.

In addition to making sure that shrinking defense budget dollars were being spent wisely, he was doing what he could to make life a little safer for Americans around the world. It was his job to see that terrorists who preyed upon Americans were themselves terrorized.

Even though the years since the end of the Cold War had proven to be more secure as far as a World War III nuclear holocaust was concerned, they had not been peaceful years. In fact, if one was to go by body count alone, the decade of the nineties had been the most deadly since the height of the Vietnam War. The last half of the nineties had been particularly bloody, when violent international terrorism reemerged as a political option.

As had been the case in the seventies and eighties, Americans were again targeted by terrorists. The U.S. Army's Delta Force and the Navy's SEAL Team Six were still viewed as the nation's premier counterterrorist agencies, but they were on such a short leash—compared to the Regan and Bush years—that a crisis of major proportions was required before they could be sent into action.

Incidents classed as "minor" resulted in American citizens being killed or maimed from time to time, but most of these acts against individuals went unpunished.

But a few men from major American government agencies—the State Department, Department of Defense, Department of Justice, FBI and CIA—felt that not responding to these incidents sent the terrorists the wrong message. So these men decided to jointly create a clandestine action agency distinct from the official United States government. A small group of carefully selected people in deep cover, known as the CAT Team—Clandestine Anti-Terrorist Team—was assembled and trained.

Whenever a terrorist attack against Americans was not addressed by official action, it would not go unanswered: the CAT Team would see to that.

In Los Angeles, however, the terrorists were homegrown. Already the media was trumpeting that the long-awaited race war was at last upon the United States. So-called minority group leaders of every color were demanding that the federal government step in to halt the violence and punish those responsible for the killings. But, as was always the case in these incidents, every group wanted to be exempt, with only the others being punished.

Some civil rights leaders threatened that America's cities would burn to the ground unless their demands were met. When their demands weren't for extralegal personal power of some sort, then they wanted federal money to distribute as they saw fit.

Against this background, the federal and state agencies were hampered to the point that no progress was being made toward putting an end to the L.A. terrorism. It was time to see if the CAT Team could discover the cause of this latest wave of seemingly mindless violence and get it stopped.

Running his hand through his hair, Steadman leaned back in his chair and shut off his modem. He had received an acknowledgment from all five members of the CAT Team and now he could finally go home for the night. Though what he would do when he got there, he didn't know. He knew he wouldn't be able to relax until Rykoff and his team hit L.A. and went into operation. But he also knew that it would look strange if he stayed in his office for the next two days. Functionaries in the Defense Procurement Agency just didn't do things like that.

Winston Steadman's job was the perfect cover for the man who single-handedly ran a counterterrorist team that didn't exist in anyone's phone book. Not only was he the CAT Team's operations officer and mission controller, he was the entire support element and headquarters staff.

His position within the Defense Procurement Agency allowed him to supply the team with the latest in high-tech weapons and equipment for their missions—direct from military stocks, no questions asked. His like-minded associates in the FBI and CIA provided the CAT Team with the most complete intelligence information the nation could provide.

Jud Rykoff was the only team member Steadman had ever met, and that was only once early on. Since then, their contact had been via modem. But that was the one of the strengths of the Team. He only got together with them electronically, which was also true for each of the active team members, who only met at the site of their missions. This way their deep cover would never be compromised by someone being seen with someone they shouldn't know.

The Team's greatest strength was that it didn't exist anywhere on paper. Since it drew no government funds, not even the Senate Select Committee on Intelligence Operations could uncover its activities. Further, the team members all had legitimate civilian jobs that could stand up to any scrutiny.

On his way through the door, as he adjusted his coat and scarf, his eyes went to the vintage print of Custer's Last Stand—a gift from Jud Rykoff that was a private joke between the two men. Rykoff and his small team were Custer and his cavalrymen, while the Indians circling them were the terrorists they fought against.

All too many times the painting reflected the grim reality of CAT Team operations, particularly this one. The forces of barbarism were loose in L.A. with a vengeance, and it looked like Rykoff and his small team would be severely outnumbered. And this time they would also have to keep out of the way of the state and federal authorities.

One of the problems with the team working inside the United States was that because of their deep cover, he could not protect them from law-enforcement agencies, either state or federal. To even try to do so would blow their covers. This time in particular they would have to be careful. Every federal cop in the western states was in L.A., to say nothing of the state and local police.

THE LEAD STORY on the six o'clock news featured Frank Buckley from the L.A. war zone again. A Hispanic gang had attacked a block of Korean business establishments in broad daylight earlier that afternoon. Roaring up in low-riders and pickups, two dozen men had jumped out, AK-74s blazing in their hands. What should have been a surprise attack, however, had been turned into a rout.

Each of the Korean businesses in that block had an armed guard from the powerful Korean Businessmen's Association security force, and a major firefight broke out immediately. Traffic along the busy street fronting the block came to a standstill as bullets swept the street as if it was a free-fire zone.

When the first police car arrived, it got caught in the cross fire and one of the officers died. The other one was seriously wounded, but not before she was able to put out a call for help. Before police reinforcements could arrive, however, the gang raiders fled in their vehicles.

The minority group spokesman on the news broadcast that night was a Mr. John Kim from the Korean Businessmen's Association. "Yes, we were expecting trouble." The American-born Kim answered Buckley's question as if the reporter was mentally retarded. "You would have to be brain-dead to live in L.A. right now and not know that there is a race war going on."

Kim turned slightly to face the camera directly. "And, since the authorities are obviously not able to protect the Korean-American community—" he shrugged expressively "—we have no other recourse but to protect ourselves. We are not going to roll over and die."

"But isn't that vigilantism?" Buckley asked.

"No," Kim said bluntly. "Vigilantism is when a group of people goes after their enemies in violation of the law. We are simply protecting ourselves, which is permitted by the American Constitution."

"Juan Gonzalez from the United Hispanic Task Force for Racial Equality and Justice has said that if paranoid Korean businessmen weren't armed to the teeth, none of this would have happened."

When Kim didn't answer, Buckley put the microphone in his face. "Do you have any reply to that?"

"Tell him to fuck himself," the Korean snapped. "His people may have started this war, but we're going to finish it."

Kim's response was bleeped when it was aired. But since he was facing directly into the camera and enunciated clearly, it didn't take a lip-reader to know what he said.

"TURN THAT GARBAGE OFF," Ramon del Castro growled. Since he'd been turned back that afternoon by the Korean security guards, the gang leader had been sulking in front of his TV set. Not even his favorite game show improved his mood.

"I'm gonna get that fuckin' gook," he muttered half to himself. "I swear by the Virgin I am."

He turned to Mario, who had taken a grazing wound in the firefight and was not happy about it. "What did that gringo say about the grenades he promised me?"

"He said that we had to pay off the first shipment before he'd talk to me about them."

"I'll get him his fucking money," Ramon snapped, "but I want those grenades. I also want you to ask him about some of those rocket launcher things. You know, the ones you always see in the movies."

"He didn't say anything about having them."

"Ask him anyway!"

"Okay."

**5**

*Burbank Airport*
*January 16*

Jud Rykoff waited in the California sun, or what little of it got through the brown smog cover, watching Erik Estevez taxi his plane into its parking spot. The pilot was the last of the team to arrive and now they could start preparing to deal with the situation in L.A.

Rykoff was dressed for January in California in a tan, military-cut safari jacket with an ascot at the neck, tan cargo pocket pants, cowboy boots and aviator sunglasses. The military look was coming back into fashion and he had always enjoyed wearing uniforms. Though he wasn't about to get his hair cut GI short to be even more in fashion. He'd had quite enough of short haircuts, thank you, during his time in the Army.

Nonetheless, he was feeling rather militant today, and the clothes fit his trim six-foot-one frame well, serving to reinforce the attitude. As much as he liked his quiet, bookish life back in Huntsville, the ex-Special Forces major was glad to be in action again.

Rykoff's involvement with the CAT Team went beyond a love of danger, though. His main reason for putting his life on the line was simple: he was a civilized man who believed that civilization needed protection from the barbarous elements in its midst.

During Operation Desert Storm and its aftermath in the Middle East, he had thought he had seen enough killing and destruction to last him a lifetime. When it was over, he resigned from the Army and sought to live the quiet life with a wife and a civilized occupation. He tried hard to make it work for him, but learned that the warrior within him had remained, unchanged and untamed.

When he was honest with himself, he realized that he never felt as alive as he did when he was on a dangerous mission. If Steadman hadn't approached him to form the CAT Team, he would probably have signed on somewhere as a mercenary.

He had no idea what he would do when he became too old to live the life of a warrior. But until that time came, he would wait for his modem to beep, calling him to another CAT Team mission.

"SORRY I'M LATE, BOSS," Estevez said as soon as his feet hit the tarmac. "Something came up at the last minute."

Rykoff raised an eyebrow, but didn't comment. Working with the CAT Team was purely voluntary, and any of them could walk away from it any time they wanted. Considering what he sometimes asked them to do, he was surprised that they were all still with him.

"They're all waiting for you, so we'd better get going."

Grabbing his bag, Estevez hurried after Rykoff. He hated being the last one to arrive at the party. Fortunately, it was a short ride to the hotel suite Rykoff had taken for their command post. Though it had been only a couple of weeks since they had all been together in Havana, Estevez felt that he hadn't seen the others in months. There was something about being together again that made this schizoid life worthwhile.

"Hi guys," he called out, smiling broadly when he walked in.

"We couldn't get our ass out of bed in time," Bao said with a smirk. "Is that it, Erik?"

He grimaced. "It's good to see you too, Mel."

"Don't mind her," Sendak said, sticking out his hand. "I'm glad to see you. I need that twenty you owe me."

MacLeod was deep into one of his electronic gadgets and just waved a greeting.

"Now that Erik's here," Rykoff said as he poured himself a cup of coffee from the brunch tray, "we need to get started. Here's the situation. For those of you who haven't been staying up to watch CNN, a major interracial war has broken out here and it's threatening to spread all up and down the coast. Right now the body count is about sixty men, women and children, and it's growing every day. So far, the combat is within the minority communities and hasn't yet spread to the white sector, nor have the warring factions taken on the cops at this point.

"In fact, this whole thing looks a lot like what was going on in Bosnia, Serbia and Croatia a few years ago. The Asians, Hispanics and blacks are fighting a three-way private war as if they're going for their own version of ethnic cleansing."

He picked up a file on the table behind him and handed it to Sendak. "Police raids on known gang hangouts have turned up caches of brand-new infantry small arms, up to and including RPG antitank rocket launchers. According to the markings on both the weapons and ammunition, the stuff was all made in the old Soviet Arms Factory Number 397, which just happens to be in the Republic of the Ukraine right now."

"What in the hell are the Ukrainians doing promoting urban warfare in California?" Estevez asked. "That doesn't make much sense to me."

"My intelligence says that they're not," Rykoff answered. "They're just selling the weapons for hard cash like they've been doing all over the world for the last five or six years now. They don't care how they're used after they've been paid for.

"The usual cast of federal agents and state police forces have not been able to find out how these weapons are getting into the country, who is paying for them or how they're being distributed. Our job is to track these weapons down and see that they're brought under control."

He turned to Bao, who was finishing off the last croissant. "Mel, you're going into the Chinese community as a photographer again. Once you make contact, I want you to express outrage at what's going on and volunteer to help out in any way you can. I know how the Asian gangs work. I know they're very secretive and don't have much use for women. But I'm hoping that your family name and Seattle reputation will get you inside quickly. Once you're inside, try to find out where those damned weapons are coming from."

Bao nodded. It was a simple mission order and one that she had performed well over a dozen times in the past, both with the Seattle PD narc squad and with the Team. Even though she wasn't targeted against the gangs themselves, she still ran a risk.

Rykoff caught Estevez's eye next. "Erik, the same goes for you. I want you to go back to the East L.A. 'hood and hang out. Maybe even flash a little cash to establish yourself, but steer clear of anything except the weapons. If you find a ton of crack or tar sitting in a warehouse somewhere, call the cops, but don't go looking for it. I know you like to pop drug maggots, but this isn't a drug operation. We're trying to stop a war instead."

Estevez had a hard-on against drug scum, but he could put it aside this time. That didn't mean, however, that he couldn't take notes on any drug action he came across and pass the information on to someone who could make good use of it. He still had contacts in the DEA who wouldn't ask too many questions.

Rykoff turned to MacLeod. "Jake, you're going in with your alter ego persona of bad-ass biker again. It's getting a little thin, I know. But since the average black gang banger is younger than his Hispanic or Asian counterpart, I can't send you in as a potential recruit. You walk the walk and talk the talk, though, and should be able to get an inside line before too long."

MacLeod had figured this was coming and had brought his metal along—a collection of solid gold rings, bracelets and necklaces that would establish him as a bad-ass black biker on the wrong side of the law. "I'll need to rent a hog," he said.

Rykoff handed him a business card. "Give this guy a call. He's expecting you."

Rykoff took a long drink of his cold coffee before continuing. "Every one of you make sure you stay away from the cops. The place is crawling with all kinds of cops—Fed, state and local—so be careful, real careful. If you get busted, I may not be able to bail you out for a while.

"Alex and I will be setting up our command post and comm center here. To keep it simple, we'll be doing everything over the phone this time, though I want each of you to carry one of Jake's personal locators. We'll have a modem and fax, as well as police scanners and all the rest of Jake's gadgets. Feed us anything you get as soon as you can, but make sure to check in at least once a day.''

Rykoff's eyes swept the room. "Any questions?"

"Why are we getting involved with this anyway?" Estevez asked. "Not that I mind, but this is supposed to be FBI, ATF and DEA stuff. We're supposed to go after terrorists, aren't we?"

"There are two answers," Rykoff stated. "The first is that, as far as I am concerned, this is a counterterrorist mission. Whoever is arming these people is killing innocent Americans the same as if he was using a car bomb. This time, though, he's simply getting others to do the killing for him. Secondly, as you know only too well, we can do things even the Feds can't get away with."

Rykoff went on to explain. "There's been a massive media invasion and an L.A. cop can't even pull a minority over for speeding without a network camera being on him and a civil rights leader screaming discrimination. Because of the massive publicity, the official agencies are hampered to the point that they can't gain any ground. When they do get a tip about an arms cache, they have to fight to get a search warrant and get permission from the civil rights commission to conduct the raid. Then, when they can finally hit the location, the media people are there waiting for them, but the guns are gone."

Rykoff's eyes swept over his team. "Their hands may be tied, but ours aren't. Once we find out who's behind these arms shipments, we're going to go after him big time. We're going to get him, get his operatives and anyone else who's working for him. We'll get his guns and then get rid of all of them at the same time. Someone has to get this shit stopped, and this time we drew the mission."

Under normal circumstances, five would be a small number of people to take on an assignment of this nature. But the team's small size had been determined by the need for absolute security. Also, their capabilities in the field were far greater than their numbers alone would indicate. This was a case where the total was far greater than the sum of the parts. There were only five of them, true. But working together, they were the most dangerous five people Rykoff had ever known.

Each one of them brought a particular deadly skill set to the team. Rykoff, Sendak and MacLeod were all products of elite-unit military training. Estevez and Bao had both worked with top law-enforcement agencies against the drug trade. With the exception of Mel Bao, they were all seasoned combat veterans. But she was no cupcake. She had cut her teeth on the combat arts and had fought her way out of more than one scrape during her drug-busting days.

Rykoff reached over to the table and picked up three manila envelopes. "I've got background packets on each of the three major minority groups involved in the fighting. You'll find FBI, DEA, ATF and state agency intelligence reports. Read these over before you go, and I'll update them for you when you phone in.

"Alex has the mission pack with the hardware and expense money. He's also got phone calling cards, plastic money and anything else you think you might need while we're here."

"How about a change of clothes," Bao said. "I didn't bring anything appropriate to wear in Chinatown."

"You're not going to wear your tiny Cuban bikini this time?" Alex grinned broadly. "I rather liked that outfit on you, myself."

She glanced out of the corners of her dark eyes. "Eat your heart out, Sendak. We're not on vacation this time. I've got to go into the Chinese community looking like my father's honorable daughter, not some shameless American hussy."

Sendak grinned. "It's a good thing there weren't any Chinese in Havana. Or I'd have missed the show."

"You can use the plastic to get anything you need," Rykoff interrupted. "Our account is fat this time."

Bao smiled. "Great. I need a new pearl necklace."

"Mission-related stuff only," Rykoff growled.

"But the pearls make the outfit and establish me as a woman of substance."

Rykoff shook his head wearily. Outfitting the men was easy compared to putting together Bao's kit. Until the Cuban operation, he hadn't known how much a few square inches of thin fabric sewn into a bikini could cost. "Okay, but only one string."

"I could use a new pair of cowboy boots," Erik said with a grin.

Rykoff ignored him. "Okay, I want to wrap this up and get you guys out into the field."

"I guess I don't get new boots," Estevez said as he got to his feet. "Bummer, man."

**6**

*Los Angeles*
*January 17*

Waiting on the crowded sidewalk for the dragon procession to come by, her cameras at the ready, Melissa Bao felt herself transported back to the streets of the Seattle of her childhood. In fact, it had been selling snapshots of the Chinese New Year celebrations to the Seattle-area newspapers that had gotten her started as a professional photographer.

She had grown to know Seattle's large Asian community even better after she joined the narcotics division of the Seattle Police Department as an undercover drug agent. That was when she had learned that not all people of Asian ancestry were her friends. That experience had also taught her that she couldn't depend on all the people she worked with to be as professional about their work as she was. The lure of drug money was a difficult one to resist, even for a narcotics cop.

A big bust she had worked for months to set up had been blown because one of the narcs had gone bad. In the resulting shootout, she had taken a round in the side that had put her in the hospital for several weeks. When she got out of the hospital, she resigned from the police force and took the settlement money to start her own photography business.

She had struggled that first year in business, and then she had met Judson Rykoff. She still remembered vividly the afternoon that he had walked into her little shop and her life. She had been behind the counter when a tall, fortyish man, good-looking in a rugged way, walked into her shop. To her surprise, he greeted her in Chinese. *"Ni Hao,"* he said, smiling.

"You speak Chinese?" she asked in surprise.

"Not really," he admitted. "It's just that I used to work with a Nung Chinese when I was in the Army."

That set off an alarm bell in Mel's mind. "How did you know I was a Nung?"

"Your father is Houng Van Bao and your family escaped to the States after Vietnam fell," he stated. "You grew up here after moving up from California. Upon graduating from high school, you joined the Seattle PD and did a couple of years in the narc squad. A drug bust went bad because of a bent badge and you picked up a bullet in the side. When you got out of the hospital, you took a cash settlement and opened this shop. So far, you haven't done too badly, but it's always tough to start up a small business. Particularly when there's so much crime on the streets."

Rykoff's face turned serious. "I also know how deeply you feel about stopping crime so the innocent can live their lives in peace. I represent a small group of people who feel as you do about criminals who prey on the innocent and I would like you to consider joining us.''

He then launched into an explanation of why the CAT Team was being formed and what their mission would be. When he was done, he held out his card. "You'll find a number on the back to call if you want to check on me. Better yet, have your father call. He'll know the man on the other end of the phone."

She took his card and promised to call him back after she thought about what he had said. That night, she went to her father's house and had a long talk with him before he made the phone call. As Rykoff had said, he knew the man he talked to and knew him well. Even so, he didn't want her to get involved because of the danger, and Mel agreed with him. But the appeal of Rykoff's proposal wouldn't go away, and then there was the special history of her family.

She had been only a small child when her Nung Chinese parents fled the communist conquest of South Vietnam in 1975. Both her father and mother came from Nung warrior families and had served with the U.S. Special Forces CIDG units during the long war. Also, both of them had close association with the Americans, and neither of them would have survived imprisonment.

After thinking it over for several days, she decided that if she had a chance to give something back to the country that had given the family so much, she should do it.

She talked to her father again and, getting his blessing, she called Rykoff the next day and her life hadn't been the same since.

Not that her life had been calm up to then. The family eventually had settled north of Seattle, Washington. There her father organized the resistance to a local Vietnamese gang who terrorized their community. But there was a price to pay. Mel Bao was twelve when she was kidnapped by the gang leader. After her father rescued her, getting wounded in the process, he started teaching his daughter to be a Nung warrior.

She was a willing and talented student of the warrior's arts with a positive talent with cold steel weapons. And from her mother, she learned to use her femininity as a weapon, both in the direct and indirect mode.

She proved to be as good a student of the feminine arts as she was at those of the warrior, and her body soon became her favorite weapon of choice. Guns could run out of ammunition or jam, and knives could break, but she always had her body. This time, though, she didn't think that she would have much need for that part of her arsenal.

Having a camera bag over her shoulder and a Nikon in her hand had always been enough to get her into most places she wanted to go. She knew that being a woman also helped, but it was the camera that did it every time. People were crazy about having their picture taken. If her Nikon were a weapon, she could be the world's most successful assassin. As it was, she was able to make a legitimate income from her photos.

STANDING ON THE Chinatown street corner next to Mel were two young Chinese men. Both were well dressed in casual clothes—rather than the baggy black pants, jacket and white shirt uniform of most Asian gangs—and they smoked while they watched the parade pass by. For most Oriental men, smoking was not the capital offense it had become in Caucasian California society.

In her role as a proper Chinese woman, she took no notice of them. But when one of them made a comment about her body, she spun on him. "You do not talk that way about the daughter of Houng Van Bao," she snapped back in Chinese.

The man smirked and slowly looked her up and down. "Just who do you think you are, missy, the Queen of Chinatown?"

Mel didn't show too much leg as she side-kicked the guy in the crotch. He fell to the sidewalk clutching his family jewels and moaning softly.

"A thousand apologies, Miss Bao," the other man said, stepping between them. "I am Dan Quan. My friend was impertinent and did not know who he was talking to, but I do." He bowed his head slightly. "I am honored to meet the honorable daughter of such an illustrious man."

"Your friend's manners do not say much for his upbringing," she snapped, without bowing back. "In Seattle, the Han have better manners than that."

Quan motioned behind his back and the man on the ground scrambled to disappear. "Again, I apologize for my ill-mannered friend. May I buy you a cup of tea to show you my sincerity?"

When she hesitated to accept, he continued. "My family owns a small tea shop up the street and my grandmother would be honored to meet one of the Bao women."

"I could use a cup of hot tea," she admitted.

Quan's family tea shop was not small, as he had stated. In fact, it was not a tea shop at all, but a large restaurant that looked prosperous. At this time of the afternoon, most of the patrons were Chinese, but she saw that the posted menu was written in English, Spanish and Vietnamese, as well as Chinese. To make it in the L.A. restaurant business, it helped to appeal to a broad clientele.

Quan's grandmother was honored to meet Bao, who bowed deeply to show her deference to the woman's age. After passing pleasantries, Quan led Bao to a table in a semiprivate room in the back of the restaurant. In the rear of the room, three men sat at a corner table minding their own business, smoking and drinking beer. They were speaking in normal tones, but Mel didn't want to seem to be listening to them. These men were wearing the black pants and white shirts favored by Chinese gang members. If this was a gang hangout, she had really lucked out.

"This is a nice place your family has here."

"My grandfather started a tea shop on this corner right after World War II," he said proudly. "And my father later built this humble establishment when I was still a child. He has retired from the day-to-day business, and I run it for him now. Does your honored father prosper in Seattle?"

"He is well," she answered. "He has a landscaping business now with many young Han working for him."

"I am happy to hear that." Now that they had talked about their respective families, he could ask her about herself. "What has brought you to our city?"

"I'm here on a photography assignment, covering the Chinese New Year celebration," she said, glancing down to her camera bag. "I'm a free-lance photographer and do work like this for travel magazines."

When the tea came, they made small talk and she admitted to having been a little apprehensive about all the reports of ethnic violence she had heard about. "But there seems to be none here," she said.

"We have been fortunate, so far," Quan said. "If our joss is good, the trouble will pass us by. I burn extra joss sticks every day to protect us."

Draining the last of her tea, she put the cup down and glanced at her watch. "Thank you for the tea, but I have to be going," she said. "I still need to find a hotel."

"My cousin runs a nice little hotel at the end of the block," he offered. "It's small, but it's clean and he doesn't allow any funny business to go on there, if you know what I mean."

She smiled. "Thank you. It sounds like just what I need."

He pushed back his chair and stood up. "I'll take you there and see that you get a good room."

"Thank you."

AFTER CHECKING IN, Bao went back out on the streets to take more pictures. When she was done, she returned to the Quan family restaurant that evening for a late dinner.

"I am honored that you have returned to our humble restaurant," Dan Quan said in his role as maître d'. "May I show you to a table."

"Nothing fancy," she said, looking around as if she didn't want to be seen in the public rooms.

"I have just the place," he said, reaching for a menu.

Quan led her to the same semiprivate room off of the main dining room where she had eaten lunch. "This is for our special customers," he said as he pulled out her chair. "And you are a special customer."

"Thank you," she said with a smile as she took her seat.

Only one other table in the room was occupied. As before, three men sat there drinking beer, but they were not the three she had seen earlier. They looked for all the world like a security detachment keeping an eye on the restaurant. She ignored them as she ordered her meal; the honorable daughter of Bao would do no other.

"Who's the skirt," one of the men asked in Chinese when Quan walked by to go back to his station.

Quan looked startled by the question. "She's the daughter of the Houng Van Bao family in Seattle," he answered quickly. "And please keep your voice down, elder brother, she speaks our honorable language."

"Is she the one who kicked Pao in the eggs today?" one of the other men asked with a laugh. "I heard about that."

Quan nodded.

"I've told him more than once not to accost strange women on the street."

"So have I," Quan said sternly. "And he will be punished for that little stunt. I will not have common gangsters connected with my family."

"Is her father the Bao who took out that Vietnamese gang in Seattle several years ago?" the other man asked.

Quan nodded.

"I've heard that he trained her in the martial arts because he had no son."

"I can believe that," Quan said. "She took Pao out with the cleanest kick I have ever seen. She didn't even raise her skirt to do it."

WHEN SHE FINISHED her dinner, Bao left the restaurant. Outside the door, she stopped for a moment and considered her next move. In keeping with her persona, she should go back to her hotel, but L.A.'s Chinatown was alive and she decided to take a walk through it. She also wanted to check in with Rykoff from a pay phone to let him know that she had found an operating base.

There were no signs of racial tension in this neighborhood. But that was because the trouble so far had been confined to the Korean and Vietnamese communities. If Rykoff was right, though, it wouldn't be long before the Ukrainian AKs would be spilling blood here, too. She had to get established before the shooting started, and it was beginning to look like Quan would be her man.

**7**

*Los Angeles
January 17*

Jake MacLeod switched off the engine of his rented Harley and put down the kickstand. This was the fourth place he'd stopped at today, but maybe he'd get lucky this time. Drinking cheap beer in grubby gang hangouts wasn't exactly his favorite way to pass time, but it was the only way he was going to get a lead on who was selling the weapons.

Jake tugged at his battered leather jacket with the Skulls' colors on the back as he walked to the door of the bar. While he usually enjoyed playing the "bad-ass black biker," this time he didn't. The current situation was too serious for role-playing. Someone was promoting a race war in L.A. and the people doing the shooting didn't even know that they were being used for someone else's purpose. But what that purpose was, he didn't have the slightest idea, and he wouldn't know until someone got a handle on who was peddling the guns.

Walking through the bar's door, he paused for a moment to allow his eyes to adjust to the dim light.

When he could see again, he headed for the bar at the back of the room, ignoring the few men seated around the tables.

"Beer," he growled as he slid onto a bar stool.

"You ain't from around here," the bartender said, stating the obvious.

"No shit."

Taking that as his cue to keep his mouth shut, the barkeep poured a draft and set it in front of MacLeod. Halfway through the beer, a man got up from one of the tables in the front of the room and walked back to the bar. "You looking for something?" he asked MacLeod.

Jake put his beer down and turned to face his visitor. "If I am, you don't look like you have it."

The man went into his rap. "I got a lotta stuff," he said with a gap-toothed grin. "I got all kind of pills, I got bo, I got hubba, I got—"

"I don't need any of it," Jake cut him off abruptly. "I don't do that shit."

The dealer looked completely confused. "What do you want then, man?"

"I want some iron, heavy iron."

"I don't deal in *that* shit, man." The drug dealer looked offended. "Guns are bad business."

"Then you can't help me," Jake said, turning back to his beer.

"But I know a brother who can."

Jake looked over his shoulder. "Who's that?"

The drug dealer glanced covertly around the room. "There's this brother, you know, and he moves a lot of iron. Let me see now, what's his name?"

Jake reached into his pocket and drew out a roll of bills. Digging into them, he pulled out a wrinkled hundred-dollar bill and handed it over.

"What are you looking for?" the drug dealer asked after he pocketed the bill.

"Blasters, Russian blasters, like everyone else in town is using right now."

"How do you know about the Russian guns?"

"I read the fucking papers," Jake snapped.

It was true that the significant fact that all the warring factions seemed to be equipped with the same Russian-designed weapons had finally hit the media. That new guy on CNN had had enough smarts to pick up empty cartridge cases from the crime scenes and compare them. Considering the intelligence of the average TV reporter, in MacLeod's opinion that alone would be sure to win him a Pulitzer this year.

"Let me make a phone call," the dealer said.

MacLeod continued drinking his beer while the man made his call. When he came back, the drug dealer was smiling. "I set up a meeting for you," he said. "There's an old garage not too far from here. They'll be waiting for you and ready to deal."

Jake knew that it couldn't be this easy. If it were, the Feds would have cracked this case weeks ago and the CAT Team wouldn't be involved. The FBI and ATF had their own black undercover agents and had probably gone through this same routine already. Maybe even at this bar. Nonetheless, even though he figured he was being set up, he had to go through with it on the off chance that he could work a connection out of it.

"If they ain't, man," he warned the dealer. "I'll be back here talking to you."

"No problem man," the dealer said. "It's cool."

"It'd better be."

WHEN MACLEOD DROVE the Harley into the garage, he saw half a dozen young blacks waiting for him. The leader of this pack was in his late twenties. The rest of his gang bangers were younger, some not too far into their teens yet. In many ways, it was the makeup of a typical black gang. All of them were armed, though, and wearing green bandannas on their heads, but none were packing AKs, so this had to be a setup.

"Who the fuck are you?" the chief punk sneered as soon as Jake turned off the Harley.

"I'm Big Jake of the Skulls," he answered as he put down the kickstand and slid out of the saddle, keeping both of his hands in sight.

The gang leader took in Jake's biker colors with a sneer on his face. "You don't look like shit to me." He turned his head to see if his followers had properly appreciated his sharp wit.

Even though this wasn't the best time or place to start something, Jake couldn't let the comment go. Not in a situation where the only thing he had going for him was intimidation and the ability to deliver it on target. He had to keep them off-balance if he wanted to walk away from this.

"Maybe that's 'cause you're such a scumbag your eyes are full of shit," Jake sneered.

"You don't dis me," the gang leader screamed, bringing his piece up. "You don't never dis me. I'm the—"

The toe of MacLeod's boot abruptly cut off the man's tirade of self-importance when it landed in his crotch with stunning force. When the punk reflexively bent over to clutch his genitals with both hands, MacLeod jerked him to his feet and spun him around to clutch him to his chest as a shield. Locking his left arm around the punk's neck, he drew his 10 mm Glock pistol with his right.

"Where I come from, scumbag," he hissed in his ear as he rammed the Glock against the back of his neck, "you only get respect from me when you earn it. You didn't earn it so I can do anything to you I want. Like maybe blow your fucking head off."

The gang bangers had been taken by surprise at the swiftness of Jake's attack. They were used to being feared, but now they faced a man without fear and were on the short end of the stick. No one had ever dared to do anything like this to them before. There was only one of him, but even with their guns, none of them wanted to see if this biker was as bad as he looked.

"Who's the second-in-command around here?" MacLeod barked.

A heavy kid with a shaved head under his bandanna looked around before answering, "Me."

"What's your name?"

"Cue Ball."

"Your real name, asshole."

"Lavonn Johnson."

"Okay, Lavonn Johnson, here's the story. You and your home boys are going to drop your pieces and get the fuck outta here while you still can. When you get back to the 'hood, you're going to ask around and find out what happens to anyone who tries to rip off the Skulls. Then you're going to take off all that gang shit you're wearing and get off the streets. If I see any one of you in that shit again, I'm going to put you down hard—so hard that your mamas are going to cry about it for a year."

MacLeod's eyes looked hard at each one of them. "You got any questions?"

"Whatcha gonna do with Red Dog?" Lavonn ventured to ask.

"He dissed me," MacLeod growled. "And nobody disses a Skull and lives to shoot off his fucking mouth about it. If he doesn't apologize real nice, I'm going to tear his fuckin' head off and piss down the hole."

The gang bangers shrank back and glanced around for escape routes. The image of Big Jake tearing a man's head off with his bare hands and urinating on what was left of his neck was all too believable.

"Book!" Jake roared. "Get outta here!"

The gang bangers dropped their guns and fled as fast as they could run.

When the last one had cleared out, Jake spun his prisoner around to face him. "Okay, asshole, tell me about the Russian guns."

"I don't have no Russian guns, man, honest."

"Then why'd you try to sucker me in here?"

The punk shrugged. "I figured we could do you and take your bike. Dingo didn't tell us who you are."

"Who has Russian guns for sale, then?"

The punk shook his head. "I don't know, man. Honest, I don't. I seen some of the players packin' 'em, but I don't know where they get 'em."

Jake clamped down on his arm again. "You and me are going to take a little ride, home boy."

"Wait, man!" The voice rose two octaves in fear. "Where are you taking me?"

"I'm going to find a nice quiet spot to dump your skinny ass after I'm done stomping it."

"Wait, man!" The punk struggled to free himself. "Chill out! I know who's got some of them guns."

Jake grinned. "Good. That might keep you alive a little longer."

Escorting the punk to the rear of the Harley, he took a pair of handcuffs from the saddlebags and snapped one onto the man's wrist, while the other cuff went around the sissy bar behind the rear seat.

"That's so I don't loose you on the turns." He smiled, but it wasn't reassuring.

**8**

*East L.A.*
*January 17*

When Erik Estevez stepped out of his car and looked around the barrio, a hundred memories came flooding back. He had spent some of his high school years in a neighborhood not much different than this, but not all of his memories of that time were pleasant.

Estevez often found himself at war with himself, though, so this was nothing new for him. Being the result of a tempestuous love match between a Mexican-American businessman and a strong-willed German artist, he had been raised in a totally schizoid environment. While his father had been fiery and emotional, his mother possessed a Teutonic temperament, always maintaining control of her emotions—except where Erik was concerned. He had been the joy of his mother's life and she of his.

He had been starting high school when his mother had been killed on the freeway by a stoned teenage driver. Her death had completely devastated him. And, to make things even worse, his father had not handled his grief well. The elder Estevez retreated to his business interests in Mexico, leaving Erik in L.A. with an aunt's family to finish high school. While his aunt had been well-meaning, Erik had had a difficult time adjusting to the hectic, emotional life-style of her family.

When he graduated from high school, his father suddenly reappeared and wanted him to go to business school. But Erik had been hurt by what he saw as his father abandoning him, and he joined the Army to spite him instead. Once he raised his hand and took the oath, however, he started looking around to see what the Army could do for him. After passing the test, he had been accepted for warrant officer helicopter-flight-training school. There he discovered the freedom of flight and it became his life.

After two years of flying choppers for the Army, he was given an opportunity to transfer into the DEA to fly for them, and he grabbed it. While he had enjoyed the Army, peacetime flying was boring and the DEA offered him a chance to get in on the action against drug dealers. He had never forgotten that his mother's death had been caused by drugs.

The one thing Erik Estevez learned during his years flying DEA choppers against the drug lords was that the earth was severely polluted with human garbage. And, from his experience, most of this scum lived long, comfortable lives because no one had the balls to see that they didn't. Try as he could, this was something he could never get used to.

Morale in the DEA had been as good as dead when Estevez flew for them. But, like the rest of the agents, he had done what he could to make a difference. For a while it had worked. Every smuggler bagged and every airplane or boat confiscated had seemed a minor victory.

His personal morale had bottomed out, though, when he saw a murder conviction thrown out of court on the grounds that the DEA had used "inhumane" force when arresting two drug runners who had killed a federal agent and wounded two others. Unable to believe he was making any difference at all, he quit the agency.

But even though he had resigned from the DEA, he hadn't backed away from his own personal mission. He just went free-lance, using his skills to identify and eliminate several local drug dealers. Eventually one of his more successful free-lance drug-war operations brought him to the attention of an ex-Special Forces major named Judson Rykoff.

He had been in his Tucson office when Rykoff walked in and hired him and a chopper for a two-hour sight-seeing flight. Once they were clear of the city, Rykoff asked him to go down to the minimum FAA-approved altitude. Once they were down on the deck, Rykoff keyed the intercom.

"That was a good job you did on those drug dealers the other night," he said. "Good clean hits, but you made it look like it was a gang shootout. Nice work."

Estevez turned to face his mysterious passenger. Who was this guy?

"Don't panic, Erik," Rykoff went on. "I'm not a cop, I'm not a Fed and I'm not with the Cartel or the Families. I run a free-lance operation myself, but I've got a lot of money behind me and I don't run the kind of risks you do because I have a team to work with. You want to hear about it?"

Estevez took a deep breath. "Let's pretend that I understand what in the hell you're talking about, mister. I don't know a thing, of course, but let's just pretend that I do. Talk to me."

By the time they returned to the airstrip, Estevez had joined the CAT Team. And since then his life had not been the same. Now he was back in the barrio on Rykoff's orders, and he wasn't too sure that he liked it.

"HEY, MAN!" A kid of eight or so had walked up to Estevez while he had been lost in thought.

He looked down at the kid. "What do you want?"

"What are you doing, man?" the kid asked.

"I'm looking for a room to rent."

"No sweat," the kid said. "My aunt, she has rooms to rent."

The kid winked. "And her husband has been dead for a year, so she's looking for a new man." The kid looked him up and down. "You make the right moves and you might get the room for free."

Estevez winced. That was just what he needed right now—a widow on the lookout for a new husband. "I just need a room, Chico. I find my own women."

The kid shrugged. "Suit yourself, amigo, but my aunt is much woman." His hands sketched female curves in the air. "I just hope she doesn't get another child," he said wistfully. "She lets herself go when she's with child."

"Why don't you introduce me," Erik said, digging in to his pocket and handing the kid four quarters.

The kid looked at the change. "Why is it that guys like you are always big spenders? I can make more than this watching cars for the whores when they turn tricks."

"I'm not a pimp, that's why." Erik said. "I'm just a guy who needs a place to stay for a couple of days."

"Across the street." The kid pointed to a small frame house in need of a coat of paint. "Follow me."

The kid ran on ahead, and by the time Erik hit the front steps he heard a loud burst of Spanish from inside the house. A woman's voice was telling the kid that she wasn't going to let any trash into her house.

The kid answered that this guy wasn't trash, but looked to be rich. He was driving a nice car and was dressed well.

Before she could say anything else, Erik called out in Spanish. "Señora, excuse me, but I understand that you have rooms for rent?"

The woman who came to the door couldn't have been much older than twenty-five. Her clothes weren't new, but they were clean and her hair was neatly done. The two-year-old boy in her arms was also clean and well dressed. The family might be poor, but poverty hadn't yet worn down her pride in herself.

"Who are you, señor?" she asked, staring him straight in the eyes. "Another out-of-town drug dealer?"

"No." Erik switched to English. "I'm Erik Estevez from Arizona, but I'm not a drug dealer. I'm in the city on business and need a place to stay for a week or so."

She looked him up and down before making up her mind. "A hundred dollars a week, cash in advance."

He reached for his wallet. "How much if I take my meals with you?"

She looked him over even more carefully before answering. "One-fifty for two meals a day—breakfast and dinner."

"That sounds fair enough." He handed her the cash. "Thank you, Señora. I promise I won't be any trouble."

"I am Señora Garza," she said as she stepped out of the way to let him through the door.

"I am pleased to meet you, señora."

The inside of the house was neat and clean. Again the poverty showed, but the pride did as well. The large room she showed him was in the front of the house. He guessed that it had been the master bedroom when her husband had been alive. Now that she was renting rooms, she was sleeping somewhere else.

"This will do nicely," he said. "I'll go get my bag from the car."

"THAT WAS VERY GOOD, señora," Estevez said as he laid his fork down. "I haven't had good home cooking in a long time. Not since I lived in L.A. as a kid."

Señora Garza didn't take up the conversation bait and ask him about his childhood. In fact, she had said very little during the meal except to encourage her young son to eat his food rather than watch the strange man eat his.

"I have to go out for a while this evening," Estevez announced. "But I'll be quiet when I come in."

"I put the chain locks on at midnight," she warned.

"I should be back by then. If I'm not, I'll sleep in the car."

Señora Garza looked startled. "No you won't," she said. "You paid for a bed and you will sleep in it tonight. I run a decent place here and I don't want anyone sleeping in a car in front of my house. You come in late, you knock on the door and I will let you in."

"Okay."

The kid who had directed him to his lodgings was on the sidewalk when Estevez went out a little before eight. "Hey," he called out. "How do you like my aunt? She is much woman, just like I said, no?"

Estevez grinned. The kid had a great future ahead of him in sales. "Señora Garza's a very nice woman," he said. "Very respectable."

"She used to be more fun," the kid said wistfully. "Before her man died."

"What did he do for a living?"

"He had a shop where he fixed TVs and stuff like that. One day these guys from the other side of the barrio, they came in to try to rob him. Well, Roberto was much man and he kept a gun behind his counter. He shot one of them, but they killed him."

"I'm sorry to hear that. It sounds like he was a good man."

The kid shrugged. "He was a good man, but he didn't let the cholos help him, you know. He said he didn't want any part of people who didn't work for a living."

"Speaking of gangs," Estevez said, "where do they hang out?"

The kid automatically tensed. "You're not a cop or nothing like that, are you?"

Estevez shook his head. "No, I'm not. I'm just a businessman from Arizona."

The kid grinned; he understood business, particularly when it involved grass, heroin and cocaine.

"You don't look like you're in that business, señor."

"Drugs? No—" Estevez shook his head "—I'm not a drug dealer."

"The information will cost you. You know, a commission for a sales lead."

Erik handed over a five-dollar bill. "That's the last time I'm paying you, Chico."

"Only for now." The bill disappeared into the kid's pocket. "Wait until you decide you need a woman, amigo. That information will cost you ten."

"In your dreams, Chico."

THE TAVERN the kid directed him to was typical for the neighborhood, and the toughs standing in front of it were typical, as well. Most of them wore plaid shirts with only the top button buttoned over khaki pants. Dark bandannas tied around their necks or worn as headbands and sunglasses completed the uniform. They stood with their arms crossed and cigarettes hanging from their mouths.

These were older Hispanics, veteranos in street slang, so he might not have the trouble with them that he would with the younger kids who were willing to take risks to maintain a macho image. If he was reading it correctly, most of the spray-painted graffiti on the walls of the tavern indicated that this was the hangout of the Eastside Cholo Kings. The name didn't mean anything to him, but he knew it did to them.

"Hey, man!" one of the veteranos called out as he approached.

Estevez turned slowly, taking his sunglasses off. "You talking to me?" he asked in English.

"Yeah, asshole," the punk answered.

One of the other gang bangers lounging against the wall turned to his buddy and made a crack in Spanish that included calling Estevez a bastard. Knowing that he couldn't let that crack go and hope to keep his standing as a man, he spun on the guy.

"At least I knew who my father was, punk."

The homie came off the wall ready to fight to defend his mother. Just then, the kid ran up. "No, Paco!" he said. "He's a good guy. He's staying with my aunt."

With the kid vouching for him, the door guard detachment stood aside and let him go in. The dimly lit tavern had half a dozen more gang bangers inside, sitting at the tables smoking and drinking beer. Right after the bartender put a beer in front of him, one of them walked up and asked what he thought he was doing.

"Other than drinking a beer," Estevez answered, "I'm here on business."

"We don't need no new connections," the man said. "We're covered."

"I'm buying, not selling."

"If you want to buy, you talk to the homie outside on the corner."

Estevez allowed a sneer to cross his face. "I'm not stupid. I don't buy drugs."

"What do you buy, then?"

"I buy information about where I can get guns. Particularly the new AKs that everyone seems to be packing around here. We need some of them back in Tucson."

"I think you'd better move on. We don't deal with that shit."

"I think I'll finish my beer."

The gang banger drew a fighting knife from his boot top. "I said vamoose."

"I think I'll finish my beer," Estevez repeated as he drew his Glock pistol from the back of his belt, laid it on the bar by his glass and smiled. "All this talk has made me thirsty."

For a moment there was silence in the club. The bartender started moving toward his cash register and the gun hidden underneath it.

"Where you from?" the gang member asked.

"Like I said—" Estevez smiled "—I'm from Tucson and I'm here to buy guns. If you don't have any," he said with a shrug, "that's fine. I'll ask someone else as soon as I'm finished here."

"I don't want no trouble around here." The man motioned to the bartender to stand fast.

"I don't either. I just want to buy some guns for the cholos at home."

"You leave and I'll make some calls."

Moving slowly, Estevez took the Glock from the bar and put it back under his belt. "You can find me at Señora Garza's."

**9**

*Los Angeles*
*January 18*

Judson Rykoff hated this part of an operation, any operation. He had all of his people in the field and now he had to sit on his thumb and wait for something to develop. Neither Erik Estevez nor Mel Bao had much to report when they called in earlier that morning. Both operatives had established quarters for themselves in their target areas and had made contact in their neighborhoods. Beyond that, though, they had made little progress.

MacLeod hadn't called in, however. "I wonder where the hell Big Jake is?" he asked more to himself than to Sendak, who was typing a report at the computer.

Rykoff would rather have been in the field with Jake, Erik and Mel than be stuck in their hotel-room command post. But there was no way he would have been able to infiltrate any of the warring factions. There were no middle-aged white gangs involved in the fighting, so far. If they didn't get a handle on this quickly, however, it would come down to that sooner or later when the fighting spread outside of the ethnic communities.

Watching Rykoff pace back and forth across the room like a tiger in a small cage was driving Alex Sendak completely up the wall. He, too, sincerely wished that Rykoff had something else to do.

"Why don't you go out for a little lunch, Jud," he suggested. "They've got real decent submarines at that place across the street."

"Good idea," Rykoff agreed. "Maybe by the time I get back, one of them will have called in with something."

"Christ!" Sendak exploded. "Will you give it a fucking rest, Rykoff. They've only been in the field for a day now. If this thing was going to be easy, we wouldn't be involved. You know that."

Rykoff stopped in midstride. "Okay, okay." He threw up his hands. "What kind of sandwich can I get you?"

"How about turkey and Swiss on sourdough, Dijon and hold the mayo.

"Go on, get outta here," Sendak repeated when Rykoff didn't immediately head for the door. I'll watch the phones while you're gone. Take all the time you want, and you can spell me when you get back."

Rykoff knew how to take a hint as well as the next guy. "Okay, okay! I'll leave you alone."

On the street corner outside the hotel, Rykoff waited for the light to turn before crossing the street. The passersby and the group of black teenagers standing at the bus top in the middle of the block seemed tense. Everyone was watching everyone else very closely. Staying alert was a way of life in L.A., but this was more than the usual street smarts. This was paranoia.

The light changed and he was just about to step off the curb when an early-eighties Chevrolet low-rider in brilliant red paint came around the corner. The muzzle of the weapon poking out the passenger window was instantly recognizable as belonging to a Russian AK-74.

Rykoff went down on his face in the gutter without even thinking about it. Concrete rash was preferable to 5.45 mm holes in his body. Had he been armed, he could have taken care of the problem with a couple of well-placed shots. But he wasn't packing a piece so that he wouldn't attract attention from already-nervous local authorities. The warning he had given the team about not being picked up went for him, as well.

The people waiting for the bus didn't see the AK until it started firing. By then it was too late. The gunman laid down on the trigger, spraying the contents of a full magazine in one long, ragged burst. The instant the bolt locked back on an empty magazine, the unseen driver hit the gas and the low-rider sped on down the street to quickly lose itself in the traffic.

Rykoff picked himself up off the sidewalk and ran down to the bus stop to assess the damage. Though a complete 30-round magazine had been fired, only three people were still down. You could give a punk a modern weapon, but that didn't mean he would know how to use it. He pushed his way through the crowd that was forming around the casualties now that the danger was over.

"Let me through!" he commanded. "I know first aid. Someone get to a phone and call 9-1-1. Quick!"

The first man he checked was dead, with three rounds drilled through his upper body. The second guy had taken a couple of rounds in the legs but wasn't bleeding too badly. The third casualty, however, was quickly bleeding to death. A bullet had clipped the teenager's artery on the inside of his upper left arm. Dark arterial blood was spurting high up into the air.

Leaving the other guy for the medics coming later, he knelt beside the wounded boy, reached up into his armpit and clamped down on the pressure point. The spurting lessened but didn't stop.

"Does someone have something I can use for a tourniquet?" he asked the onlookers. "A thin belt, a scarf, a purse strap?"

A teenager reached down and quickly stripped the laces out of his high-top sneakers. "Here you go, mister."

Taking the laces, he quickly tied a loop around the youth's upper arm. "I need a pen or a lighter, something to use to turn the tourniquet."

A hand reached down with a cheap pen. "Is he going to die, mister?"

"Not if I can help it."

Sliding the pen into the looped laces, he turned it in circles until the laces tightened against the boy's arm. The blood slowed and then stopped spurting altogether. If the kid got a transfusion before too long, he'd live. He might even be able to keep the arm after a little surgical repair.

The police and an ambulance arrived while Rykoff was sticking the end of the pen under the tourniquet to hold it in place. Paramedics rushed out to take over and Rykoff backed off to let them do their work.

While the paramedics attended to the two wounded, a cop took Rykoff aside to interview him.

"All I saw was that it was an eighties Chevy Caprice," Rykoff explained. "Painted a fancy red and wearing California plates. The windows were blacked out so I couldn't see how many guys were in the car."

"Did you see the weapon?"

Rykoff shook his head. There was no point in spending an hour explaining how he knew the difference between an AK-47 and an AK-74. They'd figure it out when they collected the empty brass from the street. "It was some kind of fully automatic assault rifle, though."

The cop closed his notebook and glanced over to the two gurneys being loaded into the ambulance. "That was a good job you did on that kid."

Rykoff shrugged. "I spent some time in the Army and learned a little combat first aid."

The cop glanced at the ambulance as it drove away. "You should be in big demand around here. This whole fucking city's become a combat zone."

The officer's voice carried a mixture of anger and frustration. Cops were supposed to keep things like this from happening, but so far they had been helpless to do anything except police up the bodies after the fact.

"You've got that shit right," Rykoff said.

Since the cop was finished with him, Rykoff walked on down to the submarine-sandwich shop. Even watching a firefight made him hungry. After ordering Sendak's sandwich, he ordered a double roast beef with extra horseradish and red onions for himself.

SETTING UP A MEETING with the second gang hadn't been easy for MacLeod, even with Red Dog's help. L.A. street gangs were professionally paranoid and this bunch was certainly no exception. Putting the muzzle of the Glock to Red Dog's ear, however, seemed to help him convince the guy on the other end of the phone to at least meet him in a deserted TV repair store in the neighborhood.

This time four of the punks were packing AKs. Bingo! He had hit the jackpot.

All he had to do now was take their leader away from his guards and wring him out. It would be a piece of cake if he had some backup. Doing it alone, though, was going to be dicey. This was where he really hated this lone-wolf shit.

"Yo, Red Dog!" MacLeod's prisoner was greeted by the only punk not packing an AK. Obviously that made him the leader of this pack of scum. "You lookin' like you got jacked up bad, my man." The punk's hands contorted into gang signs Jake couldn't read.

Since he was handcuffed to the bike's sissy bar, Red Dog couldn't shoot his signs back. All he could do was hang his head.

"What you doing with my homie, Red Dog, there?" the punk asked.

"He dissed me, man," MacLeod growled. "And he's gotta pay. Nobody disses me."

"Well, just who the fuck you think you are?"

"I'm Big Jake of the Skulls. I'm lookin' to buy some of those Russian guns."

"You like those, do you?" The punk glanced at the assault rifles in the hands of his guards.

"Well, I like Harley Hogs and I like a well-draped dude," the punk said, looking at MacLeod's solid-gold necklace. "You give me that fancy fuckin' necklace you're wearing and maybe we'll talk about them guns you want."

What was it with these guys, anyway? Didn't they know that there was money to be made without being assholes about it? No wonder they never graduated from being street punks to the big time like the old Italian Mafia had done. They were so busy trying to be macho assholes that they never figured out how to go beyond selling drugs on the corner and running a few whores. But business schools didn't appeal much to the street punk mentality.

Too bad, because he had wanted to do this deal without having to resort to gunplay. That decision, however, had been taken out of his hands.

His Glock was in his hand faster than any of the punks could bring up their AKs. Unlike the gang before, however, the sight of the pistol didn't stop them. That meant that they weren't as smart as that first bunch had been. It was too bad, but just another case of social Darwinism in action. On the streets of L.A., only the smartest survived.

The first 10 mm round MacLeod triggered smashed into the nearest punk's left kneecap, pulverizing it before tearing out the back of his knee. The second round drilled the next man in the chest. The big 10 mm knocked him over onto his back, dead before he hit the ground.

One of the guards managed to get his AK in action, but he had the selector switch pushed all the way down to the full-auto mode when he fired. After the first two rounds, the muzzle climbed far enough to take the weapon off target. But those first two rounds were enough to kill Red Dog, who couldn't drop for cover because of the cuffs.

MacLeod's third and fourth rounds took out the gunner, spinning him around before he went down. The fourth guard simply dropped his piece and took to his feet without firing a shot. The leader had dropped on the first shot and was still scrabbling across the floor when Jake jammed the muzzle of his Glock behind his ear.

"Don't shoot me!" the punk screamed.

"Shut the fuck up and don't move," MacLeod warned as his hands patted the guy down.

When he found that he was clean, he grabbed him by the collar and jerked him to his feet. He had wanted this guy and now he had him. He would have preferred to take him without having to kill his buddies, but that was the problem when dealing with amateurs packing guns. They didn't know when to use them and when not to.

Dragging the punk over to his bike, MacLeod held him with one hand while he unlocked the handcuff holding Red Dog's body to the bike and let him fall to the ground. It was too bad that he had soaked up the rounds. Again, though, he had put himself in the line of fire by trying to rip him off.

"Get on the back of the bike," he ordered.

"Where you taking me?" the punk said as he mounted.

"Right now I want you alive," MacLeod said as he snapped the handcuffs over the punk's wrists. "You open your fucking mouth one more time, though, and I might change my mind."

The punk clamped his mouth tightly shut and didn't say a word as MacLeod started the Harley and headed out to the street. He was no rocket scientist, but he was smart enough to know that a man who had just killed three of his homies as calmly as he would have swatted three flies would do him just as easily.

WHEN RYKOFF RETURNED with Sendak's sandwich, he got welcome news. "Jake's on his way in with a package for us to interrogate," Sendak said.

"We'd better hurry up and finish our lunch then," Rykoff said with a grin as he opened the paper bag. "It looks bad to be eating when you're trying to get information out of a guy. It's unprofessional, you know?"

Ripping the paper wrapper halfway off, he bit into his submarine. "Damn, those are good onions."

Sendak shuddered and carefully checked his sandwich before biting into it. He hated onions.

**10**

*Los Angeles*
*January 18*

MacLeod had no trouble at all with his prisoner on the ride to the hotel. With his hands cuffed to the sissy bar on the back of the saddle, there was no place the punk could go. In the parking lot behind the building, he was unlocked from the back of the bike and then re-cuffed. Since the gang banger was only half his size, MacLeod practically carried him up the back stairs and down the hall to Rykoff's suite.

"Just what do you have here?" Rykoff asked rhetorically when Jake came through the door with the punk dangling from his right hand.

MacLeod grinned. "Something I picked up off the street. He and a couple of his home boys thought they'd rip me off when I tried to buy a piece from them. They had the goods, but they wanted to get cute."

"Did they now?"

"This one was the only one left in any shape at all when I got done with them, so I thought you might like to talk to him. You'll be reading about the others in the body-count section of the morning paper.''

Rykoff grimaced. He had hoped to do this job without too much collateral damage, as the military put it. There were enough bodies on the street as it was. At the same time, he knew Jake wouldn't have gotten into a gunfight unless it had been absolutely necessary.

"You guys undercover cops?" The punk looked at the computer Sendak sat behind.

Rykoff smiled broadly. "No such luck, asshole. If we were cops we'd be reading you your rights and all that good stuff by now. We're not cops, but before we're done with you, you're going to wish the hell we were.''

The punk's eyes grew even wider. "What're you going to do to me?''

Rykoff shrugged. "That depends a lot on what you decide to tell me about the Russian assault rifles you assholes are packing. Give me what I want and you get to walk out of here on two good legs.''

He reached over to the table, picked up one of the 10 mm Glocks and theatrically racked the slide back to chamber a round. "Fuck with me even once and I'll blow off both your kneecaps before I start talking to you again. Fuck with me twice—" Rykoff paused for effect "—and there won't be a third time. I'll kill you in a heartbeat.''

Something about Rykoff got through to the core of the street punk's fear center in his brain. This white man would rather kill him than talk to him, and if he didn't, the big black dude would gladly do it for him. His only chance to get out of this place in one piece was to talk. Why not? He had nothing to lose by giving them what they wanted. He sure as hell didn't owe anything to the two guys who had sold the guns to him.

"First off," Rykoff said. "What's your name?"

"O. G. Killer."

Jake clamped down on the punk's neck. Why did he have to go through this with each one of these pukes. "Your real name, asshole."

"Tyrone Baker."

"Okay, Tyrone," Rykoff said. "Where'd you get the weapons?"

"This white guy offered to sell them to us." He shrugged as best he could with his arms cuffed behind him. "And they were real cheap, only a hundred bucks apiece, so I went for it. No big deal."

MacLeod and Rykoff locked eyes over the head of their prisoner. They had not expected to find a white man involved in selling expensive military weapons at bargain-basement prices. Usually a full-automatic assault rifle brought five hundred to a thousand dollars on the street. "A white man?"

"Yeah, man, real white, you know. He had blond hair, blue eyes and some kind of funny accent. He sounded like one of the bad guys in an old James Bond movie."

Finding a punk who was a fan of old movies wasn't too surprising—this was Southern California.

"Did he sound like Arnold Schwarzenegger?" MacLeod asked.

"No—" he shook his head "—he didn't talk that bad."

Rykoff smiled to himself. After all these years Arnie was still taking a lot of flak for his accent. "But he had some kind of European accent?"

"Yeah, man, something like that."

"What else can you tell me about this white guy? Did he have a name?"

"He called himself Mr. Smith. His partner's name was Jones."

"What was this partner like?"

"He was white bread, too, but he had brown hair."

"Okay," Rykoff said. "Start from the beginning and tell me everything that happened with Smith and Jones."

"Well," Tyrone said, "we was sitting around the house when this guy calls up, you know, and asks to talk to me. He says that he's got these guns and wants to know if we want some of them. I tell's him that it depends on the price. He says that they're real cheap..."

Tyrone went on to tell that after settling on a price, he had agreed to meet Smith in a remote location. The AKs had been in wooden crates in the back of an unmarked van with several wooden cases of ammunition. He had had enough money to buy a dozen weapons and the ammunition to go with them.

"And that's it?"

"Yeah," Tyrone answered. "It was an up-front thing. He took the money and we got the guns. Like I said, it was no big deal."

"And you don't remember anything else about the sellers?" Rykoff prompted him. "Like how old they were?"

"I don't know," the punk said. "They were in their forties or something like that." Tyrone thought for a moment. "Oh, yeah, that Jones dude, he was missing the little finger on his right hand."

That was more like it. "Did this Mr. Smith give you a way to contact him if you wanted to buy more of these cheap guns?"

The punk shook his head no. "He said he'd call me in a couple days to see if I needed any more ammo."

Tyrone was lying, of course. Smith had given him a number and had told him to call anytime he wanted more. But there was no way he was going to tell these three assholes that. They were bad, particularly that big black dude, but that Smith dude was even badder. Plus, maybe Smith would like to know that three guys were asking questions about him. Maybe the information would be worth something—a big something.

"This is your lucky day, Tyrone Baker," Rykoff said. "You get to live a little while longer. Maybe even another twenty-four hours."

The punk came completely unglued. "What do you mean, man? You said you'd let me go if I told you what I know, and I told you everything."

Rykoff smiled. "I said I'd let you walk. If you want to live longer than twenty-four hours there's something else you have to do."

"What's that?"

"You gather up all your new guns, all your ammunition, and take them to your local police station."

"You're crazy, man. They'll throw me in jail. That's a federal rap, having guns like that."

"You can drop them off on the front steps of the station and book, if you like. But if I don't get a report about your weapons being turned in within twenty-four hours, I'm going to come looking for you. And so will an LAPD SWAT team complete with armored cars."

The punk nodded his head. "Okay man. Chill out. I'll ditch the guns."

"At the police station."

"Yeah, man," Tyrone said sullenly.

"One last thing," Rykoff added. "If I hear that you've been talking about me or my friends here, I'll also track you down and kill you. Got that?"

The punk nodded.

Rykoff nodded to MacLeod, who snatched Tyrone around and unlocked the cuffs. "There's the door. Don't let it hit you in the ass on the way out."

Tyrone needed no second invitation.

As soon as Tyrone Baker's back cleared the door, Rykoff, Sendak and MacLeod went over what the punk had said. "Smith and Jones. Real cute." Sendak said.

"But with accents," Rykoff reminded him.

"That could be anyone, from Canadians to Israelis or even Ukrainians themselves," MacLeod said.

"There's Jones's missing finger," Sendak mused.

"Right," Rykoff said. "Let's run that and see if we have any international gunrunners who fit the description of our nine-fingered Mr. Jones. We can run the FBI, CIA and ATF files from here."

While Sendak ran the lists, MacLeod poured himself a cup of coffee from the pot Rykoff had set up on the table next to the computer. This place was quickly taking on the appearance of a military operations room. Sendak had a huge map of L.A. pinned up on the wall, and the ashtray by the keyboard was overflowing. Sendak only smoked when he was on a mission and then he chain-smoked. The tougher the mission, the more he smoked. From the look of the ashtray, Erik and Mel weren't doing any better than he was.

Of course, that was to be expected. When they had something to go after, they could zero a target in nothing flat. But when they didn't have a target, it could take time to develop one. At least, though, he had taken a few of the guns out of circulation. He felt certain that Tyrone would turn the guns in just as he had been told. He didn't think the punk wanted to try his luck twice.

MacLeod drained his coffee and stopped off in the bathroom. When he came out, Alex and Jud were bent over the computer screen. "I'm taking off again," he announced.

"Right," Jud answered, not taking his eyes off the screen. "Keep in touch."

MacLeod let himself out and went down the back stairs he had come up. There was no point in having the guys at the front desk ask him what he was doing in their hotel. The Regina Hotel wasn't the kind of place that had too many black guests wearing biker regalia checking in.

His rented Harley was waiting where he had left it. It was usually safe to leave a Harley almost anywhere. Car thieves were afraid that if they stole it, some biker would hunt them down and kill them when he found that his ride was missing. Straddling the saddle, he fired it up and rolled it back off the kickstand.

When he hit the street, he paused for a moment. Maybe he should go back and have a little chat with the drug dealer who had set him up on that first deal. He had paid good money for information and he didn't like being ripped off. It tended to set a precedent and he didn't want that. It was bad for his image.

Hitting the throttle, he lifted the front wheel off the ground. Damn, this was a good bike!

NONE OF THE FEDERAL agency files had anything on nine-fingered gunrunners. Running Smith and Jones's names through the computer records of the Immigration and Naturalization Service didn't produce anything, either. But Rykoff hadn't thought that it would. The names were so obviously phony that it would have only worked in one of those paperback novels where the terrorists are always discovered and exterminated in the last chapter.

Interpol's data banks turned out to be considerably more useful—particularly their list of known international gunrunners with only nine fingers. There was a South African by the name of Jan Holtzmann who was missing the little finger on his right hand. He was known to sell arms to anyone who had the price and had been investigated several times on gunrunning charges, but never indicted. His tracks ran all the way from the Khmer Rouge to the IRA, with side trips to Bosnia and South America. He had been a busy boy in the bull arms market of the nineties.

Tyrone had said that Smith and Jones both spoke English with European accents. South Africa wasn't in Europe, but it would serve for the purpose of identifying an accent. In fact, a Boer speaking English was difficult to pin down unless you had a real good ear for the nuances of accents.

On a hunch, he ran Holtzmann's name through the Immigration lists, but again came up with a blank. Then he ran all the South African male passport entries for the past three months and was surprised to see how many of them there were. Everything from graduate students to genetic engineers showed up as having entered the country. He deleted all those who had since returned to their own country, but was still left with a list of a several hundred men.

He then sorted the list by age. Tyrone had said that Smith and Jones were in their forties, so he eliminated those under thirty years old, as well as those over sixty. That still left him with a list of over two hundred names, of which several dozen had listed temporary California addresses on their INS forms.

"I can call all of them with the California addresses," Sendak said, "and ask if they're missing the little finger on their right hand."

"It might come down to that," Rykoff said. "But I think we'd do better if we try to get a local lead on them first. We need to find someone who has a phone number for them."

"You mean like the number for the local outlet of We Be Guns?"

"Something like that. If they're selling guns over the phone that way, they've got to have their number out there so customers can place their orders."

"We can put Bao and Estevez on that."

So as not to be obvious, none of the CAT Team members were carrying communications gear, but they were all wearing receptor watches that acted as pagers. By calling a particular number and then punching in a number, the watch's display would show a number to be called.

"Good idea. Get in touch with them."

## 11

*Los Angeles*
*January 18*

Frank Buckley was in his element again. The cops all recognized him by now and called him Mr. Buckley when he and the CNN crew arrived in their satellite-link van. They escorted him directly to the blood and bodies and kept the gawkers out of his back shots. It was nice to get the celebrity treatment and the cooperation from the police.

For the past couple of days now, the ethnic attacks had been occurring in broad daylight rather than under the cover of darkness. It was as if the warring factions had lost all their fear of being stopped or even hindered by the authorities. One of the talking heads on a major network had coined the term "Armageddon 2000" for the race war, and that was what it seemed to be turning into. Each incident brought on more killing as men, women and children were added to the list of those crying out for vengeance.

The way this was going, L.A. would become a Bosnia-style war zone before too many more days passed. The street barricades hadn't gone up in the minority communities yet, but that was the next step. Buckley didn't really mind the escalation of the fighting, though. More incidents meant more on-camera reports for him. His face was getting wide exposure as the CNN reports were fed to the major networks, as well as to foreign outlets. His name was becoming a household word in Middle America, and in his business, name recognition was everything.

Even so, there was a part of him that wanted the fighting to end in the name of humanity. The larger part, though, wanted the fighting to last at least as long as the Gulf War had. That guy back then who had been nicknamed the Scud Stud—whatever the hell his real name was—had done well for himself reporting from Baghdad while the Allied bombs were falling. He hoped to be able to do the same with his reporting from the L.A. battle zone.

If this ended without destroying the United States completely, he would be able to write a book about his adventures during the L.A. race war. Then he could leave the smog and traffic of Southern California far behind and retire as a millionaire somewhere on the northwest coast. Not too bad for a boy broadcaster from Portland, Oregon. For now, though, he had another killing to report on.

When the lights came on, he took the mike, faced the camera and waited for his cue. "This is Frank Buckley reporting from the scene of the latest mass killing in what has come to be known as Armageddon 2000."

The camera panned to show the bodies being carried out—Asians this time. "Every day Los Angeles becomes more and more of a combat zone. With each new shooting, the body count soars. Local police and even the federal agencies seem powerless to bring an end to the slaughter. This time a block of Chinese-American businesses were hit in broad daylight. The survivors claim that the attackers appeared to be Latinos. The police have not confirmed that report yet, however.

"The mayor of Los Angeles has asked the governor of California for National Guard troops to police the streets of this strife-torn city. But so far our sources indicate that the governor is reluctant to send in the guard. Publicly, Governor Johnson is concerned that sending in the guard will only escalate the violence. Concerns have also been voiced by civil rights groups about the use of armed troops to police the streets. They are concerned that the military would be all too ready to violate the civil rights of the minority community in the name of law and order. So for now it appears that the National Guard will not be called up.

"In a related story, noted African-American civil rights leader Billy Williams held a rally in front of city hall today in an attempt to end the violence."

The TV audience saw the scene shift to show the sidewalk in front of city hall, where Williams stood behind a podium and bank of microphones. The camera panned away from the podium to the sparse crowd carrying homemade signs. Most of the signs bore tired slogans about gun control and making the streets safe. None of them directly addressed the madness that had overtaken L.A.

Though the rally had been widely publicized as a "multicultural celebration" against violence, most of the sign carriers were the middle-class white professionals that predominated at every liberal rally. The minorities involved in the fighting were not well represented. Buckley didn't comment on that, but let the camera do it for him. This was a case where a picture was worth more than a thousand words.

"Williams was joined by other African-American civil rights leaders, as well as prominent members of the local African-American community. When asked if there was any truth to the rumors that Hispanic and Oriental civil rights leaders had refused to join him in his plea for peace today, Williams had no comment."

The scene shifted back to Frank Buckley for the wrap-up on the latest crime scene. Ambulance sirens were wailing in the background as if they had been cued. He couldn't have asked for a better backdrop. "As the body count mounts, Angelenos of all races ask themselves if they will be the next to die. They also ask their government why they have not put a stop to the bloodshed. This is Frank Buckley, CNN News."

As soon as he received the cut signal from the cameraman, Buckley dropped the professional reporter look from his face. While the crew packed up their gear, he signed autographs on scraps of paper handed him by the onlookers. More and more, this was becoming a routine with him, and he made sure that he always had a pen in his pocket.

He had been flattered by the requests at first, but it had soon become a chore. Then he realized that if each autograph seeker bought a copy of the book he intended to write, he would become a wealthy man. Then he started carrying a notepad for those who couldn't find a scrap of paper for him to write on. There was a lot more to being a media star than he had realized.

MEL BAO TOOK HER LUNCH at the Quan family restaurant again. She had spent the morning taking more photos in Chinatown to develop her cover. If anyone was watching her, she wanted to be doing what she was supposed to be doing. But she had to admit that it was the greatest cover any spy could ask for. Even though photography was a sideline with her now, she still enjoyed it, and L.A.'s Chinese community was a great place to find good shots.

She had established herself so well at Quan's by now that the men at the corner table paid her no attention when she walked into the semiprivate room. They had been told that she was off-limits and they respected that. Not only for who she was, but because Dan Quan had told them to leave her completely alone.

She was beginning to think that she had lucked out. Young Quan certainly seemed to be more than merely the junior partner in a family restaurant business. His mannerisms and poise were more those of a leader of men, and in this part of town, that could only mean the leader of a Tong, a Chinese gang.

But there were many kinds of Chinese Tongs. The word translated into English as "association," and most of them were harmless, noncriminal organizations such as burial clubs. Other Tongs had been formed to protect Chinese businesses from criminal gangs. Then there were the famous criminal Tongs. Some of them were into drugs, some into illegal immigrant slavery, some sold Mafia-style protection. All of them gave the Oriental community in the United States a bad name.

Most Oriental-Americans were honest, hard-working people who tried to make their fortune the old-fashioned way—by working for it. Very few of them had succumbed to the culture of violence that was now so common in the United States. She still didn't know what kind of gang Quan headed, but her bet was that it had been organized to protect his family and their shops from the violence of L.A. If her hunch was right, sooner or later he would have to buy weapons to arm his people against the new threat. When that happened, she hoped to get an in.

Mel was finishing up her tea when Dan Quan walked in, a fierce frown on his face. "Dan! What's wrong."

He pulled out a chair at her table and dropped into it. "A Mexican gang attacked a Chinese video store this morning," he said, his voice tense. "Several people were killed and the store was torched. One of my cousins worked there and he's one of the dead.''

"I am so sorry," she said.

"I had hoped that we could escape this madness that has broken out."

"What are you going to do now?"

Quan looked deep in thought. "I have to call a man," he said. "He promised that he could help us if something like this happened."

Bao's ears perked up. Rykoff wanted her to be alert to getting the phone number of the men who were offering the weapons to the ethnic gangs. If she worked it right, this could be her chance.

"Maybe I can help," she offered. "My father's name is not unknown in both the Chinese and Vietnamese communities here. I have connections, too."

Quan looked surprised at the thought that she wanted to get involved. "Are you sure you want to have anything to do with this? This is a family matter and it could be dangerous for you."

"If someone is killing honest Chinese businessmen," she said, sounding determined, "it matters to all of us. My father taught me that anything that harms any of us, harms all of us. That, he said, was what went wrong in Vietnam. Every ethnic and religious group only looked out for their own welfare and really didn't care about what happened to anyone else. The Communists used that attitude to their advantage. If the Chinese, Montagnards, Vietnamese, Buddhists and Catholics had all worked together back then, the war might have gone differently.''

"Maybe you can help us," Quan said. "I am going to get a shipment of weapons to arm my people. I know you've been trained in the Nung warrior tradition, but do you know much about firearms?''

"I learned to shoot when I was still a small child in Vietnam.''

"Good. Our women will need training. I don't have enough men to cover all of our operations. Some of the women are going to have to learn to protect themselves.''

"Where are you getting the weapons?''

He looked at her, but since the question was a natural one, he didn't think any more about it. Nonetheless, he didn't answer the question. "I'll be picking them up this afternoon," he said instead.

MR. SMITH'S PRICE for the Ukrainian AK-74s to Dan Quan wasn't the bargain-basement hundred dollars a copy he had offered to Tyrone Baker. Smith knew that the Chinese were fully aware of the price of automatic weapons on the street. To offer them at any less than full market price would arouse suspicions. He did, however, allow himself to be bartered down to a discount price for a volume order. But that was also part of dealing with the Chinese.

Smith didn't care a bit about the price he got for his weapons. He would have given them away free on the streets if he could have gotten away with it. His only purpose was to get the weapons out into the hands of people who could do something useful with them. Something like killing people of a different race simply because they were different.

After a brief demonstration, Quan and his men left with fifty brand-new Ukrainian AK-74s with three magazines each and ten thousand rounds of ammunition with them. He also left Smith with an order for a dozen RPG-9 antitank rocket launchers and a hundred rounds of armor-piercing rocket ammunition to be picked up in two days.

Smith smiled to himself as he watched them drive out of sight. Now that he'd made an inroad to the Chinese community, the orders would pour in. A couple more weeks of this and he could move on to his next assignment. The smog in L.A. was really getting to him and he longed to breathe clean air for a change. Maybe he would like Seattle better.

ALTHOUGH BAO KNEW about the Ukrainian AKs, this was the first time she had seen one of the guns that were tearing L.A. apart. When Quan led her down into the basement under the restaurant, they were being taken out of their wooden crates. She couldn't read the writing, but the wooden crates were marked with black letters and she could make out the designation AK-74 and the 5.45 mm on the ammo crates.

"They're Russian AKs," she said. "And they look like the newer 5.45 mm models."

When she saw the look on Quan's face, she explained. "Along with *Popular Photography*, I also read gun magazines."

To show Dan Quan that she knew what she was doing, she took one of the AKs from the crate and quickly broke it down. The assault rifle was covered with a thin layer of protective Cosmoline and needed cleaning before it could be used.

"They're easy to break down," she said. "And they all need to be cleaned."

"I'll get the women working on that."

"If I might make a suggestion," Bao said. "Why don't you have the men clean the guns and I'll put the women to filling the magazines with ammunition."

"Good idea," Quan agreed.

The ammunition was packed in 15-round stripper clips, and the cartons all had magazine loader guides packed with the clips. While the magazines could be filled one 5.45 mm round at a time, having the loaders made that chore much easier and faster.

Taking a cleaned magazine, Bao showed one of the women how to load it. The magazine loader guide went over the mouth of the empty magazine, and the 15-round stripper clip clipped into the other end. Pushing down on the row of cartridges in the clip slid them down into the magazine. When the clip was empty, another one was fitted in its place to finish filling the 30-round magazine.

Before long, the basement looked like an armory. As soon as every AK was cleaned, it was reassembled and checked to make sure that it was functioning properly. It was then joined up with three loaded magazines and another 150 rounds still in the boxes. That gave each shooter 240 rounds all told, a good basic load for a security guard or a street fighter.

As soon as the weapons and magazines were ready, men packed them in boxes bearing a florist supply company's name and hurried out of the basement with them. They would be in the hands of Quan's men before the hour was out. The next time one of their establishments was attacked, the Quan family would be able to fight back.

**12**

*Los Angeles*
*January 18*

While Sendak checked on the California-based South African visitors on the list, Rykoff kept sorting through it himself, searching for a pair of men who were traveling together. It wasn't good security procedure to enter the country together, but the chances were that Smith and Jones had done it anyway. It was only human nature to want a traveling companion.

It didn't take long for Rykoff to find such a traveling couple. A Hans Binkermann and an Ian Lancaster had indeed flown to the United States together on South African passports.

"I've got two guys here I want you to check into," Rykoff said. "They're listed as biogeneticists who came in on work visas sponsored by an organization in Arizona called the New Dawn Corporation."

"Isn't that a strange cover for a couple of gunrunners to use? Why didn't they come in as dentists or lawyers? What makes you think that they're our boys?"

"They're the only two on the list who came in on the same flight together and who listed the same occupation with the INS. And they flew in from Paris, not Johannesburg, which is stretching it even farther."

"They should be easy enough to check out," Sendak said. "All I'll have to do is run their credentials through all the universities that offer advanced degrees in bioengineering. And I can check the bioengineering periodicals to see what they've published."

"I hadn't thought of the periodicals," Rykoff mused. "Run those first and see what you get."

A couple of minutes later Sendak's face broke into a smile. "These guys don't exist anywhere as bioengineers or geneticists," he stated flatly. "You can't work in that field and not publish, and there isn't a single article published in any language under either of these two names."

"Bingo." Rykoff grinned. "Now we need to take a look at the corporation that sponsored them. If they're phonies, maybe the company is, too."

Researching the New Dawn Corporation was a snap. All Sendak had to do was to plug into Compuserve's Who's Who in American Corporations to get a complete rundown on the organization. Though the company was only a few years old, the file was rather extensive. The biotech business was hot and the New Dawn Corporation was near the top of the list in that field. After downloading all the data, he gave it to Rykoff to look over.

"They look legit to me."

Based on what he was reading, Rykoff had to agree, but he decided to run the company's owner, Joshua Nisi, through Steadman's confidential files. A businessman as prominent as Nisi was sure to have a file. "Move over," he told Sendak. "I need the keyboard."

Sendak turned the computer over and went to refill his coffee cup. When Jud was working on the computer, he didn't like anyone looking over his shoulder. Someday, though, Sendak vowed that he was going to learn where Rykoff was getting his classified information. Like MacLeod, he, too, thought Rykoff answered to someone in government, but the real question was who.

Whoever it was, Sendak just liked knowing that there was some kind of official backing, however anonymous, for Rykoff's off-the-wall operation. The major had impressed upon each one of them that their activities were not officially sanctioned in any way and that there was always the risk of running afoul of the law every time they went on a mission. So far they hadn't had any problems. But, if and when they ever did, it was nice to know that some shadowy influence could be called in to bail them out.

"What did you come up with on him?" Sendak asked when Rykoff pulled the hard copy from the printer.

Rykoff quickly scanned through the report Steadman had faxed him. "His real name is Bob Fullerton, but he goes by Joshua Nisi now. Nisi, by the way, is ancient Hebrew for prince."

"That's real cute," Sendak said. "Is he some kind of religious freak?"

Rykoff shook his head. "No. It says here that he's some kind of bioengineering genius with a bent for saving the world from itself."

"Why do I feel that I've heard that line somewhere before?"

"This guy is apparently making it work, though. He made himself a multimillionaire by inventing a drug-infusing enzyme to fight diseases and is putting his money where his mouth is. He's established an arid-region agriculture experimental station in Arizona as the New Dawn Corporation. The IRS reports that his taxes, both personal and corporate, are in order."

Rykoff continued reading through the report. "He doesn't have any kind of criminal record, though he did get kicked out of college when he was a sopho-more for engineering a race riot, it says here. It started out as a protest against the lowering of academic standards for minorities, but it got out of control. Several people were hurt in the melee and he got his young ass thrown out of school for not being politi-cally correct."

"He's a Nazi, in other words."

Rykoff shook his head. "No indications of contri-butions or membership in right-wing fringe groups. In fact, he doesn't seem to have even been politically ac-tive after that incident. But he has contributed to the zero-population-growth movement and is on record as supporting a limitation on non-European immigration into the United States.''

''Do you think he could be our man?''

Rykoff stared at the papers in his hand. ''On the surface, he looks squeaky-clean. Just another eccentric, wealthy science nerd with dreams of bringing utopia to earth. But there is one confirmed link between him and the Ukrainian government.''

''What's that?''

''There was a problem with a wheat disease in the Ukraine a few years ago and he came up with an inexpensive, genetically tailored enzyme to combat it. He was credited with saving the Ukrainian wheat harvest and was made a hero of the republic. This was the year before he did the other enzyme that made him all the money he's spending now.''

Rykoff thought for a moment. ''Since Ukrainian grain ships dock in L.A., maybe we should look into what they might be carrying mixed in with the cheap wheat. I should have thought of that earlier, but I figured that the Feds would have that one covered. I'd better check it out, though—the Feds have been known to overlook the obvious.''

''What do you have on his research station, that New Dawn thing?''

''That's where the picture starts becoming confusing,'' Rykoff answered. ''The locals love his New Dawn Corporation because he's provided a lot of jobs and spends money in the local economy. On the other hand, the reports indicate that he runs the place with an iron hand. His people are extremely disciplined and never cause any trouble when they go to town on Saturday night. They're also pretty closemouthed about what they do for a living and they don't complain about the company. Also, there have been no reports of problems with either drugs or alcohol in the work force."

"Good military-style discipline."

Rykoff nodded. "Yeah. And he has at least two levels of employees. Some of them wear uniforms of a sort and have been seen armed on the compound. But no one has ever seen a non-Caucasian in the company uniform."

"Sounds a little like the Waffen SS to me. Does the ATF or FBI have anything on him?"

Rykoff shook his head. "Nothing here, and the Arizona state police have also given him a clean bill. As far as they're concerned, he's just an aging eccentric running a free-love agricultural commune."

"How's that?"

"The only thing that has bothered any of the locals is that no one seems to be married up there. And, apparently, all of the women are real good-looking and are raising kids without the benefit of husbands."

Rykoff smiled. "You know how the women of a rural community are. The thought that people are living together without the pain of matrimony is enough to ruin their whole day. They're miserable in their marriages and they want everyone else to be just as miserable as they are."

Sendak laughed. "Ain't that the truth."

"All that aside, however, the big question is why this Nisi guy sponsored a couple of ringers if he's completely legit. You can get in deep shit with the INS for much less than that. And that's to say nothing about what the ATF and FBI will have to say if he's importing gunrunners."

"Why don't I travel down to Arizona and check this place out?" Sendak suggested. "I'm not doing much around here. If this Nisi guy's hiring, maybe I can see if I can get hired on and take a look around the place. Apparently his two phony bioengineers are here in L.A., but there might be something else I can learn by nosing around. If he's planning another David Koresh number, we can call the ATF in on him."

Rykoff grinned. "Good idea. But let me stack the deck in your favor first. I'll have your military records altered to indicate that you were court-martialed and thrown out of the Army for a racial incident. That way, if he's screening for neo-Nazis, you'll fit right in."

"Thanks a lot."

"I'll have them changed back as soon as we're done," Rykoff assured him. "But it seems that he screens his workers carefully. And if he's got connections, he could have access to the DOD files."

"Good point."

"Also, we'll need to create a legend for you." Rykoff thought for a moment. "I can do a divorce, a big alimony judgment and a sale of your house. That should explain why you're far from home looking for work."

"Great. If Catherine hears about that, she'll come unglued. She's already starting to make noises like she's going to pack her bags."

Rykoff frowned. Domestic problems were always a risk for clandestine operatives, which was a lot of why he wasn't living with anyone right now. He didn't like to think that Sendak had anything on his mind other than finding the source of the Ukrainian weapons that were tearing L.A. apart.

"When we get done with this, I'll send you two on a paid vacation if you think that will help."

Sendak grimaced. "I appreciate it. But I don't think it will do much good. She wants me to stay at home and quit running around all over the world, doing something "important" or not. She also hates not knowing the details of what we do. I think that's the worst part for her, being kept on the outside."

He shrugged. "But, I can't bring her in. No one's allowed to know specific details outside of us, anyway. Then, she's one of those people who simply doesn't understand that the only way to deal with the shit in the world is to stamp it out. She's completely bought into the liberal mythology that all you need to do is sit down and talk to bring peace on earth and goodwill to all men."

Rykoff didn't have anything to say in answer to that one. His own ex-wife had been one of those people, as well. And her beliefs had been the main reason they had parted. He had seen enough evil in the world to know that you couldn't talk it away—it took action. That was also why he had decided to head up the CAT Team.

As far as he was concerned, the liberal philosophy was the most dangerous enemy of the great American dream. Because life was so easy in the United States, the average American had no concept of the evil men could do when they were not stopped cold. This was not to say, however, that there wasn't more than enough homegrown, garden-variety evil right in the United States.

By almost any statistic you wanted to name, the United States was one of the most violent societies on the face of the planet. But the violence was almost always small-scale. And the cult of the victim was used to explain away the evil as being caused by poverty, racism or any of a hundred other excuses. All it took was for another mass murderer to crop up somewhere, and more people would line up to carry signs defending him and explain away his crimes than would sign up to hang him from the nearest lamppost.

"I don't know what to say," Rykoff answered honestly.

"Fuck it," Sendak said, repeating the old Airborne Ranger mantra. "It don't mean nothin'. Right now I've got a mission to accomplish and I'll just have to worry about her after we get this thing all wrapped up."

"You get started on your travel arrangements while I work on your cover story. I want you to fly into Denver this afternoon and then take a commuter flight to Boulder. You'll launch from there."

"Sounds good to me."

AS SENDAK PREPARED for his solo mission, he thought back to all the other times he had gotten his gear ready to go to war. As a kid growing up in a traditional working-class family, he had always wanted to be a soldier, a real soldier, an infantryman. His father had gone to Vietnam, and while he didn't encourage his son's love for the military, he didn't discourage it, either.

In high school Sendak had been active in sports, all sports, but couldn't wait until the four years were over and he could get started on his adult life. While he waited, he watched every war movie that had ever been made and read war novels. His favorites were the action-packed novels of Vietnam, particularly those written by Jack Hawkins and Knox Gordon about the Air Cav and the Special Forces.

The week after he graduated, he enlisted in the Army for Infantry and Airborne training. From there, he went into Ranger training and was selected for an assignment with the Army's elite 75th Rangers at Fort Steward, Georgia. His first months in the Rangers were spent in training, training and even more training.

He was beginning to think that he would never get a chance to do it for real when his unit was alerted for the invasion of Panama. They stayed on alert for three days while the Ranger companies from Fort Lewis, Washington, took care of the problem of General Noriega and company. Then it was back to training.

The 1991 Gulf War was a welcome reprieve from training, and Sendak looked forward to his baptism by fire. It came soon enough when Sendak's recon team was inserted deep behind Iraqi lines right before the bombing campaign began. Their mission was to point out targets for the bombers and do bomb-damage assessments after the raids. The four-man team had the bad luck to be inserted too close to an Iraqi patrol and they had to fight their way out of an ambush.

That was when Sendak fully appreciated the endless training he had undergone. Even though the enemy had had the element of surprise, the Rangers successfully fought off twice their number and emerged from the firefight unscathed. For the rest of the short campaign, they operated behind Iraqi lines and only linked up with an Allied armor column on the last day of the fighting.

When he returned to Fort Stewart, Sendak requested a transfer into one of the elite Delta Force Blue Light antiterrorist teams. There he trained in advance tactics and operations and again got to put his new training to good use in several of the renewed antiterrorist campaigns of the late nineties.

It was the constant training, however, that put an end to his military career. He injured his knee in a training accident that left him in the hospital for several weeks. When he was faced with being assigned to a noncombat unit, he took a medical discharge rather than stay in the Army knowing that he could never go to war again. His whole life had been about being a soldier and soldiers went to war. Even with the mountain climbing and skiing, civilian life had bored him stiff. When Rykoff had offered him a chance to be a real soldier again, he joined the CAT Team in a flash.

"Does this place have a barber shop?" Sendak asked, dragging his thoughts back to the mission at hand.

"I think so, why?"

"If I'm going to go to war, I think I'd better get a haircut."

Rykoff surveyed Sendak's long blond hair. "No, leave it. You don't want to look like you're an ATF agent."

Sendak laughed. "God forbid. We don't need that kind of problem."

**13**

*Los Angeles*
*January 19*

While Mel Bao was helping Dan Quan turn the basement of his family's restaurant into an assembly-line armory, Erik Estevez was still trying to develop a lead in his end of town. The guy who had promised to make a couple of calls for him had not panned out and he was beginning to think that he was wasting his time screwing around with the Eastside Cholo Kings. They were armed, all right, but so far he hadn't seen any of them packing Ukrainian AKs. Their weapons were mostly garden-variety gang handguns.

Rykoff was pressing him to develop a lead on the gunrunners, but it just wasn't happening. Maybe he'd have to move on to another Latino neighborhood, make new contact and start the process all over again. That was too bad; he was beginning to enjoy staying at Señora Garza's. The kid had been right—his aunt was "much woman."

So far he hadn't been able to talk her into bed, but he thought he was making a little progress. He had to admit that since her bed probably wouldn't become available without putting a ring on her finger first, it was just an exercise in futility. Still, it was the only part of this operation that was in any way enjoyable so far. The gang bangers weren't hassling him anymore, but they weren't exactly opening up to him, either. They just pretended that he wasn't there.

He was sitting at the bar of the small club drinking yet another warm Corona beer with a squirt of lime in it when he heard the roar of a car engine coming down the street, and it was coming fast. The Eastside Cholo Kings heard it, too, and ran for the door of the club, pulling their pistols from the back of their belts.

Estevez unassed the bar stool and made it to the door in time to see two AK muzzles hanging out of the driver's-side windows of an older four-door Cadillac sedan racing down the middle of the street. The shooters opened fire halfway down the block, spraying the front of the club with full-auto 5.45 mm slugs. This time the gunmen seemed to know what they were doing and were firing in short bursts.

Estevez hugged the inside of the doorframe as the bullets splashed against the outside of the concrete-block wall. He heard a grunt of pain as a 5.45 mm slug connected. Another high-pitched scream sounded over the scattered return fire from the gang bangers' pistols. Handguns against AKs wasn't exactly a fair fight. But then, only middle-class white liberals thought that life had to be fair, and there were no middle-class white liberals living in this particular barrio.

The firing cut off as the car passed, and Estevez poked his head around the edge of the door to assess the damage. Behind him, he heard the bartender talking to the 9-1-1 operator in Spanish.

Two of the Eastside Cholo Kings were down and another was standing with blood running down his arm. He stepped out to see if he could help with the first aid when he heard the kid who had welcomed him to the neighborhood yell out from across the street, screaming something about his cousin. Looking up, Estevez saw him leave the sidewalk to dash across the street.

At the far end of the block, the driver of the Caddy spun his big car around and started back toward them, the AK blazing again from the windows. Realizing that he was in the line of fire, the kid stopped in the middle of the street, too panicked to run.

When one of the gang bangers yelled out in Spanish for the kid to run, Estevez dashed out into the street. One of the Caddy's gunmen spotted him and sent a long burst of 5.45 mm slugs his way. The bullets chipped the blacktop behind him as the shooter failed to compensate properly for the speed of both the vehicle and his running target.

Putting on a burst of speed as he reached the middle of the street, Erik snatched the kid up without even breaking his stride and kept on running. When he reached the sidewalk, he dived for cover, shielding the kid with his body. Another short burst went over their heads as the car roared on down the street and disappeared.

"You okay, Chico?" he asked as he helped the kid to his feet.

The kid looked dazed, but appeared unhurt. One of his cheeks was scraped where he had slid against the sidewalk when Estevez dived for cover. But concrete rash was better than an AK bullet hole anytime.

The distant wail of ambulances could be heard approaching when Estevez escorted the kid across the street to the club. The wounded were surrounded by their friends and family and not a pistol was in sight. The empty brass had also been collected and deep-sixed so there wouldn't be any problem when the police came to investigate the incident.

Paco, the gang's leader, walked up to Estevez. "Why'd you risk your life to save him, man? You're not even from around here."

"He's just a kid, for Christ's sake," Estevez exploded. The adrenaline was still racing through his veins and he was ready to kick the shit out of someone, anyone. "Anyone would try to save a kid. What the fuck's wrong with you people? Have you been gang-banging so fucking long that you've forgotten how to be human? Jesus!"

Paco searched Estevez's eyes for a long moment. "Maybe I've been wrong about you, señor," he said softly. He was well aware of the effects of adrenaline and knew to talk quietly or risk becoming a target himself. "I've been thinking that you were an under-cover cop trying to cause trouble for us around here."

He held his hands out in a disarming gesture. "I don't want no trouble here. That's why I haven't bought any of those fancy guns everyone else is using for my men. We will protect our barrio if we have to, but we're not going to make war on anyone."

"I'm not a cop," Estevez said wearily as the reaction to what he had done finally set in. "And I don't work for any part of the government, but I want to see those guns taken off the streets. A lot of people are being killed and I want to help put an end to it."

He glanced over to where the kid was recounting his narrow escape to a cluster of younger kids. "I don't want to see Chico there killed because some asshole was able to buy an AK for a hundred dollars. Maybe when he grows up, he can get out of this fucking place and do something useful with his life. No offense, man, but being a gang banger isn't much of a life for a real man."

Paco looked at him for another long moment. "I do have a number for the man who is selling those guns," he said. "And I will give it to you."

"I'll see that it gets in the right hands and I won't mention where it came from."

RYKOFF SWORE when he tried to trace the number. "It's a fucking cellular phone."

"Who's it listed to?"

"That's the problem. It's listed to a retrans service, one of those companies that retransmit cell phone calls and other kinds of business communications. They probably also have scrambler facilities to encrypt the transmissions so no one can eavesdrop on them."

He thought for a moment, then turned to MacLeod. "You're the resident electronics expert, Jake. How do we get the frequency this cell phone company transmits on?"

"That's not the real problem," MacLeod explained. "We'll also need to get into the retrans station and try to break the codes they're using. Why don't I try to get a job working there as a repair tech. That way I can work on the encryption."

"Here's something I think will help." Rykoff reached into his open briefcase and pulled out a small plastic container. Flipping open the lid, he handed it to MacLeod.

"It's a clipper chip." MacLeod correctly identified the computer microchip resting in its bed of foam rubber.

Clipper chips were microcomputers used to break down encrypted phone transmissions such as scrambled cell phone calls. If he could run the gun dealer's calls through it, he should be able to listen in on them as easily as if he was on the extension phone.

"It's not just any old clipper chip, my man," Rykoff said. "This one will read any encryption known to AT&T and the CIA. With that little hummer you can listen in on any phone conversation in the world—

as well as tap into any data link, microwave or fiber optic. Even the Israeli stuff.''

MacLeod whistled almost soundlessly. This was a top-drawer, classified military item. Under the federal privacy laws, it was illegal for anyone in the United States to use one without a court order, even the FBI. ''Where'd you get this damned thing, anyway?''

Rykoff smiled slowly. ''What thing?''

Jake shook his head. ''Thanks a lot. You want me to use this even though you know that if I get caught with it, I'll spend the rest of my life in jail.''

''If you look it up, you'll see that it carries the part number of a common police clipper chip. Even the matrix is the same and it would take an electron scanning microscope to tell the difference.'' He shrugged. ''You get caught with it and all you'll get is a slap on the wrist for having illegal police equipment.''

''And you just happened to have this little item lying around from the days when you were doing top-secret electronic research for the CIA in your basement.''

Rykoff held a straight face. ''It's amazing what you can find in a garage sale, isn't it?''

MacLeod didn't attempt to get any more information out of him about the chip. This was the wall he always ran into when he tried to find out more about who he was actually working for. There was no way that a bookstore owner from Huntsville, Alabama, could get hold of something like that chip, no matter who he knew.

Sure, Jud Rykoff had been a Green Beret officer at one time, but that wasn't enough to explain his contacts. Except for Mel Bao, everyone was ex-military. MacLeod had been a SEAL himself, Sendak a Ranger and Estevez an Army pilot, but none of them had any old service buddies who could feed them the kind of goodies that Rykoff came up with on a routine basis.

From the very first, MacLeod had been certain that Rykoff was plugged into the federal government, and every one of their missions only strengthened that belief. For one thing, there was the weaponry the team was supplied with for their missions. It was all top-drawer military hardware, some of it still in the developmental stage.

Then there was the intelligence information that mysteriously showed up whenever they needed it. Rykoff's intelligence was the kind of stuff he had been issued to work with during his time in SEAL Team Six, the Navy's top counterterrorist unit. Anything they needed, from recon satellite photographs to blueprints of the target buildings, was always available and it was always accurate. It wasn't the sort of data that any civilian would have easy access to.

This clipper clip, however, topped it all. It shouldn't even exist.

Everything that had happened since he had joined up with Rykoff told him that the government was actually running the CAT Team, but he also knew that he would never be able to prove it. Not that he really cared one way or the other; it just would have been nice for him to know who he was putting his ass on the line for.

"If I can get in there," MacLeod said as he pocketed the chip, "this should do the trick. Let me change into my technician's clothes, go buy me a well-stocked toolbox and see what I can do."

"Be careful."

"I will."

As soon as MacLeod cleaned up, changed out of his biker's clothing and left, Rykoff dialed the number of his service and put out a message for Bao to call him. Now that they had a phone number for Mr. Smith's roving discount guns-and-ammo store, he didn't want her to blow her cover by digging for it when he no longer needed it.

DAN QUAN WAS STANDING next to Mel telling her about some of his family's business when her receptor watch beeped to tell her that she had a message. She glanced down at the number on the display and went back to listening to him.

"What was that?" he asked.

"Just the number of my service," she answered casually. "They probably have another assignment for me. I was scheduled to go back to Seattle tomorrow."

When she saw the expression cross his face, she hurried to add, "I'm not going to take the assignment, though. I told you I'd help as long as you need me and I will. I've already canceled the flight.''

"Isn't that kind of an expensive watch for a free-lance photographer to wear?'' Quan asked.

"This?'' She turned her wrist for him to see it. "I've had this for a couple of years since I did an ad layout for the manufacturer. It was part of my pay.''

"You didn't have it when you worked undercover for the Seattle police?''

She frowned and shook her head. "No, why do you ask that?''

"I was talking to my cousin in Seattle and he said that he knew you when you worked for the police. You didn't mention that to me.''

Now she had to think fast. "Yes,'' she admitted. "I worked for the Seattle police for a couple of years. Did your cousin also tell you that I got shot on a drug stakeout by a cop turned bad and that I resigned from the police force because of it.''

"He did say that,'' Quan admitted, "but I wanted to hear you say it, too.''

He glanced over to where the women were loading the last of the AK magazines. "You know that these guns are illegal for me to have, don't you?''

She nodded.

"In fact, it's a federal offense and I only let you in on it because you are your father's daughter. If it turns out that you are a cop, as well, I will go to prison and many of my family will go with me.''

"I'm not a cop anymore, Dan." She laid her hand on his bare arm, knowing full well that it was considered an intimate gesture among the Chinese. "Believe me."

His eyes searched hers for a long moment. "I must believe you," he said.

There was nothing she could say in answer to that. She just hoped that she wouldn't have to betray his trust.

## 14

*Apache, Arizona*
*January 21*

Alex Sendak turned his dusty, five-year-old Saturn
four-door sedan with Colorado plates into the parking lot in front of the Apache Bar and Grill. Grabbing his hat, he didn't bother to lock the door when he
stepped out into the heat. This was the American
West, where people were still safe behind unlocked
doors. Locking his car would instantly mark him as a
city boy and he didn't want that.

His roper-style cowboy boots were worn, but not
down at the heel, and they had been polished recently. His jeans were faded but clean, as was his tan
work shirt. Regardless of what he had said to Rykoff
about not wanting to look like an ATF agent, he had
cut his blond hair to a longish military style and he was
clean-shaven. Over his shirt he wore a vest made from
an Army-surplus, desert-camouflage BDU jacket with
the sleeves cut off. Sewn on the right breast pocket of
the vest was a small Operation Desert Storm patch
with a Ranger tab above it. A slightly battered flat-
top-style cowboy hat topped off the outfit.

The total effect he presented was that of a man down on his luck, but one who still had pride in himself and was willing to work to better his condition. It was a carefully crafted appearance and one that Sendak hoped would work. If it didn't, they would be back to square one.

It had been no trick for him to fly into Boulder and buy the car with the right plates on a used-car lot. After phoning in the plate number to Rykoff, the Colorado DMV records would show that he had owned it for several years and would record a Fort Collins address for the vehicle. The used clothing had been just as easy. A trip to the local Goodwill had scored most of it. The hat he had bought from a cowboy in a bar for twice the price of a new one. In his new guise, he should pass any muster.

Opening the door of the café, he walked into the dry coolness of an air conditioner running full blast. When his eyes adjusted to the dim light, he walked over to the lunch counter and took a seat on one of the stools. The only other customers in the place were older men with weathered, sun-darkened faces, wearing boots and cowboy hats, sitting and quietly talking, drinking coffee and smoking. He nodded at them when they turned their heads to watch him walk in. From the dusty pickups he had seen outside, Alex figured them to be local cattlemen.

The fiftyish waitress looked as if her name should have been Mom, or Ruby, but her name tag read Kate. She was the no-nonsense type you would find in any small eatery in the West. More than likely, she had followed some man into town and had stayed behind when he left. It was an old story, but a reality in this part of the country.

As he had expected, he got an interrogation along with his coffee after he ordered lunch. "You just driving through?" Kate asked.

Sendak shook his head slightly. "I wouldn't mind sticking around if I can find something to do," he said. "It's nice country."

"We like it here," she said. "Where you from?"

"I've been living up in Colorado for the last couple of years."

"That's nice country too," she said. "I drove through there once."

"It's too damned cold, though," he said. "I got tired of the winters."

Her eyes went down to the third finger of his right hand, and she saw the band of untanned skin; it looked as if he had recently taken off a wedding band. "That's something you don't have to worry about around here."

Her right hand swept out to take in the view of the desert from the window. "The coldest it ever gets around here is about fifty or so."

He smiled at that. "That's just fine with me."

When she saw that he was almost down to the bottom of his cup, she reached for the coffeepot behind her. "Fill it up?"

"Please."

Just then the cook dinged his bell and she went to get his lunch order. After she put the plate down in front of him, she left him alone to eat while she took her coffeepot around to the other customers at their tables.

"You want a little pie, for afters?" she asked when she came back to top off his cup again.

He shook his head with the slight grin of a man embarrassed by his circumstances. "They look real good," he said, letting his eyes fall on the pie rack. "But not today, thanks."

She had seen more than one good man down on his luck and nodded her understanding. "Maybe next time."

He nursed his last cup of coffee for twenty minutes before getting up and going back to the men's room. Coming out, he reached into his pocket and pulled out a quarter and two dimes. Leaving the change by his saucer, he walked up to the cash register. She rang up his tab, not charging him for his refills.

"Where are you headed next?" she asked.

"Someplace where I can find work." He fumbled with his wallet, counting through the one-dollar bills before pulling out four to pay for his meal.

"You ever do farm work?"

"Some," he answered enthusiastically. "I sure don't mind getting dirty."

"You might want to try at the New Dawn experimental station on down the road in the Chiricahua Valley."

"What's that?"

"They're a big company doing agricultural research. They've got a big farm in the middle of the valley and they hire seasonal workers about this time of the year."

He let a smile cross his face. "Thank's a lot. I'll give them a try. Where did you say they were?"

She gave him directions and a big smile as he turned to go. "You'll come back now."

"I will," he promised. "I want some of that pie next time."

Out in the parking lot, Sendak slid back into the driver's seat of his Saturn, started it up, flipped the air conditioner on full power and backed out onto the road. Bingo! He had a lead and it had only taken him a little over a day to develop it. And, best of all, if he was asked about where he had heard that New Dawn was hiring, he could say that Kate at the Apache Bar and Grill had told him. It was perfect local cover.

THE FLAT-TOPPED MESA that held the headquarters compound of the New Dawn Corporation looked out of place in the middle of the Chiricahua Valley of southern Arizona. The earth-toned buildings on the top of the mesa, however, seemed to blend in with the rocky, wind-sculpted sandstone crags. Only the occasional reflection of the sun on glass showed that the structures were man-made and not the result of a millennium of geological forces at work.

Unlike the widely publicized and scandal ridden Biosphere Two project that had disastrously collapsed in 1993, the New Dawn Corporation maintained a low-profile operation and had escaped the attention of the media. That was the way Joshua Nisi wanted it. Also, carefully selected friends in Washington made sure that the millionaire scientist was able to work in comparative secrecy while remaining completely out in the open.

Tourists driving along Highway 80 through the scenic Chiricahua Valley saw crops growing and herds of low-altitude llamas grazing on a scrub brush. The mesa in the middle of the valley was far enough from the main highway that casual visitors saw little of it as they whizzed by in their minivans full of kids and dogs touring the Old West. Anyone who turned off on the private road leading to the mesa was turned back by a chain-link fence and a guard house. The guards were polite but firm when they said that the corporation did not allow visitors into the research center. If people insisted, they were just as insistently denied entrance.

There were unconfirmed rumors that a couple of people who had attempted to enter the fenced reservation after dark had been found dead in the desert the next day. But then, the desert was always dangerous to careless visitors, by day or by night.

Nisi's New Dawn Corporation went out of the way to be a good neighbor to the locals who scratched out a living in the hard-rock desert. Once, when the son of a local farmer didn't return from a four-wheel-drive trip in the hills, Nisi immediately put search teams out and the company's choppers in the air to look for the young man and his female companion.

The corporation compound on the mesa top was a small self-contained city with modern facilities that were envied by the surrounding communities—a state-of-the-art hospital, an award-winning school, a full-service library, winning sports teams and even a small winery. To all who came in contact with it, New Dawn was a model community—which was how Nisi wanted it to be seen.

THE MAN who was responsible for all this ran a tight ship. As the founder, sole owner and CEO of the New Dawn Corporation, Nisi was building a New Dawn for humanity, or so he told his followers. Nisi was not a religious man, but he knew how to harness the fervor of religion to his cause. Not the mindless, religious fanaticism the world had seen at Jonestown and Waco, but true religious fervor based on superior knowledge and a vision of the future of humanity.

This understanding of the religious element in human nature allowed him to run New Dawn like an old-style cult commune. Life for an employee of the New Dawn Corporation was as strictly regulated as any inside a religious organization. The use of illegal drugs headed the list of causes for instant dismissal without recourse. Another cause was speaking to a nonmember of the corporation about any aspect of employment. Every employee signed a statement saying that he had read and understood the strict employment rules and waived any legal rights he might have had under any state or federal employment law should he violate the rules and be dismissed for cause.

Once an investigative reporter gained employment in the research center as a genetic technician. Before he had even finished his new employee orientation, however, it was discovered that his academic credentials and job history were bogus. Both he and the tabloid newspaper he worked for were successfully sued under new industrial espionage laws and financially ruined.

Despite the strict rules, or maybe even because of them, Nisi had never had a problem recruiting top-notch people to join New Dawn. Some came because of his name and reputation in bioengineering. Some came because they saw his work as essential if the world was to be saved from ecological disaster. Others joined up to belong to something larger than themselves. All of them treated Nisi as if he were the Messiah.

Since the famous ATF debacle at the Branch Davidian compound in Waco, Texas, in 1993, sects and cults of all stripes had been under close scrutiny by both the media and the government. The Religious Freedom Act of 1997 had also made it more difficult for the Feds to pull another Waco-style raid on anyone, even if they had just cause. While the federal act provided protection to religious cults and sects, Nisi had been careful not to do anything that would attract the attention of any federal agents. Additionally, even though it would have provided him extra protection under the law, he had not registered New Dawn as a religious organization under the act.

The New Dawn Corporation was licensed as a scientific corporation devoted to arid-climate agriculture and environmental and genetic research. Nisi hoped New Dawn would shine its scientific light on an America free of the plagues that were so quickly destroying it. But the time was not yet right for this revolution to occur.

As a man of great vision, Nisi knew that it would do no good to introduce the benefits of his advanced biological research to the world as it was today. These benefits would either be misused or wasted on people who simply weren't intelligent enough to appreciate them. Before the New Dawn could break, the twin scourges of criminal violence and drugs would have to be gone from American society. Poverty and ignorance would soon follow them into oblivion, as would sickness, including the horror of AIDS.

All that was needed to create the proper environment for his New Dawn was to eradicate the causes of these social ills that were breaking the back of this wonderful land. The barbarians who thrived and prospered while they spread the disease of destruction were the pathogens in American society. The answer, as in any medical situation, was that the pathogens had to be killed for the patient to live.

In Nisi's mind, the main pathogens were the non-European population of the United States. The minor social bacteria of psychosis, homosexuality, drug use and crime among the rest of the population would be easy to eradicate once the main infestation had been eliminated.

The traditional forces of law and order, both state and federal, were the antibodies of American society, but they had proven to be too weak to contain the contagion. Continuous attempts to strengthen these forces had been made since the 1960s, but they hadn't worked. Crime rates in the so-called minority populations had risen so dramatically that no number of police or prisons could contain the disease. And since these steps had clearly failed, sterner measures were necessary if American society was not to die, as so many other great nations had.

California was the perfect laboratory for Nisi's grand experiment, and Los Angeles the perfect place to begin. The so-called minority population was the majority, and no city in the United States had a higher crime rate. If the social pathogens in L.A. could be eliminated, they could be eliminated anywhere in the world.

Now that the superstitious insanity of the Millennium Madness had passed, the experiment was under way and, so far, was going well. As a scientist, however, Nisi was cautious. In the past century there had been other social experiments that had started well, but failed in the end. Unlike the earlier experiments of a similar nature, Nisi was confident that his New Dawn project would succeed.

Hitler's mistake had been to tie his Final Solution to military conquest. Stalin's grand social experiment had been based on a faulty economic premise. The ethnic cleansing of the nineties in what had been Yugoslavia had been flawed in that it had been tied to the personal ambitions of Serbian and Croatian politicians. The New Dawn, however, had none of these flaws. He had carefully studied the earlier failed attempts at social engineering and had noted their faults.

Plus, there were no outside forces involved this time. The barbarians would simply be committing suicide, but on a massive scale. The pathogens would be killing themselves instead of the antibodies doing if for them. As soon as L.A. was reclaimed, the experiment would expand all up and down the West Coast. From there it would sweep east until the entire United States was clear of the infection.

Then and only then would the New Dawn break and show the world what could be done in a society free from the plagues that had so crippled the twentieth century. Joshua Nisi would go down in history as the man who had saved civilization.

**15**

*Chiricahua Valley, Arizona*
*January 21*

The foreman at the New Dawn Corporation employment office at the foot of the mesa looked nothing like an Arizona farm foreman. To Sendak's experienced eye, he looked, and acted, more like an infantry sergeant major who hadn't been anywhere near a farm since he left Kansas twenty-five years before. Nonetheless, he played the game as he knew it had to be played.

"Were you in the Army?" the man asked, his eyes falling on the Desert Storm patch and Ranger tab sewn on Sendak's BDU vest.

"Yeah," Sendak answered, but refrained from adding a "sir." "Seventy-fifth Rangers."

"Why'd you get out?"

Sendak shrugged. "Things went to hell when Billy Boy gutted the Army and I figured it was time for me to leave. It just wasn't fun anymore."

If this organization was what Rykoff thought it was, he knew that his military records would be checked. He also knew that Rykoff had had them altered to indicate that he had been thrown out of the Army for a racial incident instead of having been medically discharged.

The foreman grunted. "What was your MOS?"

"Eleven Bravo with a secondary in small-arms maintenance."

"You ever done any farm work?"

"I was raised on a small ranch in Colorado."

"Where?"

"Fort Collins, north of Denver."

The foreman who looked like a sergeant major put his pen down and looked at him. "Okay," he said. "I'll give you a try. The pay scale starts at three-fifty a week, payday is every other week. Low-cost meals are available at the company cafeteria and medical benefits are with the company clinic. You'll be a probationary employee for the first three months and, if you're still here then, you get a pay raise and will be eligible for the company pension plan and two weeks paid leave."

Sendak caught the foreman's use of the word "leave" instead of "vacation" and knew his impression had been right on. This "foreman" had a military background.

"Do you have any questions?"

"Do you have a bunkhouse here? I'm a little strapped right now."

"There's an employee's dormitory available for a hundred dollars a month that will be deducted from your pay. There's also a canteen and club next to it where you can run a tab against your earnings until payday. However, being drunk during work hours or getting drunk and starting trouble is cause for instant dismissal.''

The foreman reached into his desk and drew out a booklet. ''Here's the company rules for those employees living in the compound. Read it and remember it because you will be expected to follow the rules around here.''

''I'm pretty good at following rules.''

''Get settled in tonight and report to Jim Bowers tomorrow. He'll put you to work and answer any other questions you might have.''

''Thanks, I really appreciate this.''

''Just do a good job here and that will be thanks enough.''

IN THE COMPANY CANTEEN later that evening, Sendak signed for a beer and a thick ham-and-cheddar sandwich and took them to a table at the far end of the small club. The sandwich disappeared quickly, but he nursed his beer as he took stock of the other employees.

Most of the people who drifted in were men, but there were more women than he would have expected. And, as Rykoff had said, there wasn't a dog among them. He thought back to his high school days on the farm, but didn't remember farm-labor women being that good-looking. Obviously the idealism of the company attracted a better class of people than your average rural community.

"Hey!" one of the men coming in called out. "Look, boys, we got us some new meat!"

The man had a smile on his face, so Sendak lifted his beer in a mock salute. As the foreman had said, getting in trouble would get him fired. Plus, the man had a good-natured smile on his face as he walked over to Sendak's table.

"I'm Bill Johnson," the man said, and stuck out his hand.

Sendak took his hand. "Alex Sendak. Glad to meet you."

"Just get in?"

Sendak nodded.

"Which group are you going to work with?"

"I don't know. The guy who hired me told me to see a Jim Bowers in the morning to get my assignment."

"Jim's okay," Johnson said. "I think he has his group working on the perimeter fence this week."

"You rotate jobs then," Sendak responded, taking a guess.

"Right. It keeps you from going crazy doing the same old shit over and over again."

"Let me buy you a beer," Sendak offered.

Johnson waved his hand. "No, I'll get you one this time. Since you're a long way from your first payday, you can pay me back then."

"Thanks."

While Johnson was getting the beer, Sendak concentrated on the other people in the club. For a mixed group of low-wage farm workers, they were an unusually cheerful, orderly bunch. He didn't see any of the sullen, mean losers—male or female—or drunks that he would have expected. In his experience, many agricultural workers were from the lower end of the social spectrum. These people, however, looked and acted more like white-collar workers. Either that or commune members.

When Bill came back, they talked about inconsequential things while they drank the beer. Sendak asked all the questions that any new guy in town would ask. Johnson answered his questions and told him all the things a new guy would need to know to keep his job.

When the beer was gone, Sendak excused himself and walked back to the dormitory. It was still early, but tomorrow was a workday and he wanted to be up for it.

A LITTLE BEFORE EIGHT the next morning, Sendak reported to Jim Bowers, his group foreman, and was issued a pair of leather gloves and fencing pliers. He got in the back of a pickup truck with four other guys, and the foreman drove them several miles to a corner of the chain-link perimeter fence in the middle of the desert.

They hopped out of the truck and immediately got to work making sure that the wire was tight and the posts secure in the rocky ground. The work wasn't too physically demanding, but the sun made it a real job. It had been some time since Sendak had worked in the desert and he was glad that he had his cowboy hat.

Right before noon, another truck drove up with box lunches for the crew, a cooler full of iced tea and a thermos jug of coffee. Lunch was two thick sliced-roast-beef sandwiches with all the trimmings, a plastic container of potato salad and an apple. With the cold, sweet tea to wash it down, it was as good a working man's meal as he had ever had. It sure as hell beat lunch in the Army.

"You guys always eat this good?" he asked the foreman.

"This is shit today," Bowers said, frowning. "Usually we get hot meals, but Wednesday is always these damned cold sandwiches and potato salad."

When he caught Sendak's puzzled expression, he handed him his second sandwich. "Here, you look like you could really use this."

"Thanks, I appreciate it."

After lunch, it was back to checking the fence, but the foreman knocked off exactly at five and they drove back to the compound.

BY THE END of the first week, Sendak had seen all of the compound that was open to the agricultural employees. He still didn't have a clear idea of what in the hell was going on at the New Dawn agricultural research center. From everything he had seen so far, this was a legitimate, if a bit fanatical, operation. There were no hidden terrorist training camps, no fields of pot growing in between the tomato plants and no antitank rocket launchers camouflaged along the perimeter fence.

The only thing that might point to there being a dark side of the corporation was that there were three categories of employees. The probationary workers, like himself, a larger group of full employees who wore company coveralls and a small cadre of upper-management people who included the armed security force.

Certain buildings were also off-limits to the general employees unless they had a specific level of security clearance. Considering that the company was conducting genetic research, that wasn't too unusual. Many companies had those kinds of clearance systems. The question was, what was the security clearance system protecting, genetic research or a chemical weapons factory?

WHEN THE FOREMAN released him on noon Saturday, Sendak went back to the dormitory, showered and changed into clean clothes. He was polishing his worn boots when Bill Johnson stuck his head around the corner of the door. "You want to go into town and get a couple of cool ones? There's a pretty good band at the Goat Roper tonight."

Sendak shook his head. "I'd better not. I need to watch the old dinaro until the end of the month."

"Come on," Bill insisted. "A couple of draft beers won't break you, and they don't have a cover charge."

Sendak allowed himself to be talked into it. There was a chance that Bill was a company fink who had been put onto him to check him out. If that was the case, he needed to cooperate as much as possible without being too obvious that he knew what was going on.

After grabbing a quick dinner in the employee's club, they hopped in Johnson's pickup to do the town. The Goat Roper's Tavern was an hour's drive from the New Dawn compound on the outskirts of Chiricahua. A large percentage of the pickups in the gravel parking lot bore New Dawn employee stickers on their bumpers.

Sendak followed Bill into the tavern to an empty table against the wall. When the waitress came by and greeted Bill by name, he introduced Sendak. "This is Alex," he said. "He just started working with us this week."

"Hi, Alex." The woman smiled, throwing her ample chest out. "I'm Cindy. I guess I'll be seeing a lot of you then. Most of the boys come by here every Saturday."

Sendak smiled. "I sure hope so."

"You come here every week?" Sendak asked Bill as soon as Cindy left to get their orders.

Bill grinned. "It helps break up an otherwise dull weekend. Plus—" he nodded over to where Cindy was putting a frosty beer mug on the table in front of another customer "—the scenery isn't bad."

"Hell," Alex said. "The scenery in the company canteen isn't bad either. In fact, I don't think I've seen so many good-looking women in one place in a long time."

"Better than the Army?"

Sendak laughed. "You got that shit right. The Army sure as hell wasn't getting the pick of the litter when I got out."

"How many years did you wear the green suit?"

"About ten and a half."

"Why'd you quit after that much time?"

"I got tired of the bullshit when Clinton started fucking with the military. Then there was that bullshit about gays in the military and all that UN bullshit duty and it just wasn't fun anymore. I joined the Army to fight for the United States, not shower with fags or let some asshole shoot at me without being able to shoot back because I'm wearing a UN armband. Fuck that shit."

Bill agreed, but then, he had agreed with almost everything Sendak had said so far. When Sendak tried to turn the conversation away from himself, however, Johnson wasn't quite so agreeable.

"Oh," he said in answer to how long he had worked for the company. "I've been there for a couple of years now."

Johnson was saved from more questions when the band started up and Sendak went back to watching the crowd. As he had expected from the bumper stickers he had seen outside, he recognized many of the patrons in the tavern as being from the New Dawn compound. Again he noticed that while they looked as if they were having fun, they were being very controlled about it. No one was arguing with his girlfriend, no one was getting too loud or belligerent and no one was too drunk. This was the most well-mannered country-and-western joint he had ever drunk a beer in. Places like this could give the whole CW crowd a bad name.

The band on the stage wasn't bad. They were never going to make it at the Grand Ole Opry, but the patrons didn't seem to mind all that much. After running through their renditions of the classic CW songs, they got off into their own compositions, and Sendak had to admit that a couple of them were decent—particularly the one about the guy who shoots the lawyer who was screwing his wife when he was supposed to be handling their divorce. It sounded like it was written from the heart. So did the one about the guy who claimed to really love his girlfriend even though she had wrecked his new pickup truck.

Sendak allowed himself to get a little loose that night and talked about his "divorce" and the house he had lost to his ex-wife. Bill was properly sympathetic as only another man could be on hearing of Sendak's woman troubles. Sendak thought he was maybe a little too sympathetic, but didn't let on. His legend didn't allow him to be suspicious of a friendly co-worker.

On the drive back, Sendak laid his head back against the car seat so he didn't have to talk anymore. He was tired and didn't want to make a mistake. He had done well so far and didn't want to blow it. In the morning he'd get hold of Rykoff and give him his report, even though he had nothing to add to the puzzle. Maybe he'd find something next week when his work crew moved into a different area of the vast New Dawn operation.

He knew he was on the right track, but he could see that it was going to take him a long time to find whatever it was he was looking for. He had no doubts, however, that he would find it sooner or later, even if he didn't know what it was. That was often the nature of a recon, and Sendak was a good recon man.

**16**

*Chiricahua Valley, Arizona*
*January 26*

Sendak slept in late the next morning. But he got out of bed before noon, showered and drove back to the Apache Bar and Grill for lunch. He wasn't tired of the food in the company canteen yet, but he wanted to thank Kate for the tip on the job. She was also his only non-New Dawn connection, and if things went bad he might need her to get out of a jam.

Kate was at her station behind the counter and smiled broadly when he slid onto a seat at the counter. "Howdy, stranger."

He flashed her a grin in return. "I'm ready for a piece of that pie with my lunch now. Thanks to you, I got hired on at New Dawn. I'm just doing hired-hand stuff, but it sure beats the hell outta being outta work."

He told her about his job as she filled his coffee cup and took his order. When she came back after giving his order to the cook, she seemed glad that he had found work with the company.

"I thought you'd do well there. They're a little particular about who they hire, but you looked like the kind of guy they like to take on."

"And what kind is that?"

"You know…" She shrugged. "A good man who's just had a run of bad luck."

He grinned broadly. "You have a crystal ball behind the counter that tells you all about your customers?"

"Honey," she said, leaning against the countertop behind her and smiling broadly, "when you've been slinging hash as long as I have, you either learn to read a man pretty quick or you find yourself in a heap of trouble."

"How do you mean?"

"Take yourself," she explained. "When you came in here, you were polite, your clothes were clean and you had a haircut. You can tell more about a man by how clean his clothes are than by how new they are. You also had a mark on your finger that showed that you'd worn a wedding band for a long time. I don't hold that every man who's just gotten divorced is automatically in the wrong.

"Plus," she wrapped up her philosophy according to Kate, "even though you were short, you left me a tip. Not everyone does that."

"It wasn't much of a tip," he said apologetically.

"It ain't the amount that counts," she said. "It's the fact that you did it."

"I'm sure as hell glad I did, then. Otherwise you wouldn't have told me about the company and I'd be by the side of the road somewhere now."

She gave him a long look. "You're never going to be on the side of the road. You're not that kind of guy."

"Boy, I sure as hell hope not."

When his order was up, she refilled his cup and left him to eat in peace.

"That was good," he said when she came back to clear his empty plate away. "Now, how about some of that there pie you're selling."

"I recommend the peach or the cherry."

"I'll have a slice of both."

"You want that à la mode?"

"Why not?"

"I like a big spender," she admitted with a smile as she went to fetch his pie and ice cream.

After leaving a big tip by his plate, Sendak left the Apache Bar and Grill and drove another forty miles east until he came to a gas station with a public phone booth that would take his calling card.

He felt a little paranoid as he checked the bumpers of all the vehicles at the station for New Dawn stickers, but it never hurt to be cautious when you were on a recon mission in enemy territory. And even though he hadn't yet met the enemy, that didn't mean that they were not here.

RYKOFF PUT the phone back down and looked out the window of his L.A. hotel room for a long moment. Sendak's report had been both good news and bad news. The good part was that he had successfully infiltrated New Dawn, but it was bad news in that he hadn't been able to turn anything up yet.

The operation in Los Angeles was also showing up in both the plus and minus columns. By passing on the information that Erik, Jake and Mel were gathering to the federal agencies, he had assisted with the confiscation of several gang weapons caches. Considering how much firepower was on the street right now, it was little enough, but it was a beginning.

Also, now that all sides in the conflict were fully armed, a strange thing was happening in the streets. The flood of weapons, rather than fueling the combat as it had at first, caused a strange form of détente. Now that all the gangs were armed the same way, cooler heads were prevailing because there were no more easy targets. Anyone who was shot at now was more than likely going to shoot back with the same kind of heavy firepower.

The mastermind behind this had made a serious error in his planning by arming all the factions equally. In places like Bosnia and Croatia, the men who were fighting for their particular ethnic group didn't have the criminal mentality. Regardless of what the rest of the world thought about them, they saw themselves as freedom fighters defending an honorable cause—their own culture. They would take any risk and fight to the last round because to do any less would mean the virtual extermination of their people.

The average gang banger in L.A., on the other hand, whether Hispanic, black, white or Asian, had no cause to fight for and also had no concept of personal courage or honor beyond macho posturing. His idea of a good fight was when a dozen of them could rape and kill a frightened woman and her husband, preferably in front of their crying children. Going up against people armed with weapons as good as he had wasn't to his liking.

Liberal gun-control freaks could take a lesson from this, but Rykoff knew that they wouldn't. When this mess was finally over, there would be a renewed flood of gun-control laws at both the state and federal levels that would once again take weapons away from law-abiding citizens. Even more than before, only criminals would be armed.

Although the body count in L.A. was leveling off, there were already reports of L.A.-style ethnic battles breaking out in Seattle, San Diego and San Francisco. How much of the new fighting was simply copycat activity and how much was being fueled by the same Ukrainian weapons that were flooding L.A., he didn't know. He did know that he needed a break to get this thing under control before the entire West Coast went up in flames.

The problem was that even though he thought he knew who was behind this operation, he still couldn't prove it. And, even more important, he didn't know how the weapons and ammunition were getting into the country and being distributed. He didn't know if they were all prestocked in Southern California or if they were being smuggled in on an as-needed basis. The answer to that question was the key to getting this mess shut down immediately.

While he didn't know, apparently neither did the state and federal agencies that were working on the problem. Through Steadman's input, he had a steady flow of police and federal agency reports coming in over his fax machine and modem. So far, the reports indicated that the agencies were simply reacting to the problem after the fact rather than trying to prevent it.

In all fairness, though, Rykoff knew that their hands were very effectively tied by the intense scrutiny of both the media and the minority special interest groups. The big news from the civil rights watchdogs yesterday had been a proposal to pull all of the police units, both city and state, as well as the FBI and AFT, out of L.A. for a cooling-off period. They claimed that the presence of the police was the main cause for the continued fighting.

That was one of the most incredibly stupid suggestions he had ever heard. Despite that, the way this thing was going, it might even be implemented. If it was, there would be more pressure on him and the Team to find a way to bring this war to an end.

IN HIS WAR ROOM two stories under the main building in the New Dawn compound, Joshua Nisi listened to the reports from the operative known in L.A. as Mr. Smith. Once more the South African mercenary was delivering the goods as he had promised.

The existence of the war room was known to only a select few at New Dawn, as was the true nature of Nisi's project. To most of the employees of the corporation, New Dawn was the agricultural research project it appeared to be on the surface. In that respect, the New Dawn would come when people living on marginal land all over the world would benefit from their research into crops able to tolerate arid conditions. This goal fit into the all-people-are-brothers, New Age view of the world most of the first-and second-level employees had. Those people would have been horrified to know the true purpose of their leader's work.

Nisi's select New Dawn cadre, however, had personal goals other than the benefit of humanity. They followed Nisi for their own benefit, both now and in the years to come. If the New Dawn project was even half as successful as Nisi planned, they would all be important men and women in the new scheme of things.

There were those who still liked to think that American society was too stable for a revolution like this to ever succeed. Nisi, however, looked at the true condition of American society in the year 2000 and saw that it was riddled with cancer and rot. For most of the American middle class, the vaunted American Dream that politicians loved to talk about was a nightmare filled with bitter disappointment. Working hard only meant that you were preyed upon by a government bent on taxing you out of existence. Then there was the unending fear of becoming a victim of the ever-growing criminal underclass who sucked up tax moneys by the billions.

The man who could bring an end to this nightmare would be able to do anything he wanted in the United States. A grateful public would make him President for life in exchange for peace and prosperity in their lives and a chance for their children to grow up and live productive lives free from fear. And those who helped Nisi attain his goal would share the power that would be his. They would be the real New Dawn of the United States of America.

Once the first stage of the operation was complete in California, the second stage could begin while the rest of the West Coast was being cleansed. The second stage involved releasing genetically altered plant viruses into certain geographical areas both in the United States and in foreign countries.

Each of these viruses had been tailored to work within a certain plant and create toxins that couldn't be removed. His favorite was the one that would be released into the Central American coca plantations. The neurotoxin it created would kill cocaine and crack users within ten minutes of ingestion. The same went for the opium poppy virus, which maintained the toxic effect even through refining the raw opium into morphine or heroin. Unavoidably, medical use of morphine would be affected, too. The toxin tailored for hemp worked a little differently and took an entire day to kill the user through respiratory failure.

He figured that within a year of his releasing the viruses there wouldn't be a single drug user in the entire Western world. Crime rates would fall so dramatically that most of the police forces in the United States would be out of work. But even better than that, people would be able to live their lives without fear. They would be able to put the energy that had been wasted on fighting crime to developing their true potential.

The United States had been great once, great because of the efforts of the whites who had built a civilization from the ground up. And it could be great again as soon as the hardworking majority did not have to waste time and energy on blood-sucking minority barbarians.

Though the New Dawn would come for the United States first, once other societies saw how well it worked, it would spread to the rest of the civilized world. Once more the United States would lead the civilized world, as it had before the government had changed from its leadership role to one of being a caretaker for the nonproductive and destructive elements of American society.

Before he could start using his viral tools, though, he had to thin out the social pathogens in California so they could be handled. That project was going along quite nicely. Every day the news media carried another story of death and destruction within the so-called minority communities in Los Angeles. The project was working well there, and now it was time to expand it to other cities up and down the West Coast. Both San Francisco and San Diego were scheduled for the next shipments of Ukrainian arms and ammunition.

It was ironic that the few fruits of the great failure of the Russian Communist social experiment would serve as the tools of his success. The only things of value that anyone could say ever came out of Russian communism were weapons of war. In particular, the Soviets had made damned good infantry weapons. And now that they were on the international arms market at bargain prices, he was glad to put them to work doing something worthwhile.

These were sturdy, simple infantry small arms well suited for use by untrained people. While modern Western weapons of war required that the user be both trained and at least semi-intelligent, the Soviet designs had worked well in the hands of the uneducated all over the world for over fifty years. From the jungles of Central America to the Afghan hills and the Congo River Basin, savages had gone from using crude spears to advanced Soviet infantry weapons with very little difficulty.

At least in the United States, the barbarians were more than familiar with firearms. The leading cause of death the past year among black and Hispanic males between the ages of fifteen and thirty-five was gunshot wound. And that had just been with the weapons they could steal or buy on the streets from other gang bangers who stole them.

The way Nisi saw it, all he was doing was giving these people the means to do what they wanted to do anyway, but do it more efficiently. The reports from Smith were proving this out. The body count had passed fifteen hundred and was sure to grow even faster now that the weapons distribution in L.A. was almost complete. Best of all, the unrest had spread to areas where he hadn't even started distributing weapons.

The New Dawn was coming faster than he had even dared hope.

**17**

*Chiricahua Valley, Arizona*
*January 26*

After finishing up in the war room, Joshua Nisi
headed for his private quarters on the upper level. An
initiate of the Daughters of the New Dawn was scheduled to be presented to him this afternoon and he
didn't want to keep her waiting. A big part of his job
as the leader of the New Dawn was to take part in the
rituals that welded his followers into a group bonded
by more than mere employment. While most of the
rituals were little more than a waste of his valuable
time, he went through them anyway for the benefit of
his followers.

This was one particular ritual, however, that he always looked forward to.

In his Spartan quarters, Nisi found the girl waiting
for him with the woman known as the senior sister. All
of the Daughters of the New Dawn were more than a
cut above the average American teenager, but this one
was a real prize. She was stunning.

His eyes glittered hungrily as they wandered over the
almost transparent white shift that was her only gar-

ment. The sheer material did little to hide the perfect breasts without even a hint of sag, the slight bulge of her taut belly and the silky blond tuft between her sleek thighs. His eyes then went up to her face, and he saw perfection there, as well.

She was the most perfect example of a postpubescent, Nordic-type female he had seen in a long time. Initiating her into the Daughters of the New Dawn would be any man's dream come true, but the honor of this girl's initiation was going to be his, all his.

"Has she entered her womanhood?" he asked the senior sister, knowing full well what the answer was. He had watched this one growing up for some time now, but he had not broken his own self-imposed rule. He had patiently waited until her sixteenth birthday, which was today.

"She is ready to become a woman, Joshua." The woman had a faint smile on her face as she remembered her own initiation a couple of years earlier.

The girl trembled when Nisi reached out and laid his hand on her arm to draw her closer to him. Her china blue eyes darted around the room, as if she was looking for a way out. He knew, though, that she would calm down in a few more minutes. The drug she had been given before being brought to him took a little time to work.

"Do not be frightened, my child," he said soothingly. "You have been honored by being chosen to become one of the Daughters of the New Dawn. Not every girl is pure enough to be one of the chosen, and after today you will join the women of the New Dawn, women who have thrown off the shackles of ignorance and superstition.''

The combination of his voice and the drug the girl had been given started taking effect. The fright faded from her blue eyes to be replaced by something he knew all too well.

When Nisi saw the change come over her face, he led her toward the bed in the middle of the room. "Take off your shift," he said softly. "And lie down."

The girl obeyed quickly and Nisi sucked in a deep breath. She was even more stunning than he had thought. "That will be all," he said to the other woman.

As soon as he heard the door close behind her, he quickly took off his own clothes. Though her fear was gone, the girl averted her eyes when his genitals came into view.

"Don't look away," he ordered. "You have to see the glory of human creation in its full power. Lift your eyes and gaze upon it. When the New Dawn comes and ignorance and superstition are banished, sex will again be the glory that it was intended to be."

The girl did as he commanded. The psychoactive potion she had been given had now taken full effect. Her heightened senses registered the male pheromones emanating from his body and she felt her sexual tissues swelling in response. It was nothing she had willed to happen, but was an automatic response of the hypothalamus, a pure DNA-based function of the human body. She rubbed her thighs together without consciously knowing why she was doing it.

Joshua's brain also registered the girl's female sexual pheromones. She had been instructed not to shower for twenty-four hours before her initiation and he could smell her fresh sexual scent over her earlier fear. The scent made his manhood swell, as well.

Sitting beside her on the bed, he parted her thighs and reached out with both hands for his prize. Probing fingers quickly told him that she was ready for him. Since there was no reason for him to wait even another minute, he rolled over on top of her.

The girl started panting even before he climbed in between her legs. The potion worked better on some of the girls than it did on others, but it looked like he had hit the jackpot this time. He had better get started before she came to an orgasm all by herself. He wanted to implant the experience in her mind as having been caused by intercourse with him. Later she would learn to bring herself to orgasm, but he wanted her to remember having her first one with him. That alone would make her come to him willingly the next time, without using the drug.

When he rolled off her at the end of the initiation, he glanced over at the clock on the nightstand. He had almost another hour before he had to go back to work and he intended to enjoy every last minute of it to the fullest. He had been working too much lately and relaxing far too little.

# Deal Yourself In and Play

## GOLD EAGLE'S

# ACTION POKER

Peel off this card and complete the hand on the next page

It can get you:

♠ Free books

♠ PLUS a free surprise gift

NO BLUFF! NO RISK! NO OBLIGATION TO BUY!

# PLAY "ACTION POKER" AND GET...

★ 4 Hard-hitting, action-packed Gold Eagle novels — FREE
★ PLUS a surprise mystery gift — FREE

Peel off the card on the front of this brochure and stick it in the hand opposite. Then check the claim chart to see what we have for you — FREE BOOKS and a gift — ALL YOURS! ALL FREE! They're yours to keep even if you never buy another Gold Eagle novel!

## THEN DEAL YOURSELF IN FOR MORE GUT-CHILLING ACTION AT DEEP SUBSCRIBER SAVINGS

1. Play Action Poker as instructed on the opposite page.
2. Send back the card and you'll get hot-off-the-press Gold Eagle books, never before published. These books have a total cover price of $18.50, but they are yours to keep absolutely free.
3. There's no catch. You're under no obligation to buy anything. We charge nothing — ZERO — for your first shipment. And you don't have to make any minimum number of purchases — not even one!
4. The fact is thousands of readers enjoy receiving books by mail from the Gold Eagle Reader Service. They like the convenience of home delivery...they like getting the best new novels before they're available in stores...and they think our discount prices are dynamite!
5. We hope that after receiving your free books you'll want to remain a subscriber. But the choice is yours — to continue or cancel, anytime at all! So why not take us up on our invitation, with no risk of any kind. You'll be glad you did!

## AND THERE'S MORE!!!

• With every shipment you'll receive *AUTOMAG*, our exciting newsletter — FREE.

SO DON'T WAIT UNTIL YOUR FAVORITE TITLES HAVE BEEN SNAPPED UP! YOU GET CONVENIENT FREE DELIVERY RIGHT TO YOUR DOOR. AT DEEP DISCOUNTS. GIVE US A TRY!

© 1993 GOLD EAGLE

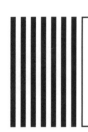

A single touch of his hand showed that she was still under the effects of the drug. Since he hadn't taken the drug himself, he guided her hands to him to give him the extra encouragement he needed right now. That was something else she would have to learn, but it looked like she understood without being told.

AFTER SHOWERING and changing clothes, Nisi went to his office to take care of the last of the day's routine business. Even though he had a well-trained staff, running an organization as large as New Dawn still took a great deal of his personal time.

Ralph Boyd, Nisi's adjutant, was waiting for him with his folder of matters that had to be taken care of today. First he dealt with routine matters—promotions, reassignments, requisitions, approvals for new experiments and the like. Then came the important business of the day.

"I think we may have a new recruit for the inner circle," Boyd announced. All employees were automatically screened when they were hired. Certain ones, however, were investigated in greater depth as possible candidates to join the New Dawn cadre. "An Alexander Sendak, ex-Army Ranger, who is working with Jim Bowers' general labor crew."

"What's his story?"

"He has a good military record," Boyd read from the paper in his hand. "Ranger and parachute qualified and a small-arms expert. In fact, he had an exemplary record until he got in trouble over a racial incident off post and was court-martialed. He then moved to Colorado, where he became a ski bum and ran a small ranch in the summer until his wife divorced him and took his house. Johnson says that he likes to follow orders and he works well with the crew. It sounds like we could use him."

"Give him his medical tomorrow," Nisi ordered. "If he passes that, let him finish his probationary period and have Johnson keep a close eye on him during that time. We'll take another look at him then."

"Yes, sir."

The adjutant thumbed through his thick folder. "The last thing I have is a cohabitation request for your approval," he said.

"Who is it and who does he want to move in with?"

"It's Ronald Billings, one of the level-two comm techs, assigned to the war room."

Nisi took the application and looked at the attached photo of the girl Billings wanted to sleep with. She was a petite teenager with milky white skin, blue eyes and long copper red hair. The name and personal stats printed on the back of the photo reminded him that her name was Debbie and that she was eighteen years old. He needed no reminder, however, of her sexual proclivities. Debbie was an oral-sex expert no man could ever forget.

The request put Nisi in a quandary. The war room staff were critical to his operation and he liked to keep them happy, but Debbie was one of his favorites and he hated to lose her services. In two months, though, he should be able to train someone to take her place. Jilly, the ethereal little blonde he had just broken in, would do quite nicely as her replacement.

"Tell Billings to reapply in sixty days." He stared at the photograph. "And tell Debbie to report to my quarters immediately after dinner."

"Yes, sir."

"Also tell Jilly that she is to attend me tonight, as well."

"Yes, sir."

"That is all."

When the adjutant left, Nisi stared at the red-headed girl's picture. That was the hardest part about his job, letting them go as soon as they were trained. If he didn't do that, he wouldn't have the control he had over his followers, and they were vital for his New Dawn to be successful.

Along with studying the great social experimenters like Hitler, Stalin and Mao, Nisi had also studied the methods of the Old Man of the Mountain, the Hindu goddess Kali's Thuggee cult and the earliest Christian church fathers.

The Syrian Old Man of the Mountain had controlled his band of trained killers by allowing them to use hashish and women under strictly controlled conditions. Their name had come down into English as the word assassin. The murderous followers of Kali had been controlled through sexual ecstasy and the ritual taste of refined sugar, a drug to them. They were also remembered in English with the word thug. In

Nisi's view, the early Christian church fathers had gained their power solely by controlling the sex lives of their parishioners, and they hadn't needed to use drugs. Nisi used all of these control techniques in New Dawn, particularly the sexual.

Sex would always be the most basic of the human needs and, within New Dawn, it was the easiest of all to satisfy once you reached the inner circle. After the Daughters of the New Dawn were trained, they were allowed to cohabit with the men of his inner circle. Some of them even cohabited with a few of the older women. Best of all, though, when you grew bored with your current partner, another one would be assigned. And there was no shortage of beautiful young women to choose from, each of them an expert in giving sexual pleasure.

In return for having their carnal desires so thoroughly satisfied, his followers were totally devoted to him and his cause. He hadn't even needed to design fancy uniforms to foster this devotion. He was surprised that no one had hit upon this particular method of social control before. It was so easy—simply give the people what they wanted most, but make it a privilege of status. No status, no nooky.

Nisi chuckled to himself at his little joke. The day would soon come when men and women from all over the nation would beg to become a part of his organization. But he had learned from Hitler's experience with the SS to keep the inner circle an exclusive club.

The New Dawn's inner circle would have to grow larger as Nisi's span of control expanded and he needed more lieutenants. His success would bring thousands flocking to his banner, but he would be careful to pick only the cream of the cream of these new followers to join the ranks of the elite. That had been one of Hitler's greatest flaws; he had not been careful enough in picking his inner circle. Drug addicts like Göring, homosexuals like Heydrich and psychopaths like Himmler had been all too common around the führer. Nisi wouldn't make that mistake. His closest followers would only be those fit to serve the New Dawn.

Nisi leaned back in his chair. The New Dawn he had dreamed of since he had been a college student was so close that he could smell it. And it smelled like victory, victory over all those who had tried so hard to keep him from developing his full potential.

After graduating at the top of his class in the small Midwestern town where he had been raised, he had gone to the university to get an education. Instead of getting an education, though, he had run face first into the not so subtle neobarbarism of the politically correct movement on campus. He had been horrified to see the lowering of entrance standards to include those who never should have been allowed into higher learning. He had come from a poor family, and even though he had almost perfect SAT scores, he had had difficulty obtaining financial aid for his education because so much of the available scholarship money was going to the so-called minorities.

Then he discovered that the "dumbing down" of classes so that the stupid could be given degrees they hadn't earned made many of his courses useless from a practical standpoint. The censorship of free speech, though, had been even worse, and speaking his mind at a dormitory meeting had gotten him expelled from his first university.

Back then, Joshua Nisi had been known as Bob Fullerton. When he had been expelled from the university in his sophomore year for speaking out on the subject of the so-called minorities, he changed his name. He chose Joshua as his first name after the man who had made the walls of Jericho fall. He intended to make the walls of academia fall in the same way. Nisi meant prince in ancient Hebrew, and he thought it went well with his new first name. After all, the man who intended to change the world would be a prince among men.

To change the world, however, required money, lots of money. In his new university, he changed his academic major from math to bioengineering. Math was fun, but no one had ever become a millionaire by discovering some obscure math formula. Bioengineering, however, was the hot ticket and serious money could be made from splicing the right genes together.

The patent on a bioengineered enzyme had made him wealthy beyond his dreams, but that had not made him feel better about the state of the nation.

Civilization in the United States was rapidly crumbling and, while he was insulated from the barbarians by his money, it was not enough. As a civilized man himself, he could not sit by and watch it die without doing something.

In other times and other places, when society had been threatened, great men had stepped forward to do what had to be done, and he saw himself as one of those great men of history. People would write books about him for the next thousand years as the man who had saved Western civilization from the neobarbarians.

**18**

*The New Dawn Complex*
*January 26*

Alex Sendak woke to find himself in what looked like the result of a bastard mating between a hospital room and a prison cell. The last thing he remembered was that he'd gone to work in the morning and his foreman told him to report to the company's medical center to undergo a routine employment physical. Apparently the examination had been a little more than routine and had turned up more than just his bad knee.

His head pounded as if he had been hit between the eyes with a baseball bat and his mouth had a horrible, scummy taste. He sat up and slowly swung his legs over the edge of the small bed. When his head stopped spinning, he took a physical inventory. The strip of adhesive tape on the back of his hand told him the whole story. Joshua Nisi hadn't needed to resort to the old rubber-hose routine to interrogate him, not when he was running one of the nation's most advanced chemistry labs.

Using pain to extract information from a subject was simply not intelligent when there were quicker and much more reliable ways to get what you wanted. Using pain to break a man down was a long, drawn-out process more suited to sadists than to intelligence gathering. Whatever else Nisi was, he was obviously too smart to waste his time being sadistic. Any of a number of modern scopolamine derivatives delivered through an IV drip would give him the information he was looking for.

Sendak wondered if the scope treatment was routine for all new employees or if he had somehow given himself away. He thought back to last Saturday night at the Goat Roper's Tavern, trying to recall saying anything that might have triggered someone's suspicions, but nothing came to mind. He also didn't think that anyone had seen him drive to the gas station to make his phone report to Rykoff.

If, however, a chemical interrogation was the standard procedure for everyone who signed on with the New Dawn, it was no wonder that no one had been able to get anything on the company. Anyone who tried would get the treatment and would reveal his or her actual motives, just as he had apparently done.

This, of course, meant that he wasn't going to walk out of this place on his own two feet. As soon as the thought surfaced, he suppressed the question about what Nisi did with the bodies of the ringers he caught. Compared to the fact that Nisi now knew everything there was to know about the CAT Team, his own death wasn't too important. Sendak had no illusions about what he had revealed under the influence of the drug. And since he had given Nisi that information, he had put his teammates in jeopardy.

Before Rykoff could take action to protect himself and what was left of the team, he would have to be warned, and that was the problem. Sendak didn't know what Rykoff's fallback position was in case the Team was discovered. But, whatever it was, he would have to go to it quickly. As it was, their asses were hanging in the wind.

Since his watch hadn't made it into the cell with him, he ran his hand over his cheek and determined that his beard hadn't grown any since he shaved Monday morning. That meant that it was still sometime Monday, maybe Monday night at the latest, and time was running out for him to do something.

He carefully looked around for a way out of his cell, but there was nothing in the small room that could be used as a weapon or a tool. While the cell had the look of a hospital room, it had been designed as a secure holding chamber. The sink and toilet were jail-style fixtures with no exposed plumbing. The bed frame was a single piece of molded plastic and the light fixtures were recessed behind thick glass covers. James Bond might have been able to find a way to get out of there, but he sure as hell couldn't.

His only hope was the old jump-the-guard-at-dinnertime routine of every spy movie. but if Nisi was smart enough to have caught him, he probably knew that routine, as well. It was his only option, though, and he lay back on the thin mattress to rest up for it. The least Nisi could have done was provide a TV set in his cells so his prisoners could watch CNN.

As SENDAK HAD FEARED, Joshua Nisi was already taking steps to take out the rest of the CAT Team. He was flattered that he had been targeted by what seemed to be the nation's number-one secret action team. This was the sort of thing that only happened in cheap paperback thrillers, and a part of his mind wanted to discount it as being one man's macho fantasy. But he also knew that the drugs he had given Sendak could not be denied. Like the sex potion he gave the girls, he was certain that the mixture he used to interrogate the candidates for the inner circle worked because he had personally designed and tested it. No matter how preposterous it sounded, whatever came out of their mouths when they were under the influence of the drug was the truth.

The thought of a clandestine action team unknown to any level of government amused Nisi. Whoever had thought that one up was good, but obviously not good enough. The cat was out of the bag now and would never be put back in. The only question he had now was whether he should destroy this so-called CAT Team or try to subvert it for his own uses. He could think of several instances where it might be very helpful to have a unit like that at his beck and call.

On second thought, though, he realized that would probably not work with these people. The team's leader, "the Major," as Sendak had called him, sounded like a fanatic, and fanatics drew other fanatics to themselves. Plus, the other three team members were so-called minorities. Even if he could subvert them, he would never be able to fully trust them because he could never bring them into the inner circle. No non-Caucasians could ever be part of New Dawn's leadership.

Since Sendak reported that his teammates were in L.A., this was a job for Smith and Jones. His fingers quickly punched in Smith's cell phone number, and when his call connected, his orders to the South African mercenary were short and specific—track down members of the CAT Team as soon as possible and kill them on sight.

His next call was to his security chief to have the new prisoner brought to his office. He wanted to see this Sendak for himself.

IN L.A., Mr. Smith put down the phone, turned the scrambler off and stared at the name and address of the hotel he had been given. That black gang punk, whatever his name had been, had also given him the name of the same hotel. When he'd told Smith about the men who had questioned him, Smith had figured them to be Feds of some kind just trying to frighten the punk.

It was too bad that he had killed the gang banger so quickly. Now he wished that he had asked more questions about this mysterious CAT Team, as Nisi had called them.

The idea of an American supersecret action team didn't surprise Smith the way it had his employer. Someone had been taking lessons from the Boer resistance groups in his homeland, but they had taken the concept one step further. In the nation once known as the Republic of South Africa—Smith could not bring himself to even think of it by the name the black majority government had given it—the Boer Resistance Commandos were fighting to retain their embattled homeland. Every white South African—man, woman or child—knew of their exploits. Here, even though this group was also apparently targeted against enemies of the state, no one knew a thing about them or even knew that they existed. How un-American.

In a land where everyone, no matter how petty or criminal their miserable lives were, clamored for their very own fifteen minutes of fame, this group alone worked without fanfare or recognition for their efforts. It was admirable and, under other circumstances, he would be proud to meet these unique Americans. But, as always, the mission came first and they had to be taken out and taken out quickly to protect the New Dawn project.

Smith was glad that he had suggested to Nisi that every new recruit to the inner circle go through the chemical interrogation procedure as part of the company medical examination. Nisi had argued against it at first, but it was the only failsafe way Smith knew to sort out the ringers from the real job applicants, and Nisi had finally seen his point. For all the hundreds of negative reports, the precautionary measure had paid off big this time.

It had paid off once before when that so-called investigative reporter had tried to infiltrate the organization. He'd had an accident involving a poisonous snake, the one the locals called the rattler. This Sendak would probably not die that easily, nor would his body be found. The secrecy of his team meant that he could disappear and no one would even inquire about him. How convenient.

Smith reached under his bed and brought out a large suitcase. This job would require specialized firepower, but he was an arms dealer and specialized weapons were his stock-in-trade. As soon as Jones returned, they would contact their Korean hit squad and start putting a plan together to take out this mysterious CAT Team.

WHEN THE GUARDS CAME for him, Sendak didn't get even the slightest chance to try the old jump-'em-and-escape routine. When the door of his cell opened, two men with drawn pistols covered him while a third came into the room.

"Stand up, turn around and put your hands behind your back," the third guard barked.

Sendak did as he was told and felt a plastic riot restraint slipped over his hands and snugged down around his wrists. Even with his hands secure, the two guards with the guns didn't holster them. The third man took his elbow and steered him toward the open door. "Come on," was all he said.

No one said a word as he was marched down a long corridor to an elevator. When he was escorted into the car, he saw that there were six floors marked on the control panel and the lighted indicator showed that his accommodations were on the fifth. When the door opened on the first floor, he was led to another elevator that had only Up and Down buttons on its control panel. When he was led out of it, he knew he was on the way to see the big man.

Alex Sendak tried not to look too impressed by Joshua Nisi's office when he was taken in. He'd have been more willing to be properly impressed were his hands not bound behind him in the riot cuffs. Even so, it was an impressive office by anyone's standards. The shuttered picture windows provided a panoramic view of the Chiricahua Valley. The harsh afternoon sun was filtered so that it fell softly on the thick carpet and the expensive art on the wood-paneled walls. Everything was in the best of taste and screamed money. Not so the geek sitting behind the executive teak desk.

Like Hitler, Joshua Nisi didn't look like a man of destiny until you focused on his eyes and found them to be the eyes of a fanatic. Unlike Hitler, though, on him the fanatic eyes looked out of place on the otherwise rather plain face of a very unremarkable man. With his neatly combed, mouse brown hair, untanned skin and cheap eyeglass frames, he looked more like the lab scientist he was than a messiah.

When Nisi didn't offer him a seat, order his restraints taken off or dismiss his three guards, Sendak knew this was not to be a social call and he waited silently for Nisi to make the first move.

"If you're as smart as you seem to be, ex-Master Sergeant Alexander T. Sendak, late of the 75th Rangers and Project Blue Light, you will have already figured out why you are in your present circumstances."

When Nisi paused, Sendak still didn't say anything. The ball was in this guy's court, so he would let him take his best shot and see if it went down.

"Oh," Nisi continued. "I forgot to mention your CAT Team, didn't I? How do you think the good major is taking your absence? How long will it be before he becomes worried and sends Big Black Jake or Erik the Pilot to check in on your well-being?"

Sendak still stood without speaking. What was there for him to say? Nisi obviously knew everything he needed to know. Everything, that is, except for Rykoff's next move. Sendak had an idea what Rykoff would do once he figured out that he had been killed or captured, but he didn't know for sure.

"You don't have anything to say about your teammates, Mr. Sendak?" Nisi smiled and looked even more like a geek. "Before tomorrow is out, I expect to hear that Rykoff, Bao, MacLeod and Estevez are among the casualties in the ethnic violence sweeping Los Angeles. It will be sad, of course, that such brave people have been killed. But it will serve to show America that no one is really safe as long as they live among barbarians. Not even people who stay in prestigious hotels to keep away from the racial violence in the streets of Los Angeles.''

Nisi stepped out from behind his desk. ''And you get to live only as long as the rest of your so-called teammates do. When I get word that they have been eliminated, you will join them because I will have no other use for you.''

Sendak didn't bother to reply to that, either. It would do no good to beg for his life and he wasn't about to give the bastard the pleasure.

At least, if Nisi wasn't going to kill him until Rykoff and the others were killed, that meant that he had a chance to get out of this alive. He was confident that Rykoff wouldn't prove to be as easy to kill as Nisi thought he was. In fact, even though all the balls were in Nisi's court, he wouldn't count Rykoff and the others out until he saw their bodies himself.

Nisi slowly walked up to him. ''I know your type, Sendak. Basically, you're a good man and I could have made something out of you. Unfortunately, though, you have sided with the barbarians, the destroyers, and I cannot understand why you have done that. You and your team are working to stop me, along with everything I'm doing to make sure that civilization is not eradicated in this country.''

"Starting a race war is promoting civilization?" Sendak asked.

"I didn't start the war," Nisi snarled. "It was started years ago when the so-called minorities were first allowed into this country. Ever since then, we have been at war with them and we have been losing. All you have to do is take a look at the rising crime statistics since the early 1960s. They have been destroying this country—one murder, one rape and one drug deal at a time—and we have been powerless to stop them."

Sendak knew that this was a speech Nisi had made many times before, but it hadn't originated with him. It was a speech as old as mankind and had been given by every dictator and mass murderer in history.

Nisi's voice fell as he went on. "Since we have not been able to stop them, I have simply given these barbarians the means to stop themselves. Now that they are properly armed, they will continue to kill each other the way they do in their own countries until there will be no more of them. Or there will be so few of them that they won't matter anymore.

"Best of all, though, is that now the average American will see what these people are really like. There has been so much liberal propaganda over the last twenty years that far too many Americans think that it is okay to watch their civilization crumble around them. They have been taught to accept crime in their streets, murder, rape and robbery in their homes as normal. They are so used to seeing their tax dollars going to support this state of affairs that they don't even realize that life can be any different."

Nisi got right up in Sendak's face. "Now, though, this will awaken them. They will see what these people are really like and a New Dawn will break over the United States. When this is all over and we have taken the nation back from the barbarians, never more will we let these subhumans across our borders."

When Nisi paused, Sendak finally spoke. "Heil Hitler!" he said softly.

Nisi recoiled and his eyes narrowed. "You're going to wish you had kept your smart mouth shut, Sendak."

Sendak had nothing further to say to this psychopathic, repulsive little man.

"Take him back to his cell," Nisi snapped.

## 19

*New Dawn Compound*
*January 27*

When they took him back to his cell, Alex Sendak's escorts didn't immediately remove the restraints from his hands. In fact, after pushing him into the cell, they crowded in with him, closed the door and holstered their side arms.

"Shooting your mouth off to Joshua Nisi wasn't a smart move, asshole." The smile on the face of the guard wasn't at all pleasant. "He deserves respect for what he has done here."

Sendak knew he was in deep kimchee, but he couldn't keep himself from having the last word. "He's a fucking Nazi," he said with a shrug.

With his hands bound behind his back, there was no way he could protect himself from the barrage of blows the guard suddenly unleashed. A hammer blow to the gut drove him backward. Two more had him up against the wall of the small cell and there was no-where to go to escape the blows. He could only duck his head and try to protect his face. When the first man was done, the second guard took over.

Finally Sendak was on his knees, his face pressed against the floor while the third man methodically kicked him in the ribs and belly. After a last kick that lifted him off the ground, the guard leaned down and cut the plastic restraint binding his wrists.

"Watch your mouth next time, asshole," the first guard said as he stepped out of the cell.

Only when he heard the door lock did Sendak allow a moan to escape his lips as he huddled on the floor. Someday he was going to have to learn to keep his smart-ass editorial comments to himself. Particularly when he was in a situation like this.

When he could move again, he dragged himself over to the edge of the narrow bed. Lifting himself up into it took everything that he had. Even though he moved as gently as he could, he felt the ends of a broken rib grate together, sending bolts of blinding pain through his right side. If one of the jagged ends of bone had punctured his lung, he was in for a rough time before he drowned in his own blood. He didn't think his captors were too big on medical care for their prisoners.

As he lay on his thin mattress, the beating of his heart sending repeated waves of pain through his battered torso, Sendak started putting his mental house in order. Having been in combat, he had already faced the possibility of death many times; all combat veterans went through that. He had also faced death several times since he had been working with Rykoff. This time was different, though.

This time there was nothing he could do to help himself; he couldn't even fight back. About the only thing he could do was to keep his big mouth shut so he didn't get beaten to death ahead of time. The fact that his captors were so willing to severely damage him did not bode well for his survival in their custody. In fact, it convinced him that Nisi would keep his promise to have him killed as soon as he had no further use for him.

Worse than his helplessness to prevent his own death was the fact that there was nothing he could do to warn Rykoff. If Nisi hadn't been blowing smoke, he was going to send a hit squad after the Team. Since he wasn't scheduled to check in with Jud until the end of the week, Rykoff had no way of knowing that he had been compromised. Sendak could only take solace in the fact that even if he was caught by surprise, Jud Rykoff was not an easy man to kill. Neither were the rest of the Team.

Nisi had a real advantage, but it might not be enough. At least Sendak hoped that it wouldn't. He wanted Rykoff to avenge his death.

SMITH AND JONES checked into the Regina Hotel with the proper amount of luggage so as not to arouse the suspicions of the desk clerk even though they paid for their room with cash. Foreign visitors often paid with cash, so they could get by on that one. The clerk didn't even mind when they specifically requested a room on the fourth floor. He had several vacancies, so it wasn't a problem.

When the desk clerk rang for a bellhop, Smith and Jones said that they would carry their own luggage. The bellhop was slightly offended, more at the tip he would miss than at the implication that he would bang up their bags. He was surprised when Smith tipped him anyway when he showed them to their room, but you could never tell what foreigners were going to do.

As soon as they were alone, Smith and Jones opened their luggage and started unloading their personal weapons. They didn't plan to make the hit at the hotel, but since Rykoff and his people were only one story and two rooms to the left below them, it didn't hurt to be prepared.

When everything was ready, Smith picked up his cellular phone and made a call to a small bar in a Latino barrio in East L.A. When the bartender answered in Spanish, Smith asked for Erik Estevez by name.

"Yeah?" Estevez answered a moment later.

"My name is Mr. Smith," the South African said. "I understand that you have been trying to reach me. What can I do for you?"

RYKOFF WAS GLAD to see Erik Estevez show up at the door of the suite. Now that Sendak was in the field, manning the command post by himself was getting old quickly. It was bad enough to be stuck with the "duty," but it was twice as bad to have to do it without having anyone else to talk to, or bitch at.

"Whatcha got?"

"I'm not sure about this one," Estevez said. "But I wanted to run it by you anyway, and I didn't want to phone it in. As you know, I tried that gun dealer's number to try to make a connection, but came up with zilch. Then, all of a sudden, I get a call today at the bar I've been hanging out in and get an invitation to buy as many AKs as I can afford. It smells like a setup to me and makes me wonder if we've been made."

"What's the deal?"

"I'm to meet this Smith guy and bring the money. He'll have the weapons and ammunition waiting for me."

"That sounds straightforward enough. Where's the meeting place?"

Estevez frowned. "That's what I really don't like. He wants to meet me at a warehouse in one of the cargo port areas and he warned me to come alone. Somewhere in the Marina Del Rey district—5065B Harbor Way."

Rykoff walked over to the large-scale map of L.A. and looked for the address.

"When's the meeting scheduled?"

"Nine o'clock tonight. I told him that it would take me that long to get the money together."

Rykoff took a grease pencil and circled the location on the map. "Did your caller have a European accent?"

"A faint one, yes, but he didn't sound British. He identified himself as Mr. Smith and he sounded like he could be one of your South Africans."

"Let's go for it." Rykoff grinned. "I want to get a look at our mysterious Mr. Smith and Jones."

"But what if it's a setup?"

Rykoff dropped the grin. "I'm sure it's a setup. But if we know it's a trap, then it isn't a trap, is it? Plus, we can invite Mel and Jake to the party in case we need a little extra firepower.

"How do you think they got onto me?"

Rykoff shook his head. "I don't know, but I'm not sure that they did. They probably think that you're some kind of undercover cop. You've been pretty high-profile and pushing hard to get their number. The guy who gave it to you probably called Smith and finked on you."

Estevez shook his head. "I don't think so, Jud. I didn't get the number until I saved that kid from that drive-by shooting I told you about. Paco owed me big time for that one and that was his way of paying me back. I really don't think he would have ratted on me."

"It doesn't really matter how they made you," Rykoff said with a shrug. "Since we know about it, the ball's in our court. We'll go in looking for trouble and if it doesn't happen, we won't be out anything."

He glanced at his watch, then reached for the phone on the desk. "I'd better call them in now so we can plan this thing."

"I'll make a fresh pot of coffee," Estevez offered.

"Great," Rykoff replied. "As soon as I'm done here, I'll call down for lunch. I could use a big roast beef with Swiss and fresh Bermudas right about now."

WHEN MACLEOD'S WATCH beeped to let him know that Rykoff wanted to talk to him, he didn't have far to go to find a phone. He was working on the central switchboard of the cellular-phone retransmission center, trying to install the clipper chip. Taking the test phone from his equipment belt, he quickly hooked it to an outside line and punched in Rykoff's number.

"What do you want?" he asked gruffly when Rykoff picked up on the other end. "I'm working."

"Call in sick," Rykoff replied. "I need you back here. Erik finally got a break and we're going to go buy us some Ukrainian guns tonight."

"Damn," MacLeod said. "I just got that damned clipper chip hooked up."

"Leave it there," Rykoff advised. "We may need it later if this doesn't pan out."

"I'll be there in under an hour."

"Take your time. I need you to make a recon on a warehouse at 5065B Harbor Way in Marina Del Rey on your way back here. Take your tool kit with you and check a fuse box or something, but I need a floor plan of the place."

"What's at the address?"

"Our target for tonight."

"Got it covered."

MEL BAO had been fully accepted by the Quan Family Tong. Both the men and the women treated her as if she was one of their own. She was taking all her meals with them now and was included in the discussions of family business, as well as security matters. When her receptor watch signaled that she had a message, she excused herself from the lunch table and called Rykoff from the pay phone by the rest rooms.

"I've just had an important call from my agent," she explained to Dan Quan when she returned. "I need to see a client. It's a big job and I need to talk to them about it. It will be a real boost for my portfolio if I can land this assignment.

"I'll be back tomorrow morning," she promised when she saw the look on his face. "We'll have breakfast."

In the past couple of days, Dan's interest in her had become serious. He wasn't going to be pleased when she finally had to move on, but it couldn't be helped. She couldn't quite see herself as the wife of a Chinese businessman, no matter how rich or how cute. She also didn't think that the reality of her life would meet with his approval.

Back in her hotel room, she quickly changed into her business clothes. She knew that the desk clerk would tell Dan if she left wearing anything else. Her "working" clothes were in Rykoff's suite with her weapons and she would change again when she got there.

On the sidewalk in front of the hotel, she was careful to hail a cab that didn't have an Oriental driver. That was another problem with getting involved with the Chinese community in a place like this. There were eyes everywhere. The last thing she needed was for Dan to learn where she was going tonight.

BAO WAS LAST to arrive at the hotel suite, and when she walked in, Rykoff and MacLeod were already suited up for war. "It looks like you finally got your hard lead," she said to Rykoff.

"Erik finally connected," he said with a nod at Estevez, who was putting on a Kevlar vest. "He arranged a gun buy tonight, and since it's obviously a setup, we're going along as backup."

"Where's Alex?" she asked when she noticed that Sendak was missing.

"He's in Arizona trying to infiltrate the company that brought our two South African gunrunners into the country. His last report was that they appeared clean so far, but a little too disciplined and organized for his taste."

"A Japanese firm?"

Rykoff laughed. "No. Actually, this mob is home-grown American, which is why he's concerned."

"What's the plan for tonight?"

"Get suited up and I'll go over it."

Taking a large suitcase from the closet, Bao opened it and took out a one-piece night-black combat suit.

Quickly stripping down to her bikini panties, she stepped into the formfitting coveralls.

Since her back was turned to him as she zipped it up, Rykoff saw that the scar from the knife wound she had taken on the Cuban mission had not yet faded. "How's your shoulder?" he asked.

Bao put her right arm through a complicated movement designed to test her full range of motion. "It's fine," she said. "I started working out as soon as they pulled the stitches and there was no real damage."

"Good. And don't forget to wear your Kevlar dainties tonight," he added. "We know these guys are packing and packing heavy. It could get interesting."

"One bullet-proof girdle coming up." She reached back into her suitcase and drew out a black, full-torso Kevlar vest, women's size small.

"This little number should do it," she said as she slipped into the vest, settled it down over her shoulders and fastened the tabs on the sides. "It's good for up to 7.62 mm NATO at fifty meters."

"We'll probably be facing 5.45 mm Russian at fifty feet or less tonight."

"It'll handle it," she said. "But I don't intend to get hit."

"Good girl."

As soon as their weapons and comm links had been checked, Rykoff gathered his team around the drawing MacLeod had made of the warehouse. "Okay," he said, "here's the setup. We're going to pay a visit to this warehouse in Marina Del Rey. Erik will be going in alone to meet Smith and Jones to make a gun buy. He's scheduled to show up there at nine, so the rest of us will go in ten minutes early to check the place out.''

He let a slow smile cross his face. "On the odd chance that this is not an ambush, we still want to police these guys up and bring them back here for a little chat. If it's the ambush I expect it to be, try to leave one of them alive, but don't take a risk to do it.''

He tapped the drawing. "Now, we know that there's at least two of them, but I'll be surprised if they don't have a few extra gunmen on hand. For this thing to work, the three of us will have to have the building under control before Erik walks in. Here's how I want to do it...."

**20**

*Los Angeles*
*January 27*

The South African mercenary known as Mr. Smith greeted Kim, the Korean gang leader, and his half-dozen gunmen in the parking lot behind the warehouse. As he had instructed, none of the Koreans had come armed. Considering that he had an armory inside the building, that would have been like taking a ham sandwich to a banquet. Plus, the last thing he needed tonight was to have his hit team pulled over for a traffic infraction and have the cops discover a car full of illegal weapons.

"What's the job tonight?" Kim asked. Since the first attack on the Latino wedding, Kim's men had made several more hits for Smith and Jones. The pay was right and the targets were always the Mexican and black street scum who had killed his grandparents. He would have gladly killed them for free, but as long as Smith and Jones were willing to hire him, it made more sense to get paid for it.

"One of the Mexican gangs think they're going to rip me off tonight," Smith said. "And I can use your help again. I'll pay you in cash or in AKs and RPG antitank launchers.''

''Which gang is it?''

''The Eastside Cholo Kings.''

Kim frowned. ''I don't think I know them.''

''They heard about my guns and decided that they wanted to get in on the action themselves. They set up a buy tonight, but I have information that they're going to hit me.''

''How many are coming?''

''There will probably only be four of them,'' Smith said. ''But they'll be well armed and they know what they're doing. From what I hear, they're quite good.''

Kim snorted. He had been going up against Mexican gang bangers for a long time now, and as far as he was concerned, they weren't worth shit. That posturing, swaggering, macho Latino bullshit was no substitute for a real pair of balls and the discipline of a true warrior. He and his men had already started their warrior training when those Mexicans punks were still shitting in their diapers.

''We can handle forty of them,'' Kim bragged. ''Where's our weapons? We left ours behind like you wanted.''

Smith led him over to a wooden crate and lifted the lid. Reaching in, he pulled out an Israeli 9 mm Uzi submachine gun. The subgun's barrel was swollen to a three-inch diameter and extended another six inches beyond what was normal for the type.

"We'll be using silenced Uzis tonight," Smith said. "I want to keep this as quiet as possible."

Kim smiled as he picked up one of the pieces and expertly cracked the bolt to check the chamber. He liked the idea of making a silent kill. The Mexicans wouldn't know what hit them. He slapped a loaded magazine in place in the handle and pulled back on the bolt handle to chamber a round.

WHILE ESTEVEZ DROVE around to the front gate of the warehouse area, Rykoff, Bao and MacLeod drove in through the rear gate in their rented van. Parking the vehicle in an unlighted area two buildings down from their objective, they silently stepped out. After they took cover against the side of the building, they locked and loaded their weapons as they checked out the immediate area.

"Comm check," Rykoff whispered over the throat mike of his comm link.

"Lima Charlie," MacLeod whispered back.

"Load and clear," Estevez answered.

"Same here," Bao transmitted.

"Let's go," Rykoff sent back. "Mel, Jake, take the point."

The approach to the building was clear. When they reached the end of the warehouse next to their target, Rykoff and Estevez stayed in the shadows to provide covering fire while Bao and MacLeod went on ahead to clear the rear of their objective.

Moving like a black cat in her night combat suit, Bao's rubber-soled boots made no sound as she slipped from shadow to shadow. Even though their target was blacked out, with the number of lights shining throughout the dock area she could see well enough that she didn't need to use her night-vision goggles. She was making her move to the rear of the building when she spotted the first of the opposition.

"Rykoff," she whispered over her comm link. "It's a setup, all right. I've got a guy halfway up the rear fire escape and he's packing what looks like a silenced Uzi."

"I've got the same keeping an eye on the loading area in front of the warehouse," MacLeod reported from the side of the building.

"Can you take yours out quietly, Mel?" Rykoff asked.

"I'm moving now," she whispered.

"Jake, wait for her."

The problem with Bao's man was that he was ten feet above her and there was no way she could go up the fire escape without him hearing her. Reaching behind the small of her back, she drew the silenced .22-caliber Ruger from her belt. Once more the old reliable methods would do the trick. All she would need to do was to catch him when he fell so the ones inside wouldn't hear the sodden thud of a falling body.

The man was leaning back against the side of the building, his head partially obscured by the framework of the fire escape. To get a clear shot, she would need to attract his attention without making him give an alarm. Activating the red-dot laser sight on the Ruger pistol, she aimed it at the railing in front of her target. As she thought he would, the man didn't recognize the red light and moved forward to see what it was. When he did, his head came into her line of fire.

Smoothly moving the laser dot from the railing to the man's temple, she triggered one round. The pistol puffed and the hollowpoint .22 round mushroomed in the man's brain. He stiffened and staggered forward, the Uzi falling from his hands. The sling over his shoulder kept the weapon from falling to the steel platform of the fire escape as he toppled over the edge.

Bracing herself, Bao broke the body's fall and eased it to the ground. "I've got mine," she reported. "He looks Korean and he was armed with a silenced Uzi. He was also packing a small radio."

"Roger," Rykoff sent back. "Jake, you're next."

MacLeod made a more straightforward kill. He simply walked up behind his man with his old Ka-bar SEAL fighting knife in his right hand. With one smooth move, he clamped his left hand over the man's mouth and jerked his head back and to the side. When his neck was exposed, the broad razor-sharp blade whipped across his neck from one side to the other, severing his carotid, jugular and windpipe in one swipe.

When the man's feet stopped kicking, he lowered the body to the ground and rolled it up against the wall. "I'm clear," he transmitted. "And I've got an open entry."

"I'm inside on the second level," Bao whispered.

Sitting in his car parked one building down, Estevez monitored the Team's comm link chatter as they cleared the rear approaches to the warehouse. As soon as they could get in position to cover the inside of the building, he'd make his move.

"You're clear to go," Rykoff transmitted. "But be advised that the opposition has hired some help. Mel thinks that they're Koreans and they're packing silenced Uzis."

"Roger," he responded as he hit the starter. "I'll be on the lookout for them."

INSIDE THE BUILDING, Smith and Jones waited impatiently. They didn't know how the CAT Team was going to make the attack, but they had all their bases covered. Having Kim's men outside should give them ample warning of anyone approaching, so they were surprised when they heard Estevez's car drive up to the front door.

Estevez checked the front of the warehouse before getting out of his car. Taking the briefcase from the passenger seat, he walked over to the partially opened door in the front of the warehouse and stopped. "Hey!" he called out. "It's Estevez! Is anyone there?"

"Come on in," a voice called out from inside.

Estevez didn't like the sound of the voice, but he had to go through with this. He just hoped that the Kevlar vest under his windbreaker was up to specs. He held the briefcase out in front of him as he walked into the dimly lit interior of the building.

In the dim light from the single bulb high on the ceiling, he saw two older Caucasians standing by a stack of wooden crates. The taller of the two had a subgun in his hand, but that was to be expected in a gun buy.

"Mr. Smith?" Estevez said, holding out the briefcase. "I've got the money."

Without saying a word, Smith raised the Uzi and Estevez threw himself face first onto the concrete, sliding for cover behind the nearest pillar.

A silenced burst of subgun fire chipped concrete behind him. "Rykoff!" he shouted over his comm link. "Go for it!"

"Flash-bangs!" Rykoff ordered.

From her position high inside the warehouse, Bao pitched a flash-bang grenade toward the South Africans before scrambling down to the main floor. MacLeod did the same from his side door and followed the grenade inside. The flash of the grenades threw sharp shadows that hid the movement of the Team.

When the grenades went off, the two South Africans dropped for cover. This wasn't going as Smith had predicted, and Jones wasn't amused. Even though Nisi had made Smith the leader of the two, Jones was the one with all the combat experience. Smith had sold weapons all over the world, but Jones had used them and he'd had them used against him more times than he liked to remember. He knew when a plan had gone bad, and this one stunk. As soon as he could see again, he started crawling for cover.

Blinded by the grenades, Smith didn't know that his partner had beat feet. Getting to his feet, he started firing long bursts from his Uzi, spraying silenced 9 mm slugs in a cone in front of him. One of the rounds ricocheted off the concrete and hit the crawling Jones in the right thigh. He bit back a cry of pain, but held his Uzi and kept on crawling.

MACLEOD SLIPPED away from the inside wall by the door and made his way through the stacked crates for the center of the building. The silencers on the opposition's Uzis kept him from spotting the gunners by sound, but the Uzis still showed a small muzzle-flash when they were aimed at him. And that small flash was all he needed.

When a spray of bullets splashed to his left, he saw a twinkle of muzzle-flashes. Carefully sighting in his H&K, MacLeod triggered three shots on semiauto fire. He was rewarded by a sharp cry of pain and the clatter of a weapon falling to the concrete floor. When the shadowy figure staggered out into his view, he put him down with a single shot to the head. "I got one," he called out.

Rykoff had kicked a door down when the grenades went off, then he rushed into the warehouse. Seeing a single man standing in the light, blazing away with his Uzi, he triggered a long burst at him. The man staggered under the impact of the rounds and went down. Rykoff ducked under cover to look for his next target. "Two down," he transmitted.

Estevez had his Beretta out and was exchanging fire with a man crouched behind a roof pillar. Neither one of them could get a clear shot at the other. When Estevez stopped to reload his pistol, Kim pulled himself completely behind the pillar to change magazines in his Uzi.

The Korean realized that this was a setup. Whoever these people were, they sure as hell weren't the Mexican gang bangers Smith claimed they were. These men were trained professionals, probably Feds of some kind, but he wasn't going to stick around for formal introductions. "Get out of here!" he yelled out in Korean. Spraying half a magazine of 9 mm rounds, he sprinted for the front door.

Bao caught a shadow making for the door and she dashed after him. She brushed against a pile of empty boxes as she ran, and they crashed to the floor. The running man spun around, bringing his weapon up to bear.

She dived for cover as he sprayed a long burst in her direction. She answered with a short burst from her H&K before the bolt locked back on an empty magazine. He fired again, but his Uzi also fell silent on an empty magazine.

Shouting a challenge, Bao leaped from her hiding place. While Kim fumbled to pull another magazine from his pocket, she spun and delivered a high kick to his chest. Driven by all the strength in her leg, the heel of her boot smashed into his chest right above his heart. Unlike in a kick-boxing movie, the Korean fell to the floor as if he had been dropped off the roof. Snatching the Ruger pistol from her belt, Bao drilled a .22 hollowpoint into his forehead.

For a moment silence echoed in the warehouse.

"Is everyone okay?" Rykoff asked.

"Roger," MacLeod sent back.

"I think I soiled my shorts," Estevez said, still shaking as he got to his feet.

"I'm okay," Bao panted.

"Spread out," Rykoff commanded. "And see if we left anybody alive to talk to."

JONES WASN'T fatally wounded, but he was bleeding badly. He had taken a stray bullet that had torn up the inside of his thigh. To Bao's experienced eye, the wound was the type that looked worse than it was as she walked up to him and kicked the Uzi out of his reach.

"Help me," Jones said.

"Keep your hands open and in sight, mister. If you move, you're dead."

"I won't do anything stupid."

"You already did."

Keeping the muzzle of her H&K trained on him, Bao knelt beside him. "Put your hands out in front of you, slowly," she said.

When his hands were in the proper position, she secured them with a set of plastic riot restraints. Only then did she take her fighting knife out of her boot sheath and cut his pants leg away to expose the wound. Just as she had thought, it wasn't as bad as it looked. Taking a pressure bandage from one of her side pockets, she tied it over the bullet holes to slow the bleeding.

"Let's get him the hell outta here before the cops show up," Rykoff growled.

"He's ready to go," she answered as she stood up.

"Where are you taking me?" Jones asked through clenched teeth as MacLeod hauled him to his feet.

Rykoff motioned with the muzzle of his H&K. "Shut up and move out."

Jones shut up and let MacLeod lead him away.

"Leave the rest of them," Rykoff ordered when he saw Estevez reach down to pick up one of the fallen Uzis lying beside a dead Korean. "And leave the weapons for the cops to find. Maybe they'll get a clue this time."

THE TEAM'S RENTED VAN had just cleared the rear gate of the warehouse complex when a caravan of police cars and two SWAT vans roared into the dock area through the front gate. They slammed to a halt in front of the warehouse and poured out of their vehicles, their weapons at the ready. When no one shot at them, the SWAT teams leapfrogged forward to the partially opened doors. Hugging the doors, they tossed flash-bang grenades inside. When the grenades went off, they stormed inside.

"That's cutting it a little too close for my tastes," Estevez muttered as he restrained himself from standing on the gas as he merged into the traffic of the Harbor Freeway. The last thing they needed right now was to get stopped for speeding.

"We got what we came for, though," Rykoff said as he turned around to look at MacLeod's prisoner. "Now maybe we can find out what in the hell's been going on around here."

**21**

*Los Angeles*
*January 27*

The wounded South African didn't give Jake Mac-
Leod any trouble on the drive from the warehouse
back to the hotel. He also allowed himself to be
dragged up the back stairs without protest. Whatever
else he was, Jones was a professional and he knew
better than to do anything that would either anger his
captors or attract the attention of the police. His only
hope to stay alive was if Rykoff's team were professionals, too, and would return the courtesy.

Only when they were safely inside the hotel room
did the mercenary finally speak. "I think I probably
should go to hospital or be seen by a doctor," he said
through clenched teeth. "I've lost quite a bit of blood,
you know."

"You're going to lose a lot more than a little
blood," Rykoff warned, "unless you tell me why you
set Estevez up to be ambushed."

Jones shrugged. At this point in the game, he owed
no further loyalty to his paymaster and it was in his
best interests to be as helpful as he could. "It was

easy," he said. "We learned about you and your team from the man you sent to Arizona to infiltrate the New Dawn Corporation. Nisi captured him and put him through chemical interrogation. He knows everything about your group that your man knew."

Rykoff was stunned. This changed everything. For the first time since the CAT Team had been activated their cover had been blown. Steadman would have to be notified immediately so damage control measures could be taken. First, though, he had to concentrate on getting Sendak back.

"When was Sendak picked up?" Rykoff asked.

"I really don't know. We got a call late Monday briefing us about you and ordering us to take you out."

"Is he still alive?" MacLeod spoke up.

"He is as far as I know," Jones replied honestly. "But Nisi didn't say much about him other than to say that he was in custody."

"You'd better hope to hell that he is," MacLeod growled. "You're going to need more than a hospital if he's dead. You're going to need a burial plot."

"I didn't have anything to do with his capture or interrogation," Jones protested. "Christ, I didn't even know about your man, or any of the rest of you, for that matter, until Nisi called Ian and told us to eliminate you."

He glanced around the suite, taking in the four of them. "I still don't know anything about you, as far as that goes."

"All you need to know about us is that we're going to wish to hell you had stayed in the veldt if we don't get Sendak back intact," Bao warned.

"Okay," Rykoff said. "Enough of that. Let's start with the beginning." He needed to get back to basics before he forgot his primary mission. "You're Hans Binkermann, right?"

The South African nodded.

"Okay, I want to know what you and Smith are doing here in L.A. and why."

"That's easy," Jones replied. "Nisi wants to get a race war started on the West Coast, but a race war confined to the wogs and the kaffirs. He has this idea of getting them to wipe each other out and then taking over once they're gone. Kind of like what we tried to do back home, but this time the factions will be well armed with his weapons. We're selling weapons and ammunition to the ethnic gangs at bargain prices."

The South African conveniently forgot to mention that he and Smith had also made the first few hits themselves to get the war started. He didn't know what Rykoff was going to do to him, but the less he knew about that particular part of Nisi's plan, the better it would be for him.

"How are the guns getting into the country?"

"The Ukrainians are bringing them in on their grain ships. Nisi has good contacts in the new Ukrainian government."

"How are they getting them past the customs inspectors?"

Jones shrugged again. "I don't really know, but it has something to do with Nisi's having friends in high places. We pick up the crates at a drop site and take them to our warehouse for distribution."

"What kind of numbers are we talking about here?" Rykoff asked.

"About ten thousand AKs and a thousand RPGs, plus five thousand rounds of ammunition per," Jones said. "And, that's just here in L.A. More are being dropped off in other port cities."

Rykoff was stunned. That was more assault-rifle firepower than an entire infantry division had on hand. "You have a list of the drop sites?"

"I can make you a list," the South African said. Full cooperation was the best chance he had of getting out of this alive.

"What's Nisi likely to do now that you and your partner are out of the picture?"

"I don't know," the South African answered truthfully. "I do know that he has other teams in San Diego, San Francisco and Seattle. He might send one of them after you when we don't report back in."

"What if you call in and say that you took us out, but Smith was killed in the process?"

Jones shook his head. "That won't work. Nisi has a line into the L.A. Police Department and would want their confirmation that your bodies had been found."

Now that there was a pause in the interrogation, Jones asked a question himself. "What are you going to do with me?"

"What's your blood type?" Rykoff asked.

"A-positive."

Walking over to the computer, Rykoff called up a menu of medical personnel in the L.A. area who were on contingency contract to the CIA. Using a code word to identify himself as a federal agent, he arranged for a doctor, a gunshot surgical kit and two units of A-positive whole blood to come to the hotel.

"Go down to the parking lot," he told Estevez, "and meet the doctor when he comes in. The code word is 'rainstorm.' Bring him up the back stairs and make sure that you aren't seen."

Estevez tucked a Glock into the waistband of his pants and pulled his shirt out to cover it. "On the way."

When the doctor entered the room he exchanged nods with the Team and went right to his patient. As with all these CIA jobs, the less he knew about what was going on here, the better he liked it. Taking off Bao's pressure bandage, he quickly got to work on his patient.

First he rigged a portable IV bag stand and plugged Jones into the first bag of blood. While that was draining into the South African, he prepared his instruments to clean and suture the bullet hole.

"Only use a local," Rykoff said when he saw the doctor reach for a vial of anesthesia and a hypodermic syringe. "I need him able to walk as soon as you're done."

The doctor switched vials, and after filling the syringe, started making subcutaneous injections to numb the surface nerves around both the entrance- and exit-wound sites. Giving the injections a minute or so to go to work, he started cleaning the wound and stitching. When he was done, he replaced the blood bag.

"He'll be okay now," the doctor said as he stripped off his bloody gloves. "No major damage was done except to muscle tissue. The dressing will need to be checked once a day and the stitches taken out in a week. I gave him an antibiotic shot and—" he held up a plastic pill bottle "—he'll need to take these as it says on the label so he doesn't develop an infection."

"He can walk—" the doctor shot a look back at Jones "—but don't walk him too much. He might tear out the stitches."

"We'll take good care of him," Rykoff promised.

The doctor left a roll of surgical tape behind when he repacked his bag. "When the blood bag's almost empty, pull the needle out and put a piece of tape over his hand."

As soon as the doctor had been seen back downstairs, Rykoff decided against interrogating his prisoner any more that evening. Jones's color was a little better now, but he was a bit groggy.

"What are we going to do with him?" Estevez asked. "We can't just let him go."

Rykoff thought for a moment. "We'll leave him here tonight and let him get some sleep. I may want to talk to him again in the morning."

"You want us to stand guard over him tonight?"

"No need to. Just cuff him. He's not going anywhere with that leg."

After writing up some notes on what Jones had revealed, Rykoff set his watch alarm to wake him at four-thirty and dropped into the empty easy chair facing the couch where Jones was sleeping. Tucking a Glock into the back of his belt, he leaned his head back and dropped off to sleep.

STEADMAN HAD BARELY gotten into his Pentagon office the next morning and booted his computer when the modem indicated that he had an incoming message. Settling into his chair, he typed "Go."

The word "Autie" appeared at the top of his monitor.

Steadman grinned again at Rykoff's code name. Autie had been Elizabeth Custer's pet name for her headline-grabbing boy general. For Rykoff to contact him this way, however, meant that he was on to something.

"Grant." He typed the name of Custer's main political enemy and President of the United States when Custer made the fatal mistake of underestimating his Indian opponents.

Rykoff quickly outlined the result of the attack by Smith and Jones. That was followed by a brief outline of the information he had obtained from Jones. After answering a few questions about the guns, Rykoff dropped a bombshell with a request for clearance to hit Nisi's New Dawn complex in Arizona.

Steadman didn't have to look up Nisi's corporation on the list of organizations that had been given a clean bill of health by the Control Group. New Dawn was well-known on Capitol Hill and even he had heard of their work.

"The New Dawn Corporation is strictly off-limits. Nisi is legit and has powerful friends. Suggest you double-check your information." Steadman hit enter and waited for Rykoff's response.

"It has been confirmed that Sendak infiltrated New Dawn and has been captured by Nisi," Rykoff sent back. "He is being held at New Dawn HQs and must be rescued. My informant reports that Nisi put Sendak through chemical interrogation and he has learned the details of the CAT Team. The entire organization is now in jeopardy."

Steadman cursed under his breath. This was the biggest problem with using the CAT Team inside the United States. He had argued that point with the Control Group when they had discussed the L.A. assignment, but he had been overruled. These same men in high places were also the ones who had put Nisi and his company on the do-not-touch list. Talk about conflict of interest, he thought. He was up to his neck in it now.

"I cannot authorize a raid on New Dawn," Steadman typed. "It is a legitimate scientific research group, not a cult. I suggest you reinterrogate your source."

"My source is good and I will not abandon Sendak." Steadman could almost hear the cold finality in Rykoff's voice. "Tell Nisi's friends that he is not what he seems. I have positive confirmation that he is behind the Ukrainian weapons shipments reaching L.A. His purpose is to encourage Serbian-style ethnic cleansing among the minority groups by arming them and then staging attacks to create a situation of increased unrest."

"Let me try to clear this with the Control Group first," Steadman sent back. "Give me twenty-four hours."

"I cannot afford to wait," Rykoff typed. "Sendak is in danger and we are going in to get him as soon as possible. Autie out."

Steadman stared dully at Rykoff's final message and then glanced up at the print of Custer's Last Stand on the wall in front of him. It had finally come, the only thing he had feared since the CAT Team had been formed—the last hopeless battle alluded to by the print.

Rykoff was an extraordinarily stable man, which was why he had been chosen to head the Team. But if he ever went rogue, and took the Team with him, they could do fearful damage before they could be stopped. This situation had been foreseen, however. The men who had given birth to the CAT Team had not been unaware of the power they were giving Rykoff and his handpicked commandos. They knew full well what kind of damage the five of them could do if they went up against the wrong targets.

With that possibility in mind, a contingency plan had been put together that would identify the CAT Team as being domestic terrorists on the federal shoot-to-kill-as-soon-as-seen list. The messages were already prepared and all it would take would be a few keystrokes to activate the program and transmit them to local, state and federal law-enforcement agencies throughout the nation.

Though he believed that Rykoff had overstepped the boundary that separated him from the terrorists he was supposed to fight, Steadman hesitated to call in the dogs. There was always the possibility that Jud was right this time. Rykoff's instincts were finely tuned and he had been right so many times before. If he was right about the New Dawn group, they deserved to be taken out before Nisi's smuggled guns plunged the entire nation into a widespread racial war. If he was wrong, though, dozens of innocent people would die—the same people the CAT Team had been formed to protect.

Steadman's fingers flew over his keyboard as he called up a program titled Little Big Horn. The code word to retrieve it was Golden Hair. Little Big Horn contained the complete dossiers of each team member laid out in wanted-poster format complete with mug shots and personal information. Within hours of his activating the program, these posters would be in every local police station, FBI field agent's desk and post office throughout the nation. The official estimation was that Rykoff and his people wouldn't last forty-eight hours after the posters went out.

He stared at the menu on the screen, unable to force his fingers to make the keystrokes that would doom Rykoff and the others. "Fuck!" he muttered when he finally exited the Little Big Horn menu.

For a moment he seriously considered deleting the program, but he didn't do that, either. He was willing to risk that Rykoff might be right this time, but there was always the next time, and the time after that. In a democracy, someone had to monitor an organization like the CAT Team, and that job had fallen on his narrow shoulders. For the first time since the operation had started, he sincerely wished that someone else had this particular responsibility.

Though it was far from the end of the Pentagon duty day, he shut down his computer and notified his nominal boss that he was sick and was going home. He would stay home with the phone shut off until he saw the outcome of Rykoff's raid on New Dawn on the evening news. That way no one could overrule him and force him to activate the Little Big Horn program. The way the CAT Team security was set up, as long as he was alive, he was the only one who had access to the program.

If he turned up dead, a procedure went into effect that would have another man in place doing his job within twenty-four hours. But he was counting on being able to stay alive at least until this was over. After that, the fate of Rykoff's team would be up to the gods and the whims of the men with the real political power in the United States.

As he took his hat and coat from the rack by the door, he took a last long look around his small office. If Rykoff was wrong, this was probably the last time he would see this office. His next residence would probably be one of those country-club federal prisons where they sent the bad boys of America's ruling class to learn not to get caught again. If he was lucky, that is. If this thing really went bad and he couldn't convince his masters that he would keep his mouth shut and take the fall, he would wind up in the wrong part of town with a bullet in his head and his name on the D.C. crime stats.

He hit the light switch and slowly closed the door behind himself. Saving the world was a lonely business. Thank God he had the company of a full bottle of Jack Daniel's and a good collection of classical music CDs waiting for him at home. The combination was a sure cure for what ailed him right now.

## 22

*New Dawn Compound*
*January 28*

Joshua Nisi was worried. Smith had still not reported
back to tell him that he and Jones had eliminated the
CAT Team. Attempts by his communications people
to contact them had not been successful, either. The
two South African professionals and their hired guns
should have been able to take care of this supersecret
team by now. They would have had the element of
surprise and prior knowledge, which Rykoff and his
people wouldn't have had.

Even so, something had obviously gone wrong, and
if that was the case, there was a good chance that this
so-called CAT Team could be coming to Arizona
soon. Although Sendak had said that he hadn't given
Rykoff anything specific when he had reported to him
last weekend, confirmation wasn't actually needed
because the fact that Rykoff had sent someone to spy
on him was proof enough that he was a target. Still,
Nisi reassured himself, he was a target who could defend himself.

He pushed the intercom button on the console at his desk in the war room.

"Yes, sir," his adjutant, Boyd, answered immediately.

"Have Lutz report to me immediately in the war room."

"Yes, sir."

The New Dawn security chief was a big man and, like the employment interviewer, had ex-military indelibly stamped on his bearing and every movement. "You wanted to see me, sir?" he said as he came to a relaxed position of attention in front of Nisi's desk.

"Yes, we may have a security problem." Since Lutz was one of the inner circle, Nisi quickly briefed him on Rykoff's team and the apparent inability of Smith and Jones to take care of them.

"You should have let me send some of my own men after them, sir," Lutz reproached his boss. "Those South Africans aren't trained for that kind of mission. They're only gunrunners."

"It's too late to worry about that now," Nisi said. "We have to deal with the situation as it is. I want the security around the compound doubled and roving patrols set out both inside and outside the perimeter wire all the way to the other end of the valley. I also want a dozen more of our people in the surrounding towns. I want them to closely watch any strangers, even those who look like they're tourists just passing through."

"What's the threat?"

"They'll be looking for four people. One is a Caucasian man in his forties. One is a black man who may be riding a Harley. Then there's a Hispanic man, a pilot. And lastly, an Oriental woman, Chinese, in fact, who may be masquerading as a photographer. Full descriptions and, hopefully, photographs will be ready soon."

"What do you want me to tell the people?"

"You can brief the first-level employees on all the details. The second- and third-level people, however, are only to be told that we have become the target of a Christian fundamentalist group that is trying to shut down genetic research facilities such as ours."

"Tell everyone to be on the lookout for these people, as well as any other strangers, and to report all suspicious activity immediately. Particularly anyone asking questions about our operations, no matter who they are. These people are dangerous and I want them shot on sight."

"We can handle that, sir."

"Let me know immediately if there are any problems."

"There won't be," Lutz promised.

As soon as Lutz left to beef up security in and around the New Dawn operation, Nisi hit his intercom button again. "Boyd," he said. "I want to talk to Sendak again. Have him taken down to the clinic and I'll see him there."

"Yes, sir."

Before joining Sendak and the medical technicians in the clinic, Nisi stopped off at his private office. Even though the war room was completely secure, there were a few things that had to be kept more than secure. Slipping into the chair behind his desk, he booted his computer.

Since this "team" was a federal operation, there was a chance that he could get them called off. He would still send people after them until they were safely dead, but he wanted to forestall any kind of attack on his compound if it was within the realm of possibility. Now that the New Dawn operation was going so well, he wanted to avoid that kind of publicity at all costs.

With the exception of his war room, there was nothing at the compound that would arouse the suspicions of the authorities. In fact, it would take a bioengineer to even understand what was going on in the labs. Nonetheless, he didn't want anyone poking around in his affairs, particularly in the aftermath of an attack on the compound.

One of the nicest things about being a millionaire was that his money could buy things and services that weren't available to the average American. Things like United States senators, who could bring behind-the-scenes pressure on various branches of the federal government on his behalf.

One of his pet senators had even been able to cut a swath through the maze of so-called environmental watchdog agencies that had tried to keep him from building the New Dawn complex in the Arizona desert. They had insisted that a long-term environmental impact study had to be made before the delicate ecology of the Chiricahua Valley could be disrupted. In this case, "delicate" meant the same sand, barren rock, sagebrush and cactus that covered most of the Southwest.

A little money in the senator's pocket—and it had been far less than it would have cost to take the matter to court—and his operation had been given the fullest blessing of every knee-jerk environmentalist group on Capitol Hill. Those who weren't based out of Washington didn't count, so he hadn't even bothered to try to bribe or pressure them.

The only problem with trying to apply congressional pressure in this case was that Sendak had insisted that he didn't know who was in overall charge of his secret team. He claimed that Jud Rykoff ran it as a private army. He also said, though, that he was convinced there was someone in the upper levels of the government who was behind Rykoff, because of the weapons, material and intelligence information they always had to work with. But he'd had no proof he could offer.

Nisi had to admit that whoever had set the CAT Team up had been smart. Not even the CIA ran their operations with the secrecy that surrounded Sendak's team. The CIA couldn't pass out bandages at a train wreck without having a dozen watch groups looking over their shoulder and claiming that it was an evil plot.

It didn't hurt to try, though. He had a senator sitting on the Senate Select Committee on Intelligence on his payroll. He would put the honorable servant of the people to work and see what he came up with. It was about time he got something of value for the money he had been lining the senator's pocket with for so long. Most of the time, he got little enough for his contributions, and he saw it as another form of tax, but this was one time that the tax would benefit him for a change instead of being wasted on people who made no contribution to the nation.

His call to Washington was put through immediately, and when the senator assured him that he was alone, Nisi quickly briefed him on the CAT Team situation. When the senator reluctantly admitted that he knew of the existence of Rykoff's team, Nisi went ballistic. "Why didn't you tell me about these people before this?" he demanded.

"We only use them for counterterrorist work outside the United States," the senator tried to explain. "And they would never be in a position to cause you any trouble."

"What happened, then?" he demanded. "Why are they investigating me?"

"I really don't know," the senator admitted. "Even though I'm part of the Control Group that oversees their activities, I didn't know they had been authorized for a mission within the country. This is completely outside of their normal authority.''

The fact that the good senator had missed the last two meetings of the Control Group was the real reason he didn't know that the CAT Team had been sent in to stop the street fighting in L.A. He had been on a junket to the Bahamas with his new favorite from his secretarial staff for most of January, celebrating the new millennium in style.

''Can you get these people turned off?''

''I think so,'' the senator said. ''I can call an emergency meeting of the Control Group and report that Rykoff has gone 'rogue.' We have a procedure for taking them out permanently if that happens.''

''Will it work?''

The senator hesitated. ''I think so. But I must admit that it's never been used before.''

''It had better work, Senator.'' Nisi's voice carried the threat that he didn't need to put into words.

''I'll get them off you one way or the other,'' the senator promised.

''I'm counting on it.''

When Nisi broke the connection he didn't feel relieved by the senator's promise. The man was a fool and couldn't be counted on to get the CAT Team off his back. When this was all over, he would have to see about finding someone to replace him, someone who paid a little more attention to business. Until then, though, he would have to take care of Rykoff's team himself.

SENDAK DIDN'T LIKE the looks of the room he was led into, but there was nothing he could do about it. Again, his hands were cuffed behind his back and he was being escorted by three men. This time, two of his guards weren't armed, but the third one walking behind was packing an Uzi. Even beat-up and restrained, they weren't taking any chances with him. Under more normal circumstances, that would have amused him, but there was nothing funny about being led into a medical facility that looked a little too much like a morgue for his tastes.

Inside the clinic, two med techs were waiting for him. "Easy," he said with a grimace when one of the techs took his right arm. "I've got a broken rib."

The tech shot a look at the guards. "Are you hurt anywhere else?"

"Just bruises and sprains. I got beat up pretty badly, but I think the rib's the worst of it."

"Let me take a look."

Sendak allowed the medic to take his shirt off and examine his bruised ribs and shoulders. "The rib's broken, all right. I'll tape it up after we're done with you here."

"What are you going to do to me?"

The medic averted his eyes. "Please lie down," he said as he reached for the straps on the table. "And put your hands down at your side."

Once he was strapped down to the table, one of the techs inserted an IV needle into the vein on the back of his left hand. It looked as if they were planning to send him on another trip into chemical la-la land. Apparently Nisi wasn't satisfied that he had told everything he knew and wanted to take him on another trip down memory lane.

It could also mean that Nisi's plan to take out the rest of the team had run afoul of reality. Even with the element of surprise working against them, Jud, Mel, Erik and Jake were nobody's pushovers. He didn't know what kind of action teams Nisi had in California, but if they weren't any better than the goons he kept here, they wouldn't have cut it going up against the Team.

If Nisi was putting him under the needle again for further questioning, more than likely it meant that they were still alive. And, also more than likely, they would be coming for him soon.

He knew that he wouldn't be able to keep from telling Nisi that he thought his friends would be coming to free him. It couldn't be prevented. If he thought it would help the others, he would try to break away and force his guards to kill him. But Rykoff would have no way of knowing if he were killed and would come anyway.

Therefore, even though he was going to warn Nisi that the CAT Team was coming, the best thing he could do was to try to stay alive in the faint hope that there was something he could do when they made their assault. Right off the top of his head, he didn't know what it would be, but he would keep his options open.

"THEY'RE COMING, they're coming," Sendak slurred his words. Even under the drug, he could feel the pain of his injuries, and he was clinging to the hope that Rykoff would come to rescue him.

"Who's coming?" Nisi asked.

Sendak smiled faintly. "They're coming."

"Why is he mumbling?" Nisi frowned. "And not giving me clear answers?"

"It's his injuries, sir," the medic answered. "He was beaten and he has a broken rib. His brain is pumping out natural endorphins to fight the pain and they're interfering with the interrogation drug."

"Will it help if you give him a painkiller?"

The medic shook his head. "If we give him anything strong enough to do any good and block the endorphins, it will block the drug, as well. All we can do is to set the rib and wait a couple of days before we try it again."

Nisi was not at all pleased at this turn of events. He had not authorized Sendak's guards to amuse themselves this way, and Lutz would answer for this incident. If he couldn't keep his people under better control than that, the security chief was going to find himself waking up in the desert with a rattlesnake around his neck.

"They're coming," Sendak repeated.

Nisi repressed the urge to beat Sendak himself. "Take him off the drug," he ordered. "See to his injuries and then call security to have him taken back to his cell."

"Yes, sir."

As soon as Nisi was gone, the medic started cleaning Sendak's scrapes and cuts. When he was cleaned up, the medic injected a dose of broad-spectrum antibiotic in case he had picked up an infection from his cell. .

By the time the medic was finished, Sendak started coming out from under the drug. "What did I say?" he slurred.

"You didn't say anything," the medic said softly. "You're okay. Try to sit up so I can tape that rib for you."

With the medic helping him, Sendak struggled to sit up and swung his legs over the side of the table. "Jesus," he said. "My mouth tastes like shit."

The medic poured him a plastic cup of a blue liquid. "Here, take this. It's just mouthwash."

Sendak gargled and spit the mouthwash back into the cup. "Thanks."

"Don't mention it. Now raise your arms so I can tape your ribs."

**23**

*Los Angeles*
*January 28*

The next morning, the CAT Team took turns getting cleaned up and going down for a real sit-down breakfast in the hotel restaurant while the others guarded their South African prisoner. Not that Jones was in any shape to go anywhere just yet. It would take him a few days to recover from the shock and trauma of the wound. He was in good enough shape, however, to eat the big breakfast Rykoff ordered from room service.

"It's time to pull the plug here, boys and girls," Rykoff said when they were all back in the suite. "Do any of you have any loose ends that you need to tie up here? If you do, handle it over the phone because I want to be moving out in under an hour."

"I need an hour or two outside," Bao said. "I can't wrap up my business over the phone."

"Why not?"

"I need to go back and talk to my contact."

"Why can't you do it on the phone?"

"Family honor," she said. "I used my father's name pretty heavily to establish myself this time and I don't want to leave him hanging. It might get back to him."

"Okay," Rykoff reluctantly agreed. Nung family honor was something he understood and he didn't want to piss off old Bao. He might need another in with a Chinese community somewhere. "Meet us at the airport as soon as you can."

"If she's going to be gone for a while," Estevez spoke up, "I'd kind of like to go get the rest of my clothes on the way to the airport instead of having them mailed to me. It's only about an hour out of the way."

"Okay," Rykoff said, sighing. "Just don't take too long saying goodbye to Señora Garza."

Estevez grinned. "I won't."

Rykoff turned to MacLeod. At least his biker persona didn't leave any unfinished business beyond turning in his rental Harley. "Jake, after you take your bike back, I want you to turn in our little van and then rent a big-cab U-Haul, at least a sixteen-footer."

"Where are we going with it?"

"You're going to load all of our gear into it and drive it to Tucson. The rest of us will meet you there tomorrow morning."

"What are you going to do about him?" he asked, jerking a thumb in the direction of the South African.

"He's going into storage until we've had a chance to get Sendak back."

"What are you going to do, rent a locker at the train station and stuff him in it?"

Rykoff grinned. "That's not a bad idea. But the Feds team is coming to pick him up and he's going into one of their safehouses. They'll keep track of him until I give them further instructions."

A half hour later, the federal agents came for Jones, and Rykoff was finally alone. Activating his computer, he called up the list of the assets Steadman had made available for his use in the western half of the United States. It was going to be very short notice to get what he needed to attack Nisi's compound, but he had confidence in the code words Steadman had provided. Code words that could not be questioned.

The first thing he needed was intelligence about the target. Within five minutes, his fax was spitting out photos, maps and blueprints of the New Dawn facility. As soon as that run was complete, he switched to looking for advance-weapons testing projects in the states bordering Arizona and hit pay dirt. The first project was coded Strongman, the second was Hot Start. A combination of the two would do nicely for what he had in mind.

After a half hour, he shut off the computer and leaned back. The job was done. Thank God for the extensive government computer network that allowed orders to be sent, and obeyed, without forged paperwork. If anything ever happened to it, the CAT Team wouldn't be able to conduct business at all.

Packing up his computer and fax printouts, Rykoff shrugged into his safari jacket and turned the lights out as he left the hotel suite. Sendak was waiting and he was in a hurry to get him out of there.

BAO WORE her photographer-in-the-field clothing when she went to say goodbye to Dan Quan at the family restaurant.

"I was worried when you didn't return to your room last night," Quan said after greeting her.

"Dan, I have come to say goodbye. My mission is done here and I have to leave now."

"So," Quan almost hissed. "You are a cop and you came to spy on my family."

"If I was a cop, would I have come back here? Think about it. I told you that I'm not a cop and I am not. But, as you know, we Baos are warriors and I am a warrior, too. This time I'm fighting against those who started this race war by selling cheap weapons to the minority gangs."

"You've come for our weapons, then?"

She shook her head. "No," she said emphatically. "No one will ever be told of the Quan family arsenal, but I must caution you about using the weapons unless you are directly attacked. The race war here is about to end abruptly and anyone who is caught with these guns will be punished. Be careful how you use them and make sure that you use them only in self-defense. In fact, I would advise you to put them away and save them for the next time you need them."

Quan was silent for a moment. "I'll be in Seattle later this year," he finally said.

"My father would be honored to meet you," she replied.

"And you?" he asked. "Will you be honored to see me again?"

She met his eyes squarely. "If I am not working, yes. But I never know where I will be from one week to the next."

"I understand," he said.

"I don't think you do," she said evenly, "but I can't explain myself beyond what I have said." She bowed her head. "I am honored to have met the Quan family. I wish you all health and prosperity."

ESTEVEZ FOUND Señora Garza at home when he stopped by for his clothes. "I was worried when you didn't come home last night," she said.

"I'm sorry I didn't call," he said, "but I couldn't get to a phone. Something has come up and I have to leave immediately to go back home."

"I will get your laundry so you can pack," she said. "I think it's dry now."

"You didn't have to do my laundry."

"You didn't have to save my nephew from the car when the men shot at the club."

Estevez had everything in his bag when Señora Garza came into his room with a pile of neatly folded laundry. "Will you come back here soon?" she asked.

"I don't know," he answered honestly, taking the laundry from her hands and laying it inside the bag. "My work keeps me very busy."

"And your work here is done, isn't it. You found where the guns are coming from."

He stopped cold and turned to face her. "What makes you say that?"

"You are some kind of cop," she stated flatly. "But you are a good man. I have seen that, too. If your work ever brings you back here, you can have this room again."

He reached for her and gently took her in his arms for a brief hug. "Thank you. It is nice to know that I have someplace to stay."

"You can call me Maria," she said softly.

Remembering Rykoff's admonition not to get too involved, he picked up his bag and headed for the door. "Take care, Maria," he said when he hit the front door. "I'll drop you a card."

She watched from behind her screen door as he loaded his bag into the rental car and drove off. Estevez kept his eye on her in his rearview mirror until he turned the corner. That was the main problem with working for Rykoff—it played hell with his love life.

Rykoff and Bao were waiting for him when Estevez drove up to the plane. "It's preflighted and the flight plan has been filed. We're ready to go as soon as you are," Rykoff said when Estevez stepped out and opened the trunk of his car.

He lugged his bag out of the trunk and set it on the tarmac. "I need to turn this in first."

"Leave it. The rental company's been told to pick it up here."

Estevez shrugged, stowed his bag and climbed into the pilot's seat to run through his checklist. Rykoff strapped himself into the copilot's seat and made a comm check with the tower.

"You said you've already filed our flight plan?" Estevez asked.

Rykoff nodded.

"Where are we going?"

"Home to Tucson."

Estevez grinned as he hit the starter switch for the engine. "Tucson it is."

RYKOFF WAS GRIM-FACED when he faced the team early the next morning in his large room in the motel along Interstate 10 east of Tucson. Everyone had had an early breakfast already, but a pot of coffee, orange juice and doughnuts were sitting on the side table.

"I wish I had Alex with me right now to help me plan this operation," he said, "but we're going to have to muddle through it on our own. In a nutshell, I'd like to have a Delta Force Blue Light team or Jake's old bunch, SEAL Team Six, to pull this one off. Unfortunately, all we have is ourselves.

"Here's the target," he said, handing out the faxed copies of the photos and blueprints of the New Dawn complex. "Nisi's headquarters complex is built both on top and inside a solid-rock mesa in the middle of the desert. As you can see on the diagram, it's five stories tall, two above ground and three under. The main problem, however, is not the architecture. According to Alex's last report, Nisi has a security force of at least fifty men and they're well armed. We can assume they will defend the complex."

His gray eyes scanned the room slowly. "Anyone who would rather not commit suicide in this manner can feel free to decline the offer. But I need to know now so I can plan this operation."

No one took him up on his offer to back out. Alex was being held and they intended to get him back, dead or alive. And if he was dead, they intended to exact vengeance on those responsible for his death. The fact that some of them could die as well didn't enter into the equation.

"If Alex wasn't being held there, I'd simply turn the information we have over to the federal authorities, who would then raid the place sooner or later. The problem is that I don't think Alex will last that long. At the first sign of trouble, he'll disappear into one of the hydroponic tanks and that'll be the last anyone will see of him.

"If Alex is going to get out alive, we're going to have to go in there after him ourselves. And we're going to have to do it quickly. Because of that, we don't have time to try to infiltrate anyone else into the compound. Also, because of Nisi's master-race plan, we don't have anyone to send anyway, other than myself. A black, Hispanic or Asian won't do and I'm not the kind of convert he wants.''

He paused. ''But, that's only if we try by the front door. We're going to go in the back way and we're going to go in shooting. Since there are only the four of us, we're going to have to take these guys out like we were one of those fictional extermination squads that go after drug lords in the paperback novels.''

Everyone grinned at that. One of Rykoff's semi-secret vices was that he wrote paperback action-adventure thrillers under the pen name Jack Hawkins when he wasn't chasing rare books. They sold fairly well in the mass market, but the team still teased him about them.

''So, to help even up the odds a little, I have a new mission pack on the way that contains three Mark III armored combat suits. These things are about as close to science fiction as you can get and still live in the real world. These suits are fully armored against everything up to .50-caliber armor piercing, they have power assists to handle the weight, and they come with full comm and data links, night vision and targeting optics.''

MacLeod whistled soundlessly. Now Rykoff was getting armored combat suits. They had only been rumored when he had been in the SEALs. Stories had come out of the Gulf War that an experimental Special Forces unit had field-tested them under combat conditions, but he'd never seen one. The thought crossed his mind that the media was going to have a field day with it when the survivors told their stories to CNN, but fuck it.

"You said you have three suits," Estevez spoke up. "Who's the odd man out?"

"You are," Rykoff said. "You have to fly our gunship and make the pickup when we snatch Alex out of there."

"What gunship?" Estevez was stunned. Rykoff had always been able to get all sorts of high-tech goodies through his mysterious channels, but never anything like a gunship.

"A fully armed XAH-66 Comanche will be ready for pickup this morning."

Estevez wanted to ask how Rykoff had been able to come up with an experimental Comanche gunship, but because he knew better, he didn't ask. All Rykoff would say was that he had picked it up at a swap meet.

"What do we do about the New Dawn employees who aren't in on Nisi's little master-race plan?" Bao asked.

Rykoff's face was a study in death personified. "If they stay out of our way, they live. If they try to stop us, they die. Once we hit the LZ and are committed, we won't have time to try to sort out the good guys from the assholes. The only chance we have to ensure that we get Alex back intact is to hit them hard and keep on hitting them until Erik extracts us."

That was about what she had expected, but she liked to have her rules of engagement spelled out before she started firing. Particularly since the people she would be shooting this time would be Americans.

"We'll have today to practice with the fighting suits and weapons and run a couple of rehearsals. We'll be going in at midnight tonight."

His eyes locked on each of their faces in turn. "Any questions so far?"

After a beat, he went on. "Since there are none, we need to get our hardware sorted out."

His eyes sought MacLeod. "Jake, I want you to pick up the mission pack and start powering up and checking out the suits. Mel, you'll go along and help Jake.

"Erik, I want you to head out now to Fort Huachuca. A ground-support crew is already on-site with your bird. They'll run you through an orientation on the Comanche and put you through a flight simulator to check you out on both the flight systems and the armament package. Once you're checked out, I want you to take a couple of familiarization flights. Then the ground crew will give the bird a final once-over and you're to fly it to our assembly area after dark."

"Any questions?"

Each of them had dozens of questions, but none that could be answered at this time. Most of them wouldn't be answered until they were deep inside Nisi's fortress.

"Let's get moving then," Rykoff growled. "We've got a lot of work to do in a very few hours and Alex is waiting."

**24**

*Fort Huachuca, Arizona*
*January 29*

Estevez whistled to himself when he saw the Comanche squatting on the sand at the deserted firing range south of the main base. He had never seen any flying machine so beautiful and yet so deadly. The chief contender in the Army's experimental light-attack-helicopter competition was the finest example he had ever seen of the old axiom that form follows function.

Though named after the greatest of the Plains Indian mounted warriors, the small gunship looked more like a shark, an air shark. On second thought, though, with its desert-sand-and-brown camouflage paint, the high T tail and hunchback main rotor housing, maybe it looked more like a flying scorpion.

Whatever the imagery, the Comanche looked like a big case of bad news in a small package. The 20 mm chain gun in the under-nose turret and the missiles loaded on the four underwing pylons showed that it was loaded for bear.

As he stood looking over the machine, an Army captain wearing a flight suit with senior pilot wings over the left breast pocket and an LHX patch with a Project Hot Start tab over the right walked up to him.

"Mr. Estevez," he said, resisting the urge to salute. "I'm Captain Rick Gentry, LHX Flight Evaluation Team."

Estevez took his hand. "Glad to meet you, Captain." His eyes strayed back to the Comanche. "That's quite a bird you have there."

"We're proud of it," the Captain admitted. "It's more than meeting our expectations. When that little hummer reaches the units, we're going to have the best light attack chopper in the world."

"I can sure as hell believe that."

"Come on into the van," Gentry said, "and we'll get you changed into a flight suit and fitted for a helmet."

The OD-painted van contained an air-conditioned training suite complete with a flight simulator and air-traffic-control station. Wherever Rykoff had found this bunch, he had hit the jackpot. Everything he needed to get thoroughly checked out on the Comanche was here in one place.

After getting changed into an unmarked Army-issue flight suit, Estevez sat down for a half-hour introduction briefing to the new helicopter.

"What was the last military chopper you flew?" Gentry asked.

"I have well over a hundred hours in C Model Apaches."

Gentry was obviously greatly relieved by that answer. He had been told that this mysterious guest pilot did have military helicopter flight experience, but he had been given no specifics beyond that.

"You'll have no trouble with the Comanche, then," he said. "It has the same type of flight controls and armament systems as the Apache. The HUD displays and target-acquisition systems are the same, plus now you'll have terrain-following radar-digital-mapping navigation tied in with the GPS system."

Estevez was glad to hear that the ship had the Global Positioning System navigation built in. With that and the terrain-following radar, there was no way he could get lost in the trackless desert of southern Arizona.

"I understand that you also have two recon personnel pods on hand," he said.

Now Gentry frowned. "Yes, we do," he said slowly. "But I have to tell you that they haven't been tested yet and I really wouldn't want to be the guy who takes the first ride in them. They're kind of claustrophobic."

Estevez grinned. "I'll let you know how they work out when I bring the bird back."

Gentry mentally shrugged. His orders were to give this guy anything he wanted from the Comanche LHX Project Hot Start package, whether it had been flight-tested or not. He'd also been promised in writing that he wouldn't be held responsible for any damage that occurred to either the chopper or the pilot on this mission.

After the introduction was concluded, Estevez put on his helmet and strapped himself into the pilot's seat of the flight-simulator module. Gentry donned his own helmet and sat in front of him in the gunner's seat.

Estevez carefully ran through the unfamiliar checklist before firing up the turbines. When he twisted the throttle on the end of the collective control stick and triggered the igniters, the simulator gave him a recording of the whoosh of ignition, the whine of a turbine spooling up to full RPM and the vibration of the real thing.

After making a routine simulated takeoff, he put the simulator through its paces, starting with simple flight maneuvers and graduating into gun runs and attack sequences. The last check in the simulator was to be a low-level autorotation.

With the altimeter reading five thousand feet, the simulator cut power to both turbines. As soon as the power went out, Estevez dropped pitch with the collective, turning the rotor blades flat to let them spin freely as the chopper fell out of the sky. As the altimeter wound down as if it was tied to a falling rock, he kept his eyes on his main rotor RPM and his feet-per-second descent meter.

Right as the altimeter needle passed 800 feet, Estevez hauled up as hard as he could on the collective. Going to full pitch on the spinning blades that quickly almost stopped the altimeter cold. The simulator bucked and then settled down to a very controlled dead-engine landing as the blades pulled enough lift from their rotational energy to keep him from crashing.

Gentry wiped the sweat from his forehead. Even in a simulator, that had been a close call. "If you have to do that for real," he said, "I'd recommend that you give it a few more feet. The checklist calls for beginning autorotation at no lower than 1200 feet."

"I just wanted to see what it could do," Estevez replied.

"You try that stunt for real, sir, and you'll probably be wearing your seat three feet up your ass."

Estevez laughed. "I'll try to remember that. Now can I fly it for real?"

Orders were orders, and Gentry had no choice but to take his guest out to the actual machine. He just hoped to hell that this cowboy kept a cool tool in his pet helicopter. Even with the waiver, if this one got smashed, he'd have a difficult time explaining it to the general.

WHILE ESTEVEZ was getting checked out in the Comanche gunship, Rykoff, MacLeod and Bao were checking themselves out in the armored combat suits at a remote desert location northeast of Tucson.

With their military background, the two men found that the suits weren't that difficult to learn to operate. The comm gear, targeting optics and data links were all things they had used before in one form or another. For the ex-SEAL MacLeod, the suit itself was like wearing a power-assisted armored wet suit. The power assists overcame any sense of weight or bulk and he was running in it within minutes.

It took Rykoff a bit longer to learn the knack of letting the servos do the work for him. But before long he, too, was scampering across the desert as if he was riding a skateboard. Bao, however, was having a bitch of a time getting used to wearing the Mark III.

All of her extensive combat training had been in Mark I human-body suits, and she couldn't get used to the encumbrance of the bulky suit. Even with the servo units to compensate for the suit's extra weight, her brain couldn't compensate and her reactions were way off. Maybe someone who hadn't spent as many years as she had in martial arts training could learn to use the damned thing, but she sure as hell couldn't.

When she stumbled and went down to one knee, Rykoff ran up alongside of her in his suit and flipped up the visor. "You okay?"

She shook her head. "Can I ditch this damned thing and go with just the optics and data-link package and forget about the armor? I'm not going to be worth a damn wearing all this junk."

Rykoff thought for a moment. If the mission was to work, they needed Bao at her best, and if the armor kept her from performing at her maximum, it would have to go. "Okay," he said. "I'll talk to Jake and see what he can do about the optics."

Tonguing his mike switch, he called to MacLeod. "Jake, we need you over here for a moment."

"On the way," MacLeod replied.

Moving as smoothly as if he had been born in armor, MacLeod had a big grin on his face when he joined them. "Man, what a ride! I think I can outaccelerate my Harley from zero to fifty in this thing."

"Mel wants to ditch her armor. She says she can't operate the way she's been trained with all that bulk slowing her down. She does want to keep the optics and data-link package, though. Can you cannibalize the suit?"

MacLeod thought for a moment. "I think I can break the helmet and power pack loose. The power cells can go in a backpack so she can still have the targeting optics, comm gear and data link."

"Thank God," Bao said as she hit the latches to open the front plate of the armor.

Without the bulky suit around her trim form, Bao felt more like herself, more in charge. She went through a short but fast limbering exercise to make sure that she hadn't put a kink in anything.

"There," she sighed. "Now I'm ready to go to work."

JOSHUA NISI READ his fax message, and he was happy to see that his contributions to the honorable gentleman from California had not been in vain. The servant of the people had really come through this time and it was a good thing for him. Had he not, Nisi would have made sure that he lost his next election. Shortly after that, he would have lost his life, as well, because he knew too much about the New Dawn operation.

As it was, though, the senator had remembered who he really worked for. He had come through with some information and now he could continue his "service to the people," as he liked to call what he did for a living.

According to the senator's fax, the Army had loaned the CAT Team a light attack helicopter, as well as three items listed as Mark III armored combat suits. Beyond being some kind of experimental personal armor, the Senator didn't have any idea what they were and wasn't cleared to check into them any closer. As far as getting the CAT Team recalled, he was still working on that one. The problem was, there was no indication that Rykoff intended to do anything except what he had been sent to L.A. to do. Until there was, it would be difficult to get the Control Group to call them off.

Overall, Nisi wasn't unhappy with what the senator had been able to get for him. Obviously the loan of the chopper meant that Rykoff had decided to hit them from the air. Fortunately that wasn't the problem for him that it would be for the average agriculture research station. With the defense package he had bought at Smith's urging, he should have no trouble dealing with a single light attack helicopter.

As for the armored suits, his security force had armor-piercing ammunition at its disposal, and he would have it issued along with all the large-caliber weapons. With the element of surprise stripped from them, he expected the CAT Team to turn into pussycats.

THE FOUR CAT Team members walked out to where the camouflaged Comanche gunship squatted on the sand waiting for them. The moon was up and there was enough light in the clear desert sky that they could clearly see the machine's menacing shape. Rykoff would have preferred not to be doing this under a full moon, but Sendak couldn't wait on the lunar cycle.

The two eight-foot-long personnel pods fixed to the tips of the Comanche's missile-laden stub wings detracted from the machine's mean appearance. But they were the key to the success of the operation. There was no way that the three of them would have been able to trek across several miles of desert without being detected, and the chopper only had two seats in the armored cockpit.

Estevez would fly them in the pods to the central compound on the mesa top, then they would rappel down and begin their search for Sendak. While they were on the ground, Estevez would loiter in the area to provide fire support if needed. If all went well, they would reappear with Sendak in tow, hook up to the retrieval harnesses and get the hell out of there.

The plan was a bit crude, but it was as good a plan as Rykoff could come up with on such short notice. It should go well if there was little or no resistance at the compound. If Nisi had a hidden private army up there, however, the plan would be in the shitter the instant the first round was fired. From that point on, it would be a make-it-up-as-you-go thing, but that was standard with any military operation. The greatest truism of military history was that no plan survived the first contact with the enemy.

Since Bao was not wearing her armor, she went first into the starboard-side personnel pod. Over her Kevlar vest she was wearing an Army-issue M-23A-3 aerial-extraction harness. This harness was a quantum leap from the old STABO and McGuire extraction rigs used by Special Forces teams in the Vietnam War and allowed an individual to hook up to a single line and be picked off the ground by a chopper and flown to safety. The harness could also be used to lower a person to the ground on a fast rappel, which was how they would make their insertion.

After Bao was safely buckled in and her pod closed around her, Rykoff hooked up and was winched up into his portside pod. When he was stowed away, MacLeod stood under Bao's pod and deployed his retrieval line. To help balance the weight, he had opted to ride on the outside of Bao's pod, hooked to the secondary pickup points. With his armor protecting him from the rotor blast and slipstream, he could ride as comfortably as if he were inside the pod.

After double-checking everyone, Estevez climbed into the cockpit, buckled his shoulder harness and settled his flight gloves tightly over his fingers. Inside his pod, Rykoff keyed his throat mike. "Let's do it, Erik."

"Roger, Major," he radioed back.

Being behind the controls of an armed gunship sent him back to the bad old days of flying for the DEA. This time, however, he wouldn't have to fight his way through a briefcase-armed platoon of defense lawyers in three-piece suits to get to the bad guys. If anyone got in their way, he could blow them out of existence and worry about the legalities of it later.

He had already run through the preflight checklist, so his gloved hand reached out to hit the starter for the portside turbine. It ignited with a whoosh and the smell of burning kerosene. As soon as the RPMs were in the green, he fired up the other turbine.

When the main rotor came up to speed, he ran his eyes over the instrument readouts one last time. Everything was still in the green. Twisting the throttle up to max RPM, he eased up on the collective control. The rotor blades changed pitch and bit into the cool night air, lifting the heavily laden Comanche off the desert floor. More pitch took the gunship up to a low hover.

As soon as the chopper broke ground effect, Estevez pressed down on the rudder pedal, snapping the ship's tail around. When the nose pointed south in the direction of Nisi's New Dawn compound, he nudged the cyclic control stick forward. As the chopper started flying in that direction, he keyed his throat mike. "As James Brown used to say, 'Look out, Baby, 'cause here I come.'"

"Just do it, Hollywood," MacLeod sent.

**25**

*Chiricahua, Arizona*
*January 29*

Estevez kept the Comanche gunship flat out at barely fifty feet above the ground all the way into the target. The sophisticated terrain-following-radar navigation system built into the high-tech bird made this high-speed, belly-hugging night flying a snap. Even though Rykoff didn't have any intelligence suggesting that Nisi had any type of radar warning system at his compound, it didn't hurt to take precautions.

He had used earlier versions of this navigation system in the Apaches he had flown for the DEA, but they had been nothing compared to the Comanche's system. The HUD—Heads-Up Display—on the inside of his cockpit glass superimposed the radar picture over what little he could actually see of the nighttime desert in front of him. When he turned his head, the HUD shifted to again show him what he was looking at. It was as close to flying in broad daylight as you could do after the sun went down.

"How's the ride?" he asked his passengers over the intercom.

Safe inside their recon pods, Bao and Rykoff loved it. MacLeod, however, had a few things to say about being jostled around facedown at over 250 miles per hour only fifty feet off the ground.

Estevez laughed. "You'd better turn your visor off so you can't see it then, big boy."

NISI STOOD in front of the status board in his war room and watched the readouts, particularly the single pip on his air-control radar screen.

Since getting the senator's report, he had taken every precaution at his command to defend his little empire. When Smith and Jones had first advised him on the setup of his war room and the compound's defenses, he had been concerned about the expense of many of the things they had recommended—things like his state-of-the-art radar system that covered both the skies and the ground surrounding the mesa. He had never really thought he would need it, but now he was beginning to appreciate its value.

The blip on the radar screen was identified as a helicopter approaching the mesa at over 250 miles per hour. If it continued on its present course, it would fly right over the helicopter landing pad at the west end of the complex.

"What do you want me to do, sir?" The young man in charge of the defensive systems was anxious to get going. Like most of Nisi's security force people, he was ex-military and liked his work.

"If it looks like it's going to land on the chopper pad, allow it to touch down. If it looks like it's going to make an attack run, shoot it out of the sky. Whatever it does, though, if it crosses the outer perimeter, don't let it get away no matter what."

"Yes, sir."

The man's fingers flew over his control board, and at the east end of the chopper pad, a radar-directed 20 mm chain gun rose from its out-of-action position. With a whine of electric motors, the three-barreled automatic cannon swiveled around until the muzzles were aimed in the direction of the approaching Comanche. To keep the gunship from picking up the pulses of its target-acquisition radar, it was slaved to the big air-control radar. Only when it was ready to fire on the gunship would it activate its own targeting radar.

WHEN THE terrain-following radar picture on Estevez's HUD showed that he was approaching the outer perimeter fence, the pilot keyed his mike. "Feet dry," he told his passengers, using the Navy code for strike aircraft reaching land on the way to their targets. "ETA four minutes."

When he received three "rogers" in return, he prepared to make his approach. According to the map and the photos he had studied, there was a chopper pad on the west side of the mesa top that looked as if it would be a good LZ for their insertion. He should be able to zoom up and be over it in a hover before anyone could react.

"Thirty seconds," he called out over the intercom.

Waiting until the last possible moment, Estevez hauled up sharply on the collective control to increase pitch to the rotor blades and sucked the cyclic all the way back against the stop. The sleek gunship pulled her nose up sharply and popped up over the edge of the mesa as if it had been shot from a catapult.

As the Comanche's nose was about to clear the top of the mesa, he shoved forward on the cyclic to push the nose back down before dumping his collective to kill the lift and tilting the rotor mast backward to halt this forward momentum. The chopper abruptly leveled off and skidded to a hover three feet off the ground in the middle of the landing pad.

Suddenly, the scream of the target-acquisition radar warning shrilled in his headphones.

Estevez was frantically pulling pitch to his main rotor and kicking down on the rudder pedal when the 20 mm chain gun opened up on him. Since the Comanche was already turning to face the threat when the gun fired, the first burst went wide of the fuselage.

A sudden lurch almost tipped the machine dangerously over onto its left side. As he leveled the machine out, he saw that the starboard recon pod had been blasted off of its wingtip mount. That was the pod with Mel inside and MacLeod riding strapped to it!

Estevez didn't have time to worry about them as he fought to control the unbalanced chopper as it staggered through the air and toppled over the edge of the mesa. He had the throttle twisted all the way up against the stop and the rotors set at half-lift, fighting to build up some airspeed before he hit the ground. The only thing that ran through his mind was the old pilot's prayer, "Please, God, don't let me fuck up now."

In his case, though, it was a prayer not to fuck up anymore. He had already lost two of his teammates, and he and Rykoff were going to die, too, if he didn't get his head out of his ass and start flying.

"What the fuck's going on out there?" Rykoff called over the intercom.

"We're taking fire from a chain gun," Estevez snapped. "Shut up and let me work."

Even though he was below the edge of the mesa, he could see the 20 mm tracer fire cutting through the air above his head. Someone had obviously taken over manual control of the antiaircraft gun, but thank God he was a piss-poor shot. And thank God again that whoever had built that gun emplacement hadn't thought about siting it where it could deliver fire closer in to the sides of the towering mesa it guarded.

Nonetheless, he was trapped where he was. His only chance was to hug the walls of the mesa until he had his airspeed built back up. Even then he was still in a bind. When he tried to escape, sooner or later, he would have to fly into the open and into a cone of fire from that gun. The Comanche was armored, but there was only so much that armor could do against a 20 mm chain gun firing AP rounds.

He couldn't fly in circles tucked in tight around the mesa forever. So, when he broke from cover, he had to take that gun out and take it out quickly. First, though, he wanted to fill Rykoff in on the situation. It wasn't fair to let him die without knowing what was going on. "Jud?" he spoke over the intercom.

"About time you checked in."

"Listen up, we're in trouble, but I think I can get us out."

"If you don't, you're fired."

"First off," Estevez continued, ignoring the comment, "we lost the pod with Mel and Jake. It got shot off and crashed in the chopper pad."

"Did they get out okay?"

"I was dodging the chain gun and didn't see."

"What's our situation now?"

"I'm in the dead zone for that gun right now. But when I break out, I've got to take it out or we're going to buy it as well."

"Do it."

Reaching down, Estevez activated the rotor-mast-mounted IR targeting system. With the masthead extended fully, he could "see" a full two meters above his actual line of sight. And if he could see the target, he could take it out with a Hellfire antitank missile.

Holding in a hover dangerously close to the mesa wall, he sought and found the chain gun's position.

Locking the missile's radar seeker to the diamond-shaped target pip illuminated on the HUD, he pulled the firing trigger on the cyclic stick.

The Hellfire missile ignited with a whoosh and leaped from the launcher. It was still accelerating when it hit the base of the chain gun's mount. The explosion of its antitank warhead pulverized the cannon, blowing what was left of it completely off its mount.

The glare of the explosion and the resulting detonation of the stored ammunition for the gun caused Estevez's helmet visor to automatically blank to preserve his vision. As soon as his visor cleared, he put the Comanche right down on the deck again and aimed his nose away from the mesa.

It was dangerous to fly so low when he didn't know what damage had been done to his ship, but since he didn't know what else Nisi might have tucked in between his genetically altered tomato plants, he had no choice.

He had just cleared the outer-perimeter fence when the oil-pressure warning sensor on the port-side turbine tripped off and the digital readout started flashing a red danger signal. He glanced down and saw that he was rapidly losing oil pressure to that turbine. Rather than let it keep running and risk having the turbine explode when the bearings ran dry and it self-destructed, he reached out and switched off its fuel feed.

He felt the rotor blades instantly slow and went into full military power on the remaining turbine to compensate. Now that he was trying to keep the Comanche in the air with only half power, he had to feed in even more pedal pressure to counter the asymmetric drag from the single remaining recon pod. He briefly considered jettisoning the remaining missiles on the other side to try to even things up a little, but just as quickly nixed the idea. He didn't want classified antitank ordnance littering the desert for any fool to take home in his pickup.

He thought he had it in the bag when the EGT warning sounded on the remaining turbine. Something wasn't right in the burner cans and the exhaust gas temperature had shot up into the danger zone. If he didn't want to burn up in the air, he had to put the aircraft down as soon as he could.

"Jud!" he called out over the intercom. "We're losing the other engine. Brace yourself, we're going down!"

Rather than attempt a gear-down landing and risk a nose over, Estevez elected to keep the wheels retracted and go in for a belly landing. The radar showed relatively flat desert in front of them and he cut back on his turbine RPM to make his descent.

Even with the radar picture to guide him, Estevez hunched his shoulders and braced himself, anticipating a hard impact. No matter what else happened, he had to keep left pressure on both the cyclic and rudder pedals to keep the right stub wing with the remaining personnel pod from scraping the ground. Feathering the main rotor blades to bleed off his lift, he let the chopper drop gently onto the desert floor rather than fly it into the ground as he would have done with a conventional aircraft.

At the last possible second, he took his hand from the collective stick and reached over to kill the fuel feed to the remaining turbine. If they hit too hard and broke something, he didn't need a fire in a fully armed gunship while he was trying to get Rykoff out of his pod.

The Comanche's belly kissed the sand and started skidding across the open ground. Since he had held the chopper level, it didn't tip over as it plowed its way across the desert floor. A hundred meters farther on, the nose hit something solid and threw Estevez against his shoulder harness. The inertial reels snapped tight, however, to keep his visored face out of the instrument panel.

For a long moment, all was silent except for the cracking and popping noises of the hot turbine cooling off. Then Rykoff's voice sounded loud over the intercom, "Get me the fuck outta here!"

"BURN IT." Rykoff's voice was hard.

"Captain Gentry isn't going to be very happy about that. That's a very valuable bird, it's not bent too badly and it could be repaired."

"It can't be helped," Rykoff said. "We can't stick around and make sure that the right people come to fetch it. I think Gentry will be much happier telling the general that it went up in flames than he would be if pieces of it appeared in the wrong hands."

"You've got a point there."

Since the Comanche was an experimental machine, there was a thermite self-destruct device built into the cockpit. There was also a missile-lock system that prevented the missiles from leaving the launch racks if the motors cooked off in the fire. After setting the missile lock, Estevez unlocked the self-destruct bar and grabbed it with both gloved hands.

"Clear!" he called out.

"Clear," Rykoff said.

"Fire in the hole!" Estevez yelled as he pulled the bar past the safety stop.

As soon as the pop of the timed igniter sounded, he was running to where Rykoff waited a safe distance away. He was skidding to a halt ninety seconds later when the cockpit of the Comanche suddenly flared with a light almost too bright to watch with the naked eye. An instant later, flames appeared and quickly engulfed the front half of the chopper.

"That's some self-destruct system," Rykoff said.

"Roger that, but we'd better get our young asses out of here before that 20 mm ammunition starts cooking off in the bays."

"I'll carry you."

Picking Estevez up as if he were a child, Rykoff cradled him in the suit's arms. "You comfy?"

"A mother's loving arms this isn't." Estevez grinned in the dark. "But let's go for it."

Rykoff started out slowly to get used to carrying the pilot's weight. Once he had the hang of it, he started putting on more speed. A hundred meters farther on, he was running at about thirty-five miles per hour. The power cell in the suit would last only three hours at this rate, but that would be enough to get them well out of the area.

"Whoa!" Estevez yelled. "Man, what a fucking ride!"

"Shut up and let me drive," Rykoff growled over the suit's loudspeaker.

## 26

*New Dawn Compound*
*January 29*

When the port-side recon pod was suddenly blasted away from the Comanche's stub wing and crashed on the chopper landing pad, Jake MacLeod took most of the impact. Even though he was protected by his armored combat suit, the crash jarred him heavily.

While he lay there stunned, lights around the landing pad snapped on, flooding the area with blinding light. Armed men ran out of the building at the end of the landing pad, the weapons in their hands pointed at him. Before he could recover and bring his own weapons into play, he was overwhelmed, disarmed and hauled to his feet.

With no way to know what was happening, Bao hit her emergency release from inside the pod to blow the seal. She was only halfway out of the pod when she saw the muzzles of a half-dozen assault rifles aimed at her. Moving slowly, she held her two hands out in front of her to show that they were empty. A hand reached down, clamped around her arm and jerked her to her feet. Other hands spun her around and forced her arms behind her back, where a plastic riot restraint was slipped over her wrists.

The first thing she saw was MacLeod surrounded by armed men. His helmet visor was open and, in the light, it looked like his face was bleeding. Whatever had happened, it was a catastrophe.

"Where are you taking us?" she asked as her captors led her away.

A rifle butt smashed between her shoulder blades, staggering her. "Shut up, bitch."

MacLeod and Bao were led into a room in the building at the end of the chopper pad. Another half-dozen armed men were waiting there, weapons at the ready. A stocky man wearing light blue coveralls with a New Dawn logo on one side and a security badge on the other stepped out from behind them.

"Listen carefully." He looked directly at MacLeod. "I'm going to have my men disarm and search both of you. At the first sign of trouble from either one of you, the woman is going to die first."

"I hear you," MacLeod answered.

"Good."

WHEN BAO AND MACLEOD were brought before Joshua Nisi, they had been stripped down to their underwear. Their arms were bound behind their backs with plastic restraints and their guards kept them covered with drawn pistols.

"The woman was a walking arsenal," Lutz said, laying a pile of assorted weapons on Nisi's desk. "She even had this in her hair." The security chief put a thin needle-blade stiletto on the table.

"And him—" Lutz jerked a thumb at MacLeod "—he was wearing some kind of science-fiction armored suit with a helmet and everything. I don't know what it can do, but I'll have some of the guys check it out."

Joshua Nisi looked at Mel Bao with more than casual interest. Oriental or not, she was stunning. She stood there in just her bikini panties as proudly as if she were wearing a court robe. Her hair had been undone and flowed down her back in striking contrast to her golden skin. Her slim hips and small breasts gave her the youthful, athletic look he so craved, and he knew that she would be the ride of a lifetime. The fact that she had been sent to kill him made her only that much more enticing.

He could tell that this was one woman who would never consider sleeping with him for any price. Since he had become a millionaire, Nisi had become so accustomed to beautiful women stumbling all over themselves to get into his bed that it had lost its charm for him. In fact, he had come to hate women who were so willing to sell themselves.

The reason he had started the Daughters of the New Dawn was so that he could have bed partners who were there for who he was, not for his money. And the drug he administered to help the Daughters get over their virginal fears of the initiation rites would also work on this Oriental beauty. But, with a delightful difference.

With the Daughters, the drug took away their fears and allowed them to experience the unknown with anticipation rather than with anxiety. Used on this woman, the drug would subvert her body, but leave her will intact. She wouldn't be able to keep herself from sexually reacting to him even though she obviously hated him.

He nodded toward MacLeod. "Put him in the cell next to Sendak. I'll question him later."

"Where do you want me to put her?"

"Send her down to the Senior Sister under guard. Tell her to prepare our captive, and I will be down shortly."

"Yes, sir."

IN THE DESERT, Jud Rykoff stopped for a ten-minute break, but the rest wasn't for him. With the servos carrying Estevez's weight, he could have packed the pilot in his arms until the suit's power cells ran out. The break was for Estevez. Trying to hold on while Rykoff ran was beating him half to death.

"How much farther?" Estevez asked as he stretched and tried to work the kinks out of his muscles. Ceramal armor wasn't the most yielding material in the world.

Rykoff called up the navigation screen on his visor and looked at the map. "It's another forty miles. I'd say about another hour."

"What are we going to do when we reach the highway?"

"I'm going to find a place to hide in the brush while you hitch a ride into Tucson, retrieve our U-Haul, drive back here and pick me up."

"Then what?"

Rykoff looked back in the direction they had come. "I'll be fucked if I know, but we're going back for them one way or the other. We'll go back to the hotel and I'll try to put something together."

He looked at Estevez. "You ready to go again?"

Estevez winced and flexed his knees. "Next time I'm going to take a cab."

"Good luck trying to find one at this time of night."

WHEN NISI WALKED into the room, Bao was fighting the effects of the drugs she had been given. Her head was buzzing, her nerves were tingling uncomfortably, particularly between her legs, and her nipples were aching. Whatever she had been given was powerful, and it wasn't like any drug she had ever read about. Though the room was cool and she was strapped naked on a medical examining table, she felt hot all over.

"How are you feeling, Miss Bao?" Nisi had a trace of a knowing smile playing at the corners of his mouth.

"It won't do you any good to fight it," he said without giving her a chance to reply. "In a few more minutes you will have no control over your sexual desires. As the vulgar saying goes, you will be ready to fuck a snake.''

When she didn't answer, he dismissed the Senior Sister and proceeded to take off his clothes, laying them carefully on the chair by the examining table. Reaching over to the counter, he picked up a foil package and opened it.

Bao felt almost relieved when she saw him put on the condom. Knowing that she would have even a thin latex barrier between her and that man was a comfort.

"It's for my protection, my dear," he explained when he saw that she had noticed the prophylactic. "Unlike with my own dear girls, I don't know where you have been or who you have been with. With the way you people are nowadays, a man can't be too careful."

"Fuck you, asshole," she panted.

"That's exactly what you are going to do, my dear," he said. "And there is nothing you can do to keep from it. Your body is mine now."

She turned her face away as he climbed in between her legs. She was going to be raped, but nothing said that she had to watch the bastard while he did it. To her horror, her body reacted to Nisi's sudden invasion. She felt herself flood with lubricant to ease his passage.

When his hands cupped her breasts a few seconds later, her legs wanted to wrap themselves around his waist. For the first time, she was glad that her arms and legs were strapped down to the table. Otherwise, she was afraid that rather than fight him off, she would cooperate with him. As it was, even strapped down, she felt her hips thrust up at him of their own accord and her back arch to press her breasts against his soft hands.

A shuddering orgasm suddenly hit her and she cried out in shame and outrage. "No! No!"

His answering shout was a cry of triumph and she felt the condom inside her swell with his ejaculation. Unable to stop herself, she thrust her pelvis up hard against him and felt another wave of pleasure sweep over her. "Oh, God! No!"

Her eyes were closed when he pulled out of her and stepped down to the floor.

"That was an interesting experience," Nisi said as he quickly dressed. "We'll have to do that again sometime soon."

To her shame, there was nothing she could say in answer to that.

WHEN THE SENIOR SISTER came back in with the guards, she couldn't meet Bao's eyes, and it was a good thing, too. Her eyes were as cold as a snake's. After unstrapping her from the table, the woman let Bao cover her nakedness with a thin smock before she was taken away to her cell.

When the guards left with Bao, the Senior Sister, once known as Debbie Browning, sat on the edge of the examining table, her hands folded in her lap. For the first time since coming to the New Dawn compound, she questioned what she was doing there.

She had originally joined up with Nisi to be a part of his vision for a better world right after she graduated from college. Within weeks, she had joined him in his bed, happy to share her body with the great man. Later she had come to believe that he needed to share his unique dream with other women, so she relinquished her place next to him at night. She had been sad, but she had thought that he was important and his happiness meant more than her own feelings.

She had also been happy when he had chosen her to be the Senior Sister of his Daughters of the New Dawn. She was glad to help the girls come to know the honor she had known in his bed. She had become convinced that the drugs the girls were given were something good that would help them overcome their fears so they could sooner know the joys she had known. Now, though, she didn't think that.

She had just been a part of a brutal rape aided by those same drugs and it frightened her. She didn't know who the Oriental woman was, but she had obviously not consented to share her body. Even though her body had cooperated because of the drugs, her will hadn't submitted. Nisi had always told her the importance of submission to the act. Even though they were young, all of the girls who were chosen to enter the Daughters of the Dawn submitted, first to take the drug and then to share their bodies with Joshua. As

Nisi himself had always said, without the submission, the sex act was rape.

And the girl who had been Debbie Browning knew about rape. She had been attacked by a street gang when she was in her senior year in high school. She had been caught after hours by half a dozen gang members and their girlfriends. The rape had been long and brutal, with the girls taking their turns with her, as well. Physical recovery had taken weeks, but the psychological scars never healed. After the rape, Nisi had been her first lover, if he could be called that.

What Joshua had done wasn't right, and although she didn't know what she could do about it, she knew she had to do something. If she didn't, she would be just like those girls back at her high school who had held her down and laughed while she had been violated.

BAO LAY ON THE BUNK in her cell and fought to overcome the aftereffects of the drugs she had been given. She had been trained to raise the adrenaline level in her body on command and found that it helped cut through the fog in her brain and cooled the burning in her body. She panted to increase the oxygen in her blood so it could burn the toxins and drive them from her system.

When her breathing was back under control, she stripped off the smock she had been given and stepped up to the built-in sink. Though there were no washcloths—or towels or soap—she turned on the water and washed her entire body as best she could with her bare hands. With the water dripping from her body, she stuck her head under the faucet and thoroughly washed her hair, as well.

When she slipped back into the smock, her skin and hair were as clean as she could make them. But she wouldn't feel completely clean as long as that bastard continued to breathe the same air she did. To have been raped was bad, but every woman ran the risk of being raped. It was a part of being female. To have been drugged, however, was the ultimate obscenity. To have been robbed of her control over her own body wasn't something she could ever take lightly.

If she hadn't been drugged, she would have cooperated with her rapist simply to keep herself from being hurt. That was just common sense and was part of the woman-warrior training she had received from her mother. When a woman was in a position that took all her options from her, the only intelligent thing she could do was not to fight it. To fight under those circumstances was to risk being hurt or killed. It made more sense for the woman to cooperate in the hope of gaining her freedom later than to risk death when she was helpless.

Nisi had better kill her while he still had the chance. If she ever got out of this cell, she was going to kill him with her bare hands and it wasn't going to be a pretty death. He would learn that the Bao woman was not to be treated that way. Nor was any woman, for that matter.

First, though, she had to get out of the cell, and to do that, she was going to have to use her body. This time, though, she would be in control of anything she did, and nothing a woman did of her own free will was shameful.

Taking off her smock again, she began drying her hair with it so she would be ready the next time someone came to get her.

## 27

*Chiricahua Valley, Arizona*
*January 30*

Joshua Nisi stared at the burned-out wreckage of the Comanche gunship. He wasn't an expert on helicopter crashes, but it looked to him like the gunship had made a fairly soft landing. The hundred-meter gouge in the sand showed that the chopper had skidded on her belly before coming to rest against the half-buried boulder.

Though the damage was not great, the chopper had caught on fire somehow. The fire had completely destroyed the cockpit section of the machine and had burned through the stub wings with their missile pylons. It had not, however, burned the pod on the left wing tip that matched the one that had been dropped during the aborted attack. The pod was open and it was empty. Rykoff and the pilot had escaped.

"We have some tracks," Lutz reported. "It looks like there were two men, and they tried to walk out to the west."

Nisi glanced in the direction the security chief pointed. Twenty-five miles away was State Highway 66 which headed for Interstate 10 to the north. Since it had only been six hours since the attack, they shouldn't have gotten too far. "Get airborne and look for them."

"Yes, sir."

"When you find them, try to bring them back alive, but don't take any chances. I don't want them reaching the highway. Is that clear?"

"Yes, sir."

While the chopper was searching for Rykoff and Estevez, Nisi had to get back to his compound to make a phone call. Infiltrations he could deal with himself, but attacks by armed gunships and men in science-fiction battle armor was just a little too much. His senator had better be able to do something about these people, and do it fast. He also needed to interrogate the man who had been captured with the girl.

If he knew where Rykoff and the pilot were, he wouldn't wait for the senator to call the dogs off. He'd kill them himself.

EVEN THOUGH STEADMAN had told himself that he was going to stay completely away from the current CAT Team mission until it was over, he just couldn't do it. Not when he heard about the helicopter crash in the Chiricahua Valley in Arizona.

According to the CNN news report, an unidentified helicopter had buzzed the New Dawn headquarters last night and collided with an unlighted radio antenna mast. Though apparently damaged, the chopper had been able to fly away, then reportedly crashed in a remote part of the valley. A rescue team was on the way to the crash site now to search for survivors.

This concerned him greatly. Knowing the kind of heavy hardware Rykoff had secured for his assault, to have had it turned back so easily indicated that there had been some kind of major disaster at the New Dawn complex. Rykoff and his people were good, but even the best sometimes ran out of luck.

A company spokesman in a blue uniform came on the tube to claim that New Dawn had been receiving threats from a far-right fundamentalist Christian group that was opposed to genetic research of any kind. He said that while the identity of the people in the helicopter was still unknown, he attributed the incident to this group.

The CNN reporter then mentioned other scientific facilities that had been having problems with anti-science fundamentalist Christian organizations. The report switched to a remote, where another reporter did a short interview with a man claiming to be from the organization behind the threats. The spokesman ranted and raved about the dangers of an arrogant, ungodly, humanistic science working to overturn God's holy laws, but Steadman wasn't convinced. The man simply didn't have the wild-eyed lunatic quality that marked the truly God crazed. But if that guy was a ringer, and Steadman was ready to bet his federal pension that he was, what was he hiding and who was behind the cover-up?

Whoever was behind this had to have enough horsepower to bend the media to his will, and CNN didn't bend easily. As Steadman had discovered, Joshua Nisi had powerful friends in high places. The way this incident was being handled strongly suggested that at least one of Nisi's friends had access to the highest levels of government. Maybe even to the group of men who were behind the CAT Team. If that was the case, Rykoff had stumbled onto a real hornet's nest and was in extreme danger.

If one of the men in the CAT Team Control Group was also working with a madman who was trying to start a race war in the United States, Rykoff and his team were as good as dead. The nation was also in deep shit, but Steadman had to concentrate on one thing at a time. If he could first bail out Rykoff, maybe he could still take care of Nisi and his plan for Armageddon.

Taking a seat behind the antique desk in his den, Steadman booted his computer. While he waited to hear from Rykoff, he would dig deeper into Nisi's background and see what he found. When he left his Pentagon office, he had switched his computer over to the land-line link that allowed him to work from home without using the phone lines. That ultrasecure mode had been installed to allow him to direct the CAT Team and access his files in complete security.

It took him a while to find what he suspected, but now he had it. Senator John Parks from California was a very good friend of Joshua Nisi. Apparently the senator had visited the New Dawn compound more than once, even though it wasn't in his home state. Since he was on the Senate Select Committee on Advanced Technology and Science, that wasn't too far out of the ordinary. But when it was tied to campaign contributions and critical votes on the Senate floor that seemed to favor New Dawn, it smelled like the senator was in Nisi's pocket.

This same senator was also a member of the Control Group that oversaw the CAT Team's operations. The question now was how could he use this information to help Rykoff and his team?

He was pondering this when the phone rang. When he didn't answer it, it kept on ringing. After a dozen or so rings it fell silent.

On a hunch, Steadman logged into the CAT Team program and looked for other recent log-ins. As he expected, there had been several attempts to get in beginning early that morning that had been turned back by the security system. Then, a half hour ago, someone had used an override command Steadman hadn't known existed to log in. From there, this person had accessed the Little Big Horn program.

He leaned back in his chair for a long moment, cursing himself for not having deleted that program when he had the chance. Now it was too late.

STEADMAN STOOD and looked out at the bleak day outside his window. January was always miserable in D.C., but the weather suited his mood perfectly. If Little Big Horn was in operation there was a good chance that his own name had been added to the hit list. And, unlike Rykoff, he couldn't run and try to hide. He had to stay at his keyboard until Jud contacted him so he could warn him.

Regardless of his job as the mission controller for five of the most dangerous people in the world, Steadman had never liked guns very much. He had never served in the military and he had never even been hunting. The *Bambi* movie he had seen as a child had hit home big time.

His personal inclination hadn't prevented the purchase of a Smith & Wesson .357 Magnum revolver ten years or so ago as a home defense weapon. He had even signed up at a gun club and had taken a course on marksmanship and gun safety so he would know how to use it. There wasn't much point in having the weapon around the house if he didn't know how to use it. He hadn't had call to use it yet, but this looked like the time when he might need to.

Walking into his bedroom, he took the .357's cylinder open to check the load. Five brass cartridge case ends were visible in the six chambers of the cylinder. Ever mindful of his gun safety course, he had always kept the hammer down on an empty chamber so dropping it wouldn't cause an accidental discharge.

That was a fine safety precaution for home defense, but this was his life he was defending now.

Going over to his closet, he opened the door and rummaged around on the top shelf until he found the box of .357 caliber hollowpoint ammunition he had purchased with the pistol. The salesman at the gun store had told him that putting one of those rounds in the "center mass of the target" would drop a man where he stood. He didn't know what the center mass of a target was, but he took the man's word for it that the ammunition was powerful.

Taking a round from the box, he loaded it into the empty chamber and snapped the cylinder back into the pistol's frame. He was putting the box of ammunition back on the closet shelf when he thought better of it. Reaching to one of the hangers, he took a battered old safari-style jacket he had owned for years and shrugged into it. The pistol went in one of the jacket's big pockets and the box of ammunition in the other. He didn't have a Western gun belt with cartridge loops, or even a holster, but this would work just as well. He would simply wear the safari jacket until this was over one way or the other.

Now that he was armed, Steadman felt a little better. With the pistol and the house security system set on audible alert, he would at least have a fighting chance. Probably not much of a chance in the real world, but at least he would go down fighting. Jud Rykoff, if he were still alive, would be proud of him.

BACK IN THEIR ROOM at the motel, Rykoff prepared to try to link up with Steadman in Washington. It had taken most of the night to walk out of the desert and for Estevez to find a ride into town to retrieve their van. Now that they were back, he wanted to report to Steadman before they did anything else—even sleep. When he completed the link and entered his ID word, a code word appeared on the screen—"Sitting Bull."

Instantly he punched out the Alt, Control, Delete sequence on the keyboard to break the modem link and reboot his machine. "We've been made," he said. "Pack up. We've got to get out of here ASAP."

Estevez turned away from the window where he had been keeping watch on the parking lot outside the motel. "What's the problem?"

"Get your gear," Rykoff snapped. "We'll talk about it on the road."

Neither man said anything as they quickly stuffed their few belongings and got back into the U-Haul van. Rykoff didn't bother to check out of their room. He had paid with a credit card, so they would get their money one way or the other. Unfortunately, the card he had used was in his name. He just hoped that the people who were after them wouldn't get around to checking credit card receipts too quickly.

Rykoff drove the van away from the motel at exactly the speed limit to the outskirts of the city. Either too fast or too slow could attract attention and the last thing they needed right now was to attract the attention of the police. Even a traffic stop would put them in jeopardy if the cop ran their ID through the "wants and warrants" check in the computer.

"Don't you think it's about time that you gave me the full story about our merry little band, Jud?" Estevez said as soon as they cleared the city limits and were headed out into the open desert to the south. "Since I'm on the run, I'd really like to know who I'm running from and why."

For a moment Rykoff said nothing as his eyes scanned the side roads. "That's a reasonable request," he finally said. "If you're on the run from your own people, I guess you have the right to know why you'd better keep on running."

He took a deep breath. "It started right before I met you. A half-dozen men in Washington decided that our country had taken enough shit from terrorists and something positive had to be done to turn things around. Even though it looked like Clinton didn't have a hope in hell at the polls in 1996, there was always the off chance that the American people would shoot themselves in the foot again and reelect that fool.

"Regardless of who the new president would be, though, the system had broken down completely and they were afraid that it would take too much time to put it back in order. With the increase in terrorism we were experiencing then, something had to be done immediately or no American would ever be safe again. One of the men involved in this plan was a general I had worked for during the Gulf War and he contacted me at the university. I thought about his proposal, and since I was at loose ends, having just been divorced from Pamela, I resigned and accepted the job of putting the Team together.

"You know most of the rest of it. It took about a year to locate and interview enough people to come up with the four of you and put the Team into operation."

"What I don't understand is how in the hell you've been able to keep this secret from the Feds."

Rykoff laughed and began telling him about Steadman, the faceless civil servant in the Defense Procurement Agency who was the mastermind behind their operations. The man who spent every day of his working life looking at an antique print of Custer's Last Stand.

When Rykoff was done with the twisted tale, Estevez stared out the windshield. "That Steadman guy must have a real pair on him."

Rykoff laughed. "He'd love to hear you say that. He's the least likely man you've ever seen to run an operation like this. He has no military background at all and has spent his entire life working with computers. What he does have going for him, though, is that he's very good at what he does and he has a world-class devious mind. If it's in a computer anywhere in the federal or any of the state governments, he can find it, access it and twist it to his use. He even reads the President's outgoing mail. It may take him a little while to sort this out, but I know he'll get it done."

"What's our next move?"

"First we're going back after Jake, Mel and Alex. We'll sort the rest out after that. I want to find a pickup with a camper so we can ditch this U-Haul. It's too easy to run the computers and find out that we rented this thing. From there, an APB will have every state trooper in the West looking for us."

"If you're thinking of taking the fighting suits with us, you'd better look for a pickup with a horse trailer on the back. Campers aren't too popular around here."

"You've got a point there," Rykoff agreed. "Where do we find one?"

Estevez broke out the road map. "There's a border crossing not too far from here." His finger traced a route. "We could drop into Mexico and see what we can find down there."

"I don't know about going to Mexico," Rykoff said. "If they've called the dogs in on us, they've probably notified the border patrol, as well. Opening the back of a horse trailer and finding those suits in there is really going to ring their chimes."

"I suppose."

Estevez went back to his map. "How about dumping the suits somewhere around here and then taking the empty van into Mexico to make the swap?"

"That's not a bad idea," Rykoff said. "That way if we run into trouble again the suits will be safe. Without those suits, we're never going to get them back now."

"Do you really think it's going to work even with the armor?"

"It has to." Rykoff's jaw was clenched. "If we don't get them out of there, they're going to die."

Neither man bothered to mention that there was a good chance that their teammates were already dead. But even if they knew for a fact that they were, there was still vengeance to be exacted and they would exact it.

One way or the other, the CAT Team was going to go out with a bang, not a whimper.

**28**

*Nogales, Mexico*
*January 30*

The Mexican cattle ranch Rykoff had been directed to didn't look all that different from any ranch on the American side of the border. On both sides, the ranch hands were Latino, the rangy cows looked just as scruffy, and the smell was identical.

The ranch's owner, Señor Estavano, didn't look all that different from his American counterparts, either. A well-worn straw cowboy hat sat on his gray head, and his wind-battered face could only have been that of a man who had spent his entire life squinting into the sun. While his work jeans and shirt were worn, the boots on his feet were fairly new. If he had nothing else, a rancher on either side of the border had to have good boots.

"I understand that you might have an old pickup truck I could buy," Rykoff said after shaking the rancher's hand.

"Yes, señor," the rancher said, pointing to a shed with several derelict pickups around it. "I have several old trucks. What are you looking for?"

The battered, two-tone-green pickup next to the shed was exactly what Rykoff was looking for. He didn't remember what year's make it was, but it had apparently spent all of its life in the desert because there was almost no rust showing through the sun-checked, faded paint. The evidence of its hard life as a farm truck, however, could be seen in the dents on every body panel, including the roof of the cab.

"I'd like to buy that GMC pickup over there, if it runs well."

The rancher's eyebrows went up. "My Jimmy truck. She runs real good. Why do you want to buy it? Do you want to take it to California and sell it, maybe?"

"No." Rykoff shook his head. Now that the United States had been picked clean of rolling antiques, the car-collector crazies were stripping Mexico, too. "I'm taking it back to Arizona. I like 'em. My father used to have one just like that."

"Okay, señor." The rancher nodded, not believing a word Rykoff had said. "You can buy the Jimmy truck for eight hundred dollars."

"How do you want it? Cash or American Express checks?"

"The checks will be fine."

Laying the folder of traveler's checks against the side of the truck, Rykoff signed eight checks and handed them over.

"*Gracias, señor.*" The rancher folded the checks neatly in half and stuffed them into his shirt pocket.

"Okay," Rykoff said. "Now I need a horse trailer. Do you have one here I could buy?"

"Do you want a new trailer or an old one like the truck?"

"An old one."

The horse trailer the rancher led him to was old, maybe older than the pickup. But both tires had air in them and the trailer hitch looked serviceable. "How much?" Rykoff asked.

When the rancher gave his price, Rykoff winced and started signing traveler's checks again.

"Now," Rykoff said as he handed them over. "Do you have a horse I could buy to put in the trailer?"

"What kind of horse, señor?" The rancher opened his arms to take in the corrals. "I have many horses here."

"I need a cheap horse."

"I don't understand."

"I want a horse that doesn't cost very much. I'm running out of money."

That was something the rancher could easily understand. This loco gringo was paying good money for beat-up old pickups and horse trailers and now he wanted a beat-up old horse to go with them.

"Come with me, señor."

In a side pasture, the rancher whistled and a black horse came trotting over to him. "This is a good horse," the rancher said, scratching the horse's chin. "His only problem is that he is older now and not much to look at. But, like the truck, he is still strong."

"How much do you want for him?"

When the checks ran out, Rykoff reached into his wallet for enough cash to make up the proper amount.

"One more thing," Rykoff said as he turned to walk back to the truck. "Do you have a man, a cowboy, who would like to change clothes with Erik here?"

Throughout the transaction, Estevez had stood silently, watching Rykoff spend their contingency money. He probably could have gotten them a better deal on their purchases if he had conducted the negotiations in Spanish, but Rykoff was on a roll and he knew better than to get in his way.

The rancher looked Estevez up and down. The pilot was wearing new jeans and a good shirt worth a week's pay for one of his men. "One moment, please."

The rancher went back into the barn and yelled out a man's name. The cowboy who appeared was almost exactly Estevez's size and was dressed in well-faded, torn jeans, a worn blue chambray work shirt and a battered straw hat like his boss's.

"Will these clothes do, señor?"

"They'll do nicely if he's willing to trade."

"I'm keeping my own boots," Estevez growled.

"That's okay, señor." The cowboy smiled. "I no think they fit me."

Quickly stripping down to his shorts, Estevez stepped into the Mexican cowboy's battered jeans, pulled them up over his legs and fastened the belt. "Not a bad fit."

While Estevez was changing clothes, the rancher had his men hitch the trailer up to the back of the pickup and load the horse inside. As a bonus, he threw a couple of bales of hay into the trailer.

"Thank you." Rykoff shook the Rancher's hand.

"My pleasure."

The rancher shook his head as he watched Rykoff and Estevez drive out of sight. Crazy gringos. He counted through the traveler's checks one more time, kissed them and stuffed them back into the pocket of his shirt.

"Ramon," he called out to his foreman in Spanish. "I'm going into town and probably will be back late."

"Okay." Ramon winked. "Give Señora Esmerelda my regards."

The rancher cackled. "I'll give her more than my regards tonight, my friend, much more."

THE LAST THING Rykoff wanted to do while he was still in Mexico was to try to get in contact with Steadman again. Even though he had been given the code word to run, he wanted to know exactly how bad it really was and if going back to the New Dawn compound was at all practical. Even if it wasn't, he would still go back to try to free his teammates, but he needed to know if he had any chance of pulling it off or if it was simply going to be a suicide run.

"Let's find a place we can stop for a couple of hours," he told Estevez.

Pulling into an American-style motel within sight of the border crossing, Rykoff sent Estevez in to get them a room under a false name. Once inside, he had the pilot stand guard outside their room. When he was alone, he took out his computer, fitted the phone in the modem cradle and booted. This time he ignored Steadman's warning code and logged on anyway with a priority code word.

Steadman came back immediately and Rykoff briefed him on everything that had happened since they had last talked. It was a one-sided conversation, except when Steadman told him about discovering the connection between Nisi and the senator on the CAT Team's Control Group.

"Can you slow that bastard down long enough for me to get my people out?" Rykoff sent back. "I'll take care of him when I'm done here."

"I'm isolated at my house," Steadman typed. "And I can't do it over the modem."

"Forget procedure," Rykoff sent. "Call the general at his office."

"That's an open line," Steadman reminded him.

"If we have a bad guy in the CG, it doesn't matter anymore. We're blown anyway."

Steadman had no choice but to agree with Rykoff's assessment of the situation. He had spent so much time trying to keep the Team under cover, it was hard for him to admit that it had all been for naught. "What do I tell the general?"

Rykoff quickly typed a set of instructions for him to follow. "I'll get back in touch later after you've had a chance to talk to him. Autie out."

After shutting down and putting the computer back in its case, Rykoff leaned back against the pillow. He couldn't remember when he had last had a full night's sleep and it was starting to catch up with him. Setting his watch alarm for two hours, he was asleep before he rolled over.

When Estevez let himself into the room an hour later to get Rykoff to spell him so he could get their lunch, he let his boss continue sleeping. Both of them were exhausted and they had more than a full night ahead of them. He'd let Rykoff drive back across the border and get his sleep on the way to their new base camp in Brisbee.

STEADMAN DIDN'T THINK that the light-colored sedan parked down the street belonged to anyone in his exclusive little residential enclave. In fact, he was certain of it. No one in Glen Acres would dare to drive anything that plebeian. The owners' covenant specifically stated that the car parked in your driveway had to cost at least three times your annual mortgage payments. Also, the darkened windows on the sedan were a dead giveaway. The sharks were gathering. Maybe Rykoff's suggestion to talk to the general would work. Even if it didn't, it sure beat the hell out of waiting around for the sharks to break in and eat him.

"General Hawkings," he said when the general came on the line. "This is Winston Steadman, from Defense Procurement. Jud Rykoff suggested that I give you a call."

"How is he?" The general's voice was guarded.

"Not well, I'm afraid, sir, and that's why I'm calling. He wanted me to remind you about a party at the Riyadh Hilton, a case of Rémy Martin, a certain naked female reporter from CBS and a raid by the Saudi religious police. He says that he needs you to return the favor."

There was a long silence on the other end of the line and Steadman wondered if he had overstepped the boundaries. Jud had said that the general owed him a big one and had a good sense of humor besides, but apparently that wasn't the case. If the general had gone over to the opposition, Jud's fate was sealed, as was his own.

Suddenly the phone erupted with a burst of laughter. "That rotten son of a bitch," the general said. "He promised that he'd never say a word about making that girl and the booze disappear that night."

"I've got a priority package from him I'd like to deliver to you as soon as possible."

"Why don't I meet you at the Wall in an hour." Like the Brandenburg Gate had been in Berlin, the Vietnam Memorial Wall in D.C. was a favorite spot for clandestine meetings.

Steadman glanced out the window at the sedan parked up the street. "Can you make that in two hours, General. I may have a little trouble getting away."

"Sure."

"How will I recognize you?"

"I'll be the only three-star general there with a staff car and my aides."

"Good enough, sir. Two hours then."

STEADMAN HAD a difficult time making his appointment with the general. Getting away from the sharks in the car hadn't been easy. The sedan was parked where it had a good field of vision over most of his property. There was only one place where he thought he could slip away without being spotted.

Putting himself into a Jud Rykoff mind-set, he checked the lay of the land at the back of the house. He decided that if he could make a fifty-meter crawl to the wooded plot at the rear of the house, the men in the car wouldn't be able to see him. Being January, the trees had shed their leaves months ago, but even so, once he was another fifty meters or so inside the tree line, the bare trunks should hide him well enough.

Back in his bedroom, Steadman changed into a pair of blue jeans and put a long black raincoat over the safari jacket. After making sure that the pistol and ammunition were secure in his pockets, he went out into the attached garage. There was a woodshed built against the back wall of the garage that had a trapdoor leading inside so he could fetch wood without going outside in the cold.

Propping the trapdoor open, he started piling the wood inside and quickly made an opening large enough to wiggle through. Once in the woodshed, he scrambled over the piled wood and peeked around the edge of the opening into his backyard. When he didn't see anyone lurking in the bushes, he crawled out into the open.

He had never been through military basic training, but he had seen enough movies to know how to do the army low crawl. Getting down on his elbows and knees in the dead grass and mud of his winter lawn, he started dragging himself down the gentle slope toward the woods. As he had thought, the rise in the ground between him and the car was enough to block the line of sight of whoever was watching.

When he reached the wood line, he continued crawling until he was certain that he was well hidden. A half hour's hike took him to the main road on the other side of the woods. Ditching the raincoat before he left the trees, he tried to brush the worst of the mud from his jeans before he walked out to stand at the bus stop.

He kept a sharp eye out while he waited for the bus in case the whole neighborhood was under surveillance, as well. He was relieved when the blue-and-white bus pulled up instead of another sedan with blacked-out windows.

When Steadman took an aisle seat and slouched down like the rest of commuters, it wasn't difficult for him to put a look of boredom on his face. He hated riding in buses. Despite his relaxed exterior, though, he kept a sharp eye out for light-colored sedans all the way into D.C.

## 29

*Washington, D.C.*
*January 30*

When he stepped off the bus at the Vietnam Memorial stop, Winston Steadman found the man he was looking for almost immediately. Even with the crowds at the Wall, the general was not hard to spot. "General Hawkings," Steadman said, walking up to him. "I'm sorry I'm late."

"Winston!" The general held out his hand, not noticing the mud on Steadman's shoes and pants. "I'm glad you could make it." Though the two had never met, they had worked together over the modem for several years.

"Let's talk in the car," the general said as Steadman stepped up to shake hands.

Once inside the staff car, the general dismissed his driver and the two men sat alone. "Exactly what in the hell is going on," he snapped. "Every time I have to leave town for a couple of days the shit hits the fan. Has Rykoff gone completely mental?"

"No, sir," Steadman said. "This time the trouble is within the Control Group."

"You'd better be able to prove that one, mister." The general had personally vetted every member of the CAT Team's Control Group, and if there was a problem with any of them, he wanted to know about it ASAP.

"I can prove it," Steadman said evenly. "And I can prove who's gone bad."

"Give it to me from the beginning."

The general listened carefully as Steadman started running through the sequence of events surrounding the CAT Team's L.A. mission. The general didn't stop him until he started talking about New Dawn. "Exactly who is this Nisi guy?"

Steadman quickly outlined Nisi's recent résumé, including his connections with the Ukrainian government and his long-time financial support of Senator Parks.

"I never did trust that bastard," the general growled. "Even for Capitol Hill, he's always been a little too slimy for my tastes. I always wondered how in the hell he got picked to be chairman of the Senate Select Committee on Intelligence. He had to have been fucking somebody or letting someone fuck him."

The general shook his head. "I can take care of his sorry ass later. Give me the rest on Rykoff."

Steadman related Sendak's capture, Rykoff's gunfight with the South Africans, and his heliborne assault on the New Dawn complex.

"What did you give Rykoff for the assault?"

"He got a Comanche gunship from the LHX program and three of the armored combat suits from Project Strongman."

"And that wasn't enough to do the job?"

"Nisi had a radar-guided 20 mm antiaircraft gun Rykoff didn't know about."

"What happened?"

When Steadman told him about the aborted raid, the general looked as if he had just heard that his favorite dog had died. "He lost both the Comanche and one of the powered suits?"

Steadman nodded. "He was able to destroy the gunship, but the suit is still at the New Dawn complex. Along with three of his team," he added.

"When Rykoff gets back in contact with you," the general ordered, "tell him to stay hidden until I can get the Little Big Horn operation turned off and to check in every twenty-four hours for further instructions."

"I don't know if he'll do that, General," Steadman said honestly. "He's completely focused on getting Bao, Sendak and MacLeod out of there, no matter what it takes. He's planning to hit the complex again tonight."

"I was afraid of that." The general shook his head. "The simple bastard. Short of going through with the Little Big Horn program, though, I can't see any way to stop him at this point. I sure as hell hope that he's got his shit together this time."

"If that's all, General, I'd better get back to my house so he can contact me."

"Wait one." The general placed a quick call on his cell phone. "I have a car on the way for you," he said when he was finished. "And there will be four of my men in it. They'll take you home and stay with you until I get this mess sorted out. If the senator's people try to give you any trouble, they'll handle it."

"What are you going to do?"

The general smiled, and it wasn't a pleasant smile. "First, I'm going to call off the dogs so Rykoff can make his play without having to dodge the Feds."

He paused and the smile grew even more sinister. "Then I'm going to pay a visit to the honorable senator from California, have a little chat with him about his consorting with an agent of a foreign government with the aim of overthrowing the United States. We call that sort of thing treason around here."

"But you can't bring him to trial without exposing the activities of the CAT Team."

The general smiled broadly now. "Who said anything about a trial?"

RYKOFF AND ESTEVEZ used their ID cards from the DEA at the border crossing, and they were allowed back into the United States without so much as a second glance. The INS Border Patrol had seen much stranger things than two drug agents crossing the border in a battered old pickup with Mexican plates pulling a horse trailer loaded with an elderly horse. One time they'd had a traveling circus complete with elephants and tigers cross on DEA paperwork.

In their motel room in Brisbee, the first thing the two men did was go over their weapons, including the SPAS semiautomatic assault shotgun Rykoff had chosen as his main weapon. One of their stops on the drive back had been at a big gun store where Rykoff had purchased their entire stock of 12-gauge Dragon's Breath shotgun rounds.

The Dragon's Breath round had originally been developed as a howitzer projectile designed to defend base camps against human wave attacks. Loaded with a combustible magnesium mixture, the 155 mm version reportedly was able to burn a path two hundred meters wide and almost two miles long through any kind of terrain.

Worried about the public perception of such a weapon as "inhumane," the Army decided not to develop the Dragon's Breath round beyond the test phase. In the mid-nineties, however, the concept reappeared in the form of a 12-gauge-shotgun round sold as a novelty item. And what a novelty they were. The Dragon's Breath round turned any shotgun into a flamethrower with a hundred-meter range.

Along with the SPAS, Rykoff prepared an H&K MP-5 9 mm subgun and his 10 mm Glock pistol. With the powered armor, he had no need of fighting knives; a stiff-fingered punch of the suit's glove would go all the way through a man's chest.

"Hadn't you better feed and water that animal out there?" Estevez asked when he was done with his own mission prep. "He's been locked up in that trailer all day."

"Jesus," Rykoff said. "Can you do that for me? I need to talk to Steadman."

"I don't know a damned thing about horses." Actually the pilot didn't like animals larger than himself and had never been around horses at all.

"It's no big deal," Rykoff said. "Take a trash can full of water out there for him and hold it in front of his nose. When he's done drinking, break up one of those hay bales and give him half of it."

"Don't we need to exercise him or something?"

"At his age, he doesn't need exercising."

While Estevez was seeing to the horse, Rykoff turned on his computer and logged on to Steadman's modem. "Autie," he typed.

"Terry," Steadman sent back. General Alfred Terry had been in overall command of the operation against the Indians that culminated in Custer's disaster at the Little Big Horn. By the time Terry's column reached the battle site three days later, the Indians had all decamped for the Canadian border to the north. The use of his name as a code word meant that the situation had gotten better instead of worse. That was good news for a change. Steadman must have gotten through to the general.

"Send update."

"I contacted Hawkings and he wants you to go to ground and wait for him to handle Nisi and the senator. The problem is being taken care of on this end, but it will take a couple of days.''

"Negative," Rykoff sent back. "If Nisi gets wind of someone closing in on him, he'll kill his captives to cover his tracks. I have to go in tonight."

"Hawkings said you would say that and he wanted me to tell you to get that lost armored suit back no matter what."

"I will if I can. But he'd better have a company cleanup team standing by in case I don't make it."

"Good luck."

"Autie clear."

When Estevez came back in, he had a steaming bag full of hamburgers and fries. "I figured we could use a little food, as well."

"Good idea." Rykoff tore open the bag and set to work. After choking down two burgers and a large fries washed down with a soft drink, it was time to go to war.

"It's dark out there now," Estevez said from the edge of the drawn curtains. "We can get going."

First Rykoff took the armored combat suit's power cells from the portable charger and reinstalled them in the suit. The power cells weren't fully charged, so he had only six hours, maybe seven, in the suit, if he didn't exert himself until he had to. It wasn't much time, but even if the suit completely lost power and he had to strip down to his underwear, he was still going in tonight.

With Estevez's assistance, Rykoff got back into his powered armor. After the long walk through the desert, he now thought of the armor as a good friend. After quickly running through the checklist, he headed for the door with a faint whine from the servos. He had to bend his head down and step sideways to clear the doorframe.

Estevez had the trailer backed up to the door and the ramp down, so Rykoff was able to climb right on inside without being seen. In the back of the trailer, he closed the suit's built-in air filters and gently shoved the horse over to give himself more room. "I'm ready," he transmitted. "Let's get it."

"I STILL THINK this is suicide," Estevez said over the mike of his comm link, concealed in the bandanna tied around his neck.

"Just be glad you're not back here with this damned horse," Rykoff growled from his hiding place inside the horse trailer.

"Heads up," Estevez said. "I'm coming up on the guard shack."

Rykoff moved to the rear of the trailer and undid the rear door from inside as Estevez gently braked to a halt in front of the closed security gate.

The New Dawn guard had his assault rifle at the ready when he walked up to the driver's side of the pickup. "This is private property, pal. You'll have to turn this rig around."

"Señor," Estevez said with a heavy Mexican accent. "Maybe you have a little water for my horses?"

"Outta here, Pancho." The guard motioned with the muzzle of his H&K. "We don't have any water."

"Please, señor," Estevez pleaded. "My horses, they need water. My truck, she broke down and it take me much time to fix her. The horses, they no have water for many hours, maybe they die."

Rykoff was monitoring Estevez's performance over the open mike of his comm link. To add a touch of realism, he reached out and goosed the old horse under the tail. Though he was an old horse, he resented the indignity. Whinnying loudly, he kicked out at the end of the trailer.

The guard was from the Southwest and had a soft spot in his heart for horses—particularly horses who had fallen into the hands of some dirt-poor Mexican who was probably taking them to the slaughterhouse to be turned into canned dog food. "Okay," he said. "I'll get ya some water."

Water from the complex's well was piped to the guardhouse, so he took a trash can, filled it and handed it to Estevez. The guard walked around to the back of the trailer in case the Mexican needed any help with the animal.

The sight of a seven-foot matt-black-armored apparition coming out of the back of the trailer froze the guard into immobility. When he went for his subgun, Rykoff reached out, wrapped the suit's powered glove around his neck and squeezed. The armored glove pinched through the man's skin, crushing his larynx. Rykoff stopped squeezing before he popped his head off and quietly laid the corpse on the floor of the trailer.

"Call the other guy back here," he transmitted to Estevez.

Estevez stepped out from behind the trailer. "Señor," he called out. "Your friend, he needs help."

"What's wrong?" The second guard started toward him, his Uzi at the ready. Realizing that he was suddenly alone now, he started turning back for the guard shack. Drawing the silenced Beretta from under his shirt, Estevez took a two-handed combat stance and triggered a single shot.

The pistol puffed and a 9 mm hole instantly appeared in the guard's coveralls, centered directly over his heart. He gasped once and crumpled to the ground, the subgun falling from his hands.

Rykoff stepped out from behind the trailer, reached down, grabbed the guard by the front of his coveralls and started to add him to the body collection in the back of the trailer.

"Wait," Estevez said when he spotted the clip-on employee badge on the front of the guard's coveralls. "Maybe we can use this."

"Good point."

The much-abused horse was spooked at the smell of the fresh blood, so before Rykoff stowed the second body inside, he let down the ramp at the rear of the trailer. Climbing in over the bodies, Estevez untied the

horse, led him down the ramp and turned him loose.
The animal would stay close to the source of water and
someone was sure to find him in the morning.

"Now," Rykoff growled as he stepped into the
guard shack. "Where's the controls for that gate?"

Estevez stepped past him and laid his hand on a
control lever plainly marked Open and Close. "You
mean this thing here?"

He pulled the lever back to the open position and
the gate slid aside.

Rykoff flicked the SPAS off safe. "Let's go," he
said.

Nisi's little kingdom was about to be invaded.

**30**

*New Dawn Compound*
*January 30*

Jud Rykoff jogged along behind the trailer as Estevez slowly drove into the New Dawn compound. The powered combat suit easily let him keep pace with the pickup while he scanned their surroundings for threats and targets. A few employees were walking back and forth between the buildings, but none were armed and they paid no attention to the familiar sight of an old pickup pulling a horse trailer.

"This is far enough," Rykoff transmitted when he saw the employee parking lot next to the company canteen. "Park it over there with the rest of those pickups."

When Estevez stepped out of the cab of the truck, he could hear country-and-western music coming from inside the club and the sound of occasional laughter. Those merrymakers would be the third-level employees who had no idea what Nisi was up to. And if they knew what was good for them, they'd leave it that way. Rykoff was in no mood to take too many prisoners tonight.

Leaving the battered cowboy hat and bandanna behind on the seat, Estevez slipped into his own Levi's brush jacket. Now he looked considerably more prosperous than he had before, almost as if he belonged in a place like the New Dawn. To dress up the image even more, he clipped the dead guard's badge onto his left breast pocket flap. He didn't look very much like the man in the small photograph on the badge, but it might serve from a distance.

Nisi's security force was still an unknown quantity. Before he had been captured, Sendak had reported that there were quite a few of them and that they were armed with pistols. But the two men they had taken out at the guard shack had proved that they had some heavier firepower. Since Rykoff was the one in the armor, he would be the storm trooper designated to deal with that.

Estevez was wearing his Kevlar body armor, but his job was to stay out of firefights and try to find where their teammates were being kept. Nonetheless, he wasn't going in there barehanded. His H&K subgun and its magazine carrier went into the sports bag with the flash-bang grenades, and he tucked his silenced Beretta pistol into the back of his belt under his brush jacket.

The blueprints Rykoff had secured before the aborted helicopter raid hadn't shown anything marked as holding cells anywhere in the complex. But there was little point in their checking out the buildings clustered around the base of the mesa. Nisi wouldn't want everyone to know what he was doing and was sure to have his jail buried out of sight inside the main headquarters complex. And that meant they had to ride the outside elevator leading up onto the top of the mesa.

"Let's go, Erik," Rykoff said impatiently.

"I'm coming, I'm coming."

Rykoff kept to the shadows, pacing Estevez as he walked directly toward the checkpoint in front of the entrance to the elevator. If Nisi was expecting company, he was sure to have the elevator well guarded. But if the employee badge could at least get Estevez close to the guard shack, all the better. If not, Rykoff would simply stand back and take the place apart with the SPAS.

The badge worked, but with the increased security Nisi had ordered, Estevez had to step up to the window of the checkpoint instead of simply being waved on inside.

"Hi," he said cheerfully, turning slightly to the side in an attempt to try to hide the picture on his badge. "Garcia, engineering. There's a problem with the water recycler and I got a call to check it out."

The man behind the window was waving him through when the second man in the booth balked. "Wait a minute," he said. "I used to work in engineering and there ain't any water recycler up—"

Estevez's silenced 9 mm round took him in the chest as his hand was going for the alarm button. The man behind the window only had time to look startled before he joined his comrade in death. That was a body count of four so far tonight and they weren't even inside yet. If things kept up at this pace, this operation was going to make the Waco incident look like a minor traffic accident.

"Let's go," Rykoff said as he stepped out of the darkness.

ONCE THEY WERE INSIDE the elevator leading up to the mesa, Rykoff and Estevez saw that there were stops on three different levels. "You get off at the lowest level and make your way on down," Rykoff said. "The cells will be as far out of sight as possible. I'll go on up to the top and create a diversion for you."

Estevez reached into his sports bag and made sure that the safety was off on the H&K. "Got it."

When the elevator stopped, and Estevez stepped out, he had his hand in the bag. "It's clear."

"Good luck," Rykoff transmitted as the door closed behind him.

There was a sign directing Estevez to another group of passenger elevators serving the inside of the complex, and he headed in that direction. He was approaching the elevators when one of the doors suddenly slid open and two men in police-style riot gear stepped out with their Uzis pointed directly at him.

"Whoa," Estevez said, holding his hands out in front of him as he took a step backward.

"Who are you?" one of the men asked when he saw the employee badge on his pocket.

"Bill Garcia, engineering."

"You seen any intruders on this level? Anybody who doesn't belong here?"

Estevez shook his head as he slowly slid his right hand into the open top of the sports bag. "Nope."

"We're on a red alert," the other guard growled. "So you better either get your ass to your duty station or get the hell outta here. Now!"

"I'm going," Estevez said, turning around and heading off down the hall.

When the guards got back into the elevator, Estevez decided to double back and take the stairs so he didn't run into any more of them.

WHEN RYKOFF REACHED the top floor, he stepped out of the elevator to find himself facing a four-man security squad. The sight of an armored figure straight out of a science-fiction movie sent the guards into a frenzy. There was no way he could be friendly, so they didn't waste time asking for explanations. They just started firing.

The storm of 9 mm fire sparkled as it ricocheted off the matt-black ceramal armor of Rykoff's combat suit. With the servos helping him keep his balance, the force of the blows didn't affect him, beyond royally pissing him off. Generally, it wasn't considered to be good judgment to piss off a man who was wearing a powered combat suit.

Rykoff spun around to face his assailants, letting his H&K fall loose on its sling as he reached down for the SPAS assault gun hanging off his right side. His attackers were wearing Kevlar body armor and helmets, but that was no big deal. The SPAS's magazine was loaded with the 12-gauge Dragon's Breath rounds and they were in for a big surprise, riot gear or not.

Rykoff triggered the SPAS and the assault gun roared in his hand. The light-sensitive visor of his combat suit's helmet instantly went blank to protect his eyes as the entire length of the hallway was transformed into a raging inferno. The screams of the guards sounded loud over the crackling of the flames.

"Fuck with me, will you," Rykoff muttered as he reslung the SPAS, took up his H&K again and continued on down the corridor.

BAO HEARD the alarms go off in the corridor outside her cell and smiled. Jud was coming for them, just like she had known he would. Now she could get serious about doing something so she could join the party. Specifically, she had to join up with Jud before he wasted Nisi. That bastard was hers and hers alone and she wasn't going to forgo the pleasure of killing him if there was any way she could help it.

The problem was that she had nothing in the cell to use as a weapon or a tool. Nothing, that was, except for the one weapon that could never be taken away from a woman.

The guards who came for her were sure to be armed, but a flash of bare breast or, even better, bare parted thighs leading to exposed pubic hair would give her the momentary edge she needed. Male hormones were wonderful things and they would force the guards to look at her naked flesh. Whether they wanted to or not, they wouldn't be able to stop themselves from doing it.

If the guards were gay, though, she'd be in deep shit. But she didn't think Nisi was the type to want homosexuals working for him. He was sexually unbalanced enough that he probably couldn't handle it.

ALARMS WERE SOUNDING in the war room when Joshua Nisi rushed in from his private office next door. "Turn that damned alarm off!" he shouted.

When he could hear again, he turned to the duty officer. "What's the situation?"

"I think we have an intruder inside the complex," the duty officer reported. "The checkpoint at the bottom of the elevator doesn't answer."

Nisi was outraged. The senator had promised him that Rykoff and Estevez would be in custody by now, facing terrorist charges. He'd take care of that simple bastard in the morning, but first he had a commando or two to deal with.

"Where are they now?"

"We don't know, but Lutz's men have been alerted and they're going after him."

"Get Lutz on the phone."

"Yes, sir."

"Do you have the intruder spotted yet?" Nisi asked Lutz when the duty officer turned over the phone.

"We're still working on it, but I think he's heading down to the lower levels."

"Get some men down there and have that woman brought here in the war room immediately," Nisi ordered. "I think her friends have come for her."

"I'll send someone down for her right away."

"We have a fire in level three, sir." The duty officer sounded panicked. "The sprinkler system just went on."

"Did you hear that, Lutz?" Nisi snapped. "Do something about it!"

"I'm on it."

BAO WAS WAITING and more than ready when two guards came for her. The first one into the room had his side arm holstered, but the second one had his pistol ready in his hand. As she had expected, neither one of them equated a half-naked woman with danger.

"Nisi wants to see you," the first man said, unable to take his eyes off her crotch.

She slowly got to her feet, letting the sides of the unbuttoned shift swing open, exposing her breasts. The guard stepped aside as she stood up, giving her a clear shot at the guy with the pistol in his hand. Going into a crouching spin, she lashed out with a kick aimed at the guard with the pistol in his hand.

Though she was barefoot, her kick to the guard's crotch carried enough force to crush his testicles and give him a hernia. He didn't have too long to suffer from it, however. Her follow-through forearm blow crushed his larynx and stopped his scream of pain. Dropping to his knees, he clawed at his throat with frantic fingers as his face turned a deep mottled red.

The other guard was still fumbling with his holster when she spun around and broke his collarbone with the edge of her right hand. Before he could bring his left arm over to reach for the weapon, she struck him across the bridge of the nose with a complicated two-part blow.

The first strike broke the bridge of his nose and the second drove the splintered bone up into his brain. The needle of bone slicing through his gray matter did a good job of scrambling his neural synapses. He stiffened, his eyes rolled back into their sockets and he crumpled to the floor twitching.

Bending down over him, Bao placed one of her hands around the side of his skull, her palm cupped over his ear. The other hand went on the other side of his head and she gave a sharp upward twist. With a wet crunch, his skull rotated off his cervical vertebra, severing his spinal column and killing him instantly.

Seeing that her first victim hadn't suffocated yet, she reached over and gave him the same neck-popping treatment. His feet kicked twice and he, too, was dead.

Snatching the second guard's 9 mm Beretta pistol from the floor, she checked to make sure that a round was chambered before she buttoned her shift. There was no point in giving away her advantage until she needed it again.

The guards weren't carrying extra magazines with their holsters. But even though the guards' side arms were of different makes, they both fired 9 mm ammunition. She dropped the magazine from the first guard's Smith & Wesson and quickly thumbed the thirteen rounds from it so she could reload her Beretta's magazine when it ran dry, then she dropped the rounds in the pocket of her smock.

Now she was ready to play.

BAO WAS WORKING HER WAY down the empty corridor when she saw a woman step out of a side room. It was the same woman who had set her up for Nisi's rape. With three bounding strides, Bao was on her, the muzzle of her pistol against the bridge of her nose.

"Don't say a word," she cautioned as she shoved the woman back into the room and closed the door behind them.

The woman stood stock-still and didn't flinch from the touch of the cold steel. "I'm sorry," the woman whispered, tears coming to her eyes. "Joshua shouldn't have done that to you. It wasn't right."

"Where can I find him?" Bao snapped.

"Are you going to kill him?" The woman's eyes narrowed.

"Yes."

The Senior Sister took a deep breath, wishing that she'd had this woman's courage after she had been raped. It would have made a big difference to the rest of her life. "I will take you to him.

"First, though," she pointed out, "you need to wear something else. The guards will stop you if they see you in that." She dropped her eyes. "It's too revealing. I have a sister's smock over there. It's a little big, maybe, but no one will notice you in it."

"Give it to me," Bao said. "But remember that I'll kill you too if you do anything stupid."

"I won't."

After taking off her smock, Bao slipped the plain white shift down over her head. As the woman had said, it was too big for her, but it did give her a full range of movement.

"Okay, let's go."

Back out in the hall, Bao followed behind the woman as if she was one of Nisi's little playthings going for her nightly romp. She kept her head down, but her eyes were alert and her hand was on the pistol in the pocket of her shift.

## 31

*New Dawn Compound*
*January 30*

While Rykoff was toasting the upper levels of the New Dawn headquarters complex, Estevez cautiously continued on down the stairs to the engineering level. He could hear the alarms ringing in the corridors beyond the stairwell, but so far he had the stairs all to himself, which suited him fine. The last thing he needed was to run into another security patrol.

At the bottom of the stairs, the fire door leading off the landing was labeled Engineering Division—Keep Closed At All Times. Since there was no window to peek through, Estevez tightened his grip on the H&K in his bag, silently opened the door and slipped through. Inside was a cavernous room with pillars instead of walls holding up the ceiling. To his left were wire-enclosed storage areas. To his right were five doors set into the wall, which could be to holding cells.

He walked over to them and was looking at the locks when a man in security-guard coveralls stepped out of the dimly lit far end of the room. "Hey!" the guard shouted. "What do you think you're doing? Get away from there!"

Estevez swung the sports bag around to cover him. "I'm just looking for—" Estevez began, when he saw the guard go for his holstered pistol.

The chatter of Estevez's H&K blasting through the thin nylon of the bag on full-auto sounded over the ringing of the alarm. The guard went down, but several of his comrades rushed toward Estevez, their weapons blazing fire. Diving for cover behind one of the pillars, he sent a burst toward them as he keyed the mike to his comm link.

"I've found the holding cells," he called Rykoff. "They're all the way down on the engineering level."

"I'm on the way," Rykoff replied.

"You'd better hurry it up, man. I've got about a dozen of the bastards cornered down here and I'm running out of ammunition."

Rykoff could hear small-arms fire in the background over the comm link. "Keep under cover, I'll be down there ASAP."

"I'm in the east end past the storage rooms."

As Rykoff made his way down to Estevez, he kept up a running conversation with him over the comm link. "I'm at the engineering fire door," Rykoff said. "Have you got any flash-bangs?"

"When do you want them?"

"Now!"

Estevez squeezed his eyes shut and covered his ears after tossing one of the grenades. The flash and the loud explosion stunned the guards, and when they could see again, the sight of Rykoff's combat armor advancing toward them sent them into a frenzy. He was blocking their exit and their only chance was to try to fight their way past him. None of them even contemplated surrendering to anything that looked like that.

A storm of 9 mm and .45-caliber fire sparkled on Rykoff's armor, sending ricochets singing all around the room. Striding toward them, he shook off their fire and raised the SPAS. The assault gun roared once, a tongue of flame leaping from the muzzle, and then roared again. The far end of the room dissolved into dripping molten flame.

Again the screams of the burning men sounded loud over the crackling of the flames. Dropping the SPAS, Rykoff swung his H&K into play and sprayed the end of the room with a full magazine. Estevez joined him with his own subgun. Most of the screams were cut off abruptly, but one poor bastard continued to wail his agony until he sucked the flames into his lungs.

"Where's those cells?" Rykoff asked.

"Back the way you came in," Estevez said, then shook with a fit of coughing. The air was quickly filling with smoke and the smell of charred flesh as the flames consumed the bodies. Before long, this entire level would be uninhabitable.

Estevez pointed out the five cell doors, one of which appeared to be unlocked. "Jake! Mel! Alex!" Rykoff called over his suit's loudspeaker.

"Yo!" MacLeod shouted out.

"In here!" Sendak's muffled voice sounded from the cell next to his.

The cell doors were fitted with electronic locks controlled by plastic key cards. Rykoff knew better than to waste his time searching the bodies for a card that hadn't melted. He simply reached down and took hold of the lock with his powered glove. One servo-assisted twist and the entire lock unit came off in his hand.

Pulling the door open, he saw a grinning Jake MacLeod standing at the far end of the cell. "What took you so long?"

"Sorry," Rykoff answered. "We had to stop and buy a horse."

"A horse?"

"I'll explain later," Estevez said.

Sendak's cell opened as easily, but he was halfway bent over as he walked out.

"Are you hurt?" Rykoff asked.

"I'm okay," Sendak said, choking in the smoke. "It's only a broken rib."

"You sure?"

"I'm sure," Sendak said. "Erik and Jake can help me if I need it. Let's get going."

"Have either of you seen Bao?" Rykoff asked on the way to the door.

Both men shook their heads. "I haven't seen her since we were captured," MacLeod said. "Nisi said something to the guards about taking her to his quarters."

"Ah, shit!" Rykoff spit. Neither man had to say what he was thinking. It also went without saying that if she had been raped or molested, Nisi would spend a very long time dying.

"Take 'em on outside ASAP," Rykoff told Estevez. "I'm going back up after Mel."

"I'll come with you," MacLeod offered.

"No," Rykoff replied. "You help with Alex. I can take care of this."

ON THE UPPER LEVEL, the Senior Sister turned a corner in the corridor and stopped. "His office is down at the end of the hall." She pointed to a large carved-wood door.

This branch of the corridor was paneled in rare hardwoods and covered with expensive carpet as befitted the entry to a CEO's office. The art on the walls, however, reflected the owner's uneducated tastes, as none of the pieces were really top-notch. But that was to be expected.

"You can go now," Bao told the woman softly. "I'll take it from here."

"He shouldn't have done that to you," the woman repeated, looking down at the floor, unable to meet her eyes. "And I shouldn't have helped him do it."

"Don't worry about it," Bao said gently. "I'll take care of him now."

"I'm so sorry."

"My friends have come for me," Bao cautioned her. "So you had better get out of here as fast as you can, and take the girls with you. Get them off the mesa because we're going to completely destroy this place.''

The woman fled as Bao strode up to Nisi's door. The massive, ornately carved door had an electronic card lock, but the doorframe couldn't resist her side kick.

Nisi spun around when the door crashed open. He had a cell phone in his left hand and a pistol in the right. His face registered shock when he realized who had interrupted him and he hesitated just long enough for Bao to leap across the space between them. A high kick sent the pistol spinning out of his hand.

"Raping me was bad enough," she said softly. "But you humiliated me and you enjoyed humiliating me. Now I'm going to humiliate you before I kill you."

Bao's callused foot lashed out, slamming into the side of Nisi's knee. The snap of the joint shattering sounded clear in the sound-proofed room. Nisi's wail of pain was high and girlish. He dropped to the floor, writhing.

She stepped up to him again, cocked her right leg and kicked him in the pit of the stomach. Her kick lifted Nisi halfway off the floor and sent him skidding up against the wall.

The next two kicks went deep into his unprotected belly, rupturing internal organs. That alone would have been enough to kill him in a few minutes, but Bao wasn't finished with this man. Not by a long shot.

When his left hand scrabbled across the rug toward the pistol he had dropped, she stomped on it, shattering the fragile bones in the base of his hand. Almost as an afterthought, she broke his other knee.

The pain was sending Nisi into shock, so Bao reached down and pinched a nerve in his elbow to bring him around. His eyes snapped open and his mouth gaped as he gasped for breath.

"Now," she said, "I'm going to make sure that you never rape anyone again."

Nisi's scream could be heard on the next level down.

RYKOFF WAS on the second level when a man broke blindly from around a corner and almost ran into him. He reached out, grabbed the terror-stricken man by the back of his coveralls and spun him around. "Oh, God," the man wailed as Rykoff lifted him off the floor. "Please don't kill me."

"I'm looking for a woman who doesn't belong in this place." Rykoff's voice was harsh over the suit's speakers. "She's Chinese, about five-three and in her late twenties. You seen her?"

"I saw the Senior Sister taking a woman up to Nisi's office," the man said, fighting to keep his composure. "She had dark hair and dark skin, so she might be the one you're looking for, mister."

"Where's his office?"

"One floor up, down at the end of the corridor. You can't miss it."

"What's the fastest way to get there?"

The man looked at Rykoff's combat suit and pointed down the hall. "I'd say take the stairs, mister. I don't know if you'll fit in the elevator."

Rykoff put him back down on the floor. "I'd get the hell out of here if I were you."

The man didn't say a word as he spun around and fled.

BAO WAS SO INTENT on ruining Nisi that she didn't even notice Rykoff come through the open door behind her. "That's enough, Mel." His amplified voice cut through the tumult of adrenaline. "He's dead."

She spun on Rykoff, her hands held in the attack-defend position. "He's not dead enough."

Rykoff stood his ground. To approach her when she was in this state of mind was to invite an attack. Even in his powered suit, he didn't want to have to fight her off. "Come on, Mel," he said gently. "We have to go now. The rest of the guys are waiting for us."

Even through the suit's speaker, his voice was low and soft. It washed over her like a cool rain dampening the fires that raged in her blood. With a shudder, she took a deep breath, sucking the air into the bottom of her lungs like a newborn baby.

With her heightened senses, she could smell the room as if she had the nose of a wolf. She could smell the metallic, plastic odor of Rykoff's fighting suit over the sharp smell of cordite from the barrel of his H&K submachine gun. Under that she could smell the lingering stench of Nisi's fear, the urine that had spilled from his bladder and the blood that covered her hands and arms. She could even smell the fox-rank scent of her own battle-driven sweat.

With the last of her breath, she finally smelled smoke and realized that the complex was burning down around her.

"We have to go now, Mel," Rykoff repeated. "I'll carry you."

Dropping her arms to her side, she slowly walked over to where he stood. Reaching down, he scooped her up with his left arm and pressed her to him. She buried her face against his matt-black armored chest and put both her arms around his neck.

Cradling her in his left arm as if she were a kitten, Rykoff held the SPAS in his right. He still had half a dozen Dragon's Breath rounds in the magazine and dearly wanted a chance to use them on someone.

"I've got her," he transmitted to Estevez. "She's okay and we're coming out."

"Fan-fucking-tastic!" Estevez sent back.

"Meet us outside by the base of the elevator."

"Roger."

When they reached the end of the corridor leading back to Nisi's office, Rykoff turned around and sent a Dragon's breath round back the way they had come. The wood-paneled walls and expensive carpet burned nicely.

IN THEIR PANIC to escape the fire that was now raging through most of the headquarters complex, not many of the New Dawn employees even noticed that there was a man in an armored combat suit in their midst. Those who did, however, took one look and shrank from Rykoff, particularly the survivors of Nisi's security force. Most of the few who still had their weapons instantly dropped them and fled. Those who didn't died in short order.

Rather than risk being trapped in the elevator by a power failure, Rykoff carried Bao down the stairs. So far, the complex's air-conditioning system was extracting most of the smoke, but it wouldn't be too long before the flames cut the power and anyone left inside would die of smoke inhalation. The powered armor made short work of the run down the stairs to the door at the base of the mesa. Once he was well clear of the entrance, he turned back to face the stair's landing.

"Erik," he called over the comm link. "Are you guys all clear?"

"We're outside."

"Good. I'm going to finish flaming this place."

Bringing the SPAS up, he triggered a Dragon's Breath round directly back into the landing. A gout of flame engulfed the landing and shot back up the stairs.

As Rykoff carried Bao to safety, he saw someone bringing the company's sole fire truck up to try to fight the blaze. He was determined that Nisi's works would disappear from the face of the earth and he didn't want anyone trying to save any of it. Unslinging the SPAS, he triggered the last of the Dragon's

Breath rounds at the fire truck. The tongue of molten flame engulfed the truck's cab. The two men inside barely managed to escape the inferno.

Dropping the now-empty assault shotgun, Rykoff swung his H&K into play, but he had no takers.

"Over here!" Estevez called out from the darkness.

When Rykoff joined them, he saw that MacLeod and Sendak had armed themselves with Uzis the guards had dropped, but there didn't seem to be any more threat. The few people they could see were watching the fire and they weren't armed. By now the flames were shooting from the mesa top.

"Let's get out of here," Rykoff said, weary at last. Even with the powered armor taking most of the physical load, combat was always exhausting. "We'll take the pickup."

He held Bao out to MacLeod. "Take her. I can't fit in the cab." He jerked an armored thumb back toward the trailer. "I get to ride back there with the horse shit."

As Estevez drove away, the towering flames from Nisi's complex flickered in the pickup's door mirrors. Somewhere in the fire was the body of the man who had wanted to cleanse the United States, but ended up being cleansed himself, by fire.

**32**

*Los Angeles*
*February 4*

Frank Buckley looked almost disappointed as he wrapped up his final broadcast from Los Angeles. Now that the flow of Ukrainian arms had been halted, the police were going after the gangs one at a time and disarming them. The federal government's general amnesty was also drying up the number of AKs still on the streets as gangs turned in their weapons rather than be busted by the LAPD or the Feds. For the past several days, no one had been reported dying in gang-related incidents anywhere in the greater L.A. area. To all extents and purposes, the race war that had been dubbed "Armageddon 2000" was over.

Now that the L.A. story was no longer the top of the news, Buckley was transferred to Florida to cover a puff piece about the return of Cuban-Americans to their homeland. As far as he was concerned, the new assignment was a long step down from the immediacy of the race war that had given him his national exposure. Still, working for CNN sure beat the hell out of being a faceless voice trying to make sense out of an

L.A. traffic jam. He had made it onto the airwaves with the nation's most important news channel. All he had to do now was stay there, and that meant taking the assignments he was given without bitching about them.

When Buckley wrapped up and his face faded from the screen, the scene shifted back to the central newsroom in Atlanta.

"In other news," the news anchor read from her prompter, "the apparent suicide of Senator John Parks has shaken Capitol Hill to the core. His colleagues will remember the California senator for his unceasing work to promote high-tech industry within the United States."

The scene shifted to show the senator addressing a national conference of computer software manufacturers. "We can only prevail as a nation if once more we lead the industrial world in applied high technology and not try to play catch-up."

When the screen showing the senator's birth and death dates faded, the anchor continued. "Washington police have completed their investigation into the senator's death and have confirmed the earlier reports that his death was a suicide. Earlier speculation that the senator didn't own a handgun have now been disproved. So have the reports that the pistol, a Russian-designed, semiautomatic 9 mm model, was from the Ukrainian weapons that have flooded into Southern California. It is now known that the pistol was given to the senator by a Vietnam War veteran friend.

"In a related story, the confirmation of the death of Joshua Nisi, the biotechnology genius behind the bioengineering research company known as New Dawn, was announced today. The corporate headquarters located on the top of a mesa in the remote Chiricahua Valley in southern Arizona was the scene of a mysterious fire four days ago. Investigators are still sifting through the wreckage, trying to determine the cause of the blaze that almost completely destroyed the facility."

The camera rolled taped footage of the smoldering wreckage on the mesa top. "The remoteness of the site prevented fire equipment from the neighboring communities from responding in time to prevent the destruction of the company headquarters. A spokesman for New Dawn said that Nisi's body was discovered yesterday and was identified from dental records...."

"Shut that off," Mel Bao growled. "I've heard about all I can stand."

Jud Rykoff hit the clicker, and the wall-size TV screen in his living room went back to showing a European landscape. The two of them had just finished a home-cooked meal in Rykoff's small but comfortable Huntsville home and were watching CNN while they shared a bottle of a vintage brandy.

He had been surprised but pleased when Mel had taken him up on his offer of the hospitality of his house while she recovered from her ordeal at Nisi's hands. He had enjoyed having her around and caring for her while she worked her way through the aftermath. It had been almost a week now, and last night had been the first night she had slept all the way through without waking up.

"He got away with it, didn't he?" Mel's voice was bitter. "No one's ever going to know what really happened in L.A. Over two thousand people died because of him and now the bastard will go down in history as one of the good guys."

Rykoff reached over and laid his hand on her shoulder. This time she didn't shrink from his touch.

"No, he won't," he said. "The people who count know what really happened and how it happened. I can assure you that after today you're never going to hear Nisi's name spoken again. There won't be any memorials for him or any scholarships in his name. He'll be erased from history as if he had never existed."

"Who did the job on the senator?"

Rykoff grinned. "We were all going to draw straws for the privilege. But Alex really wasn't in any shape to do it yet and Jake wasn't going to be able to get into the right places so it came down to me and Erik."

He shrugged. "But I opted to stay here with you and he was happy to do it for me. Oh, yes, he also sends his best wishes."

"Are you going to erase the senator from history, too?"

"Actually, no." Rykoff shook his head. "But he wouldn't have liked the way he's going to be remembered. He's going to be exposed for having accepted bribes to change his vote on the Senate floor and for having used his power to influence critical legislation in favor of his paymaster. We won't erase him from history, but he's going down on the long list of senatorial assholes. In the next couple of weeks, you're going to see his own party open investigations into his dealings and you're going to see a couple of pieces of his legislation overturned."

Bao turned on the couch to look him full in the face. "How do you make things like that happen?" She looked perplexed. "I don't understand."

His eyebrows shot up and he turned his right thumb toward his chest. "Me? I don't make anything happen. I'm just a middle-aged bookstore owner from Huntsville, Alabama, who writes paperback thrillers as a hobby. The only people I know in Washington are a few guys in the Congressional Library who buy books from me."

"Books like Machiavelli's *The Prince?*"

He smiled wolfishly. "You ought to read it. It's a fascinating study of political reality back in the days when everyone played the game for keeps, and it still makes sense today."

"Do you have a copy around here?"

"As a matter of fact, I do, one of the first English translations."

"Would you read it to me?"

"I'd be honored to introduce you to the greatest political adviser of all time."

She looked at him from under her eyelashes. "Would you read it to me in bed?"

Rykoff's head snapped around as if he had hit the end of a two-hundred-foot bungee cord. "Are you sure you want to do that?"

"Sure," she said with a slow smile. "I've always liked dirty politics."

**American hostages abroad have
one chance of getting out alive**

# BLACK OPS #3

## DEEP TERROR

### created by MICHAEL KASNER

Americans are increasingly in danger, at home and abroad. Created
by an elite cadre of red-tape-cutting government officials, the
Black Ops commandos exist to avenge such acts of terror.